REVIEWS OF BOOKS BY BARRY GRILLS

I And You, And Me And Her

"The story unfolds at a solid pace... very well-drawn and believable." (*Whistler Independent Book Awards*)

"Stories about men in love with women they can't have ... very detailed and vivid" (*BookLife Prize*)

Too Late The Hunter

"I'm very much enjoying *Too Late The Hunter* ... It's a great read. It's also a very relatable novel." (Dr. Brian Burtch, Professor Emeritus, School of Criminology, Simon Fraser University, and author of *Get That Freak: Homophobia and Transphobia in High Schools*)

"An enjoyable and fascinating novel . . . the writing is lyrical and fresh; and, at times, completely brilliant." (*Whistler Independent Book Awards*)

"Psychological thriller... Grills writes masterful description! His phrases gave me goosebumps more than once... a bingeworthy novel!" (Marla J. Hayes, author of *Cassidy's Deadly Exit)*

"Lovely writing... naturally flowing narrative... *Too Late the Hunter* takes the reader to the heart of the human problem... [and] tackles the bigger job that real novels need to do, that is, to look at an enduring human issue... without prescribing a position that must be taken... integrating different perspectives over a wider and non-contiguous span of time... in a seemingly fluid manner that doesn't feel either contrived or clunky to the reader." (Ric de Meulles, author of *Junkshop Angel)*

Oblivion

"The author writes well and is, like his protagonist, a good communicator... [with] tone and style." (*Whistler Independent Book Awards*)

Roadkill

Shortlisted for the 2018 *Whistler Independent Book Awards*; Finalist for the 2018 *Next Generation Indie Book Awards*

"Set in a compelling dystopian future ... the story develops greater urgency as it progresses. Writing in fluid, lyrical sentences, Grills demonstrates a clear facility with language and tone ... alluring descriptions... striking prose and an enticing premise allow this novel to stand out within the larger category of dystopian fiction" (*BookLife Prize*)

"I absolutely loved *Roadkill.*" (Donna Sinclair, author of *Saving The Future*)

"A thinking person's speculative fiction." (Erich Weingartner, editor of *A Journey of Faith Across a Turbulent Century: Memoirs of a Refugee Pastor*)

"Highly imaginative and richly described ... adventure, suspense, romance, and action ... a masterful piece of dystopian storytelling ... I highly recommend *Roadkill* to all readers, regardless of their preferred genre. It's definitely a five-star read." (K. L. Davidson, author of *Ten Thousand Fields*)

Every Wolf's Howl
"Surprising, poignant, affectionate, and amusing memoir." (*Prairie Fire Review of Books*)

"An accomplished author of stories... Barry Grills... in his first memoir... [writes] a moving story of friendship and transformation, and anyone who has ever longed to companionate with wild creatures will be transfixed" (*Winnipeg Free Press*)

"An innovative story told backward ... *Every Wolf's Howl* proves a successful literary endeavour" (Stacey May Fowles, *Quill & Quire*)

Cock-Eyed Voice: Stories
The short story "A Game with Adonis" ... [is] "so successful the reader squirms in self-recognition" (*Books in Canada*)

"These stories are vintage gold... with a unique and pointed voice... A treat for readers." (Jennifer Rouse Barbeau, author of *Dying Hour*)

The Pack

Barry Grills

Books by Barry Grills

Fiction
The Pack (Fluid Grouse Enterprises)
Infamy (Fluid Grouse Enterprises)
An Ecstasy (Fluid Grouse Enterprises)
The Last Light Spoken (Fluid Grouse Enterprises)
Cock-Eyed Voice: Stories (Fluid Grouse Enterprises)
Too Late The Hunter (Fluid Grouse Enterprises)
Oblivion (Fluid Grouse Enterprises)
I And You, And Me And Her (Fluid Grouse Enterprises)
Roadkill (Fluid Grouse Enterprises)

Non Fiction
Every Wolf's Howl (Freehand Books)
A New Day Dawns (with Jim Brown) (Quarry Press)
Falling Into You (Quarry Press)
Ironic (Quarry Press)
Snowbird (Quarry Press)

The Pack

Barry Grills

FLUID
GROUSE
enterprises

Barry Grills

For information about permission to reprint, record, or perform sections of this book, write
Fluid Grouse Press, 635 Scollard Street, North Bay, Ontario, Canada P1B 5A2

This novel is a work of fiction; any resemblance to its characters by persons living or dead is
purely coincidental

Library and Archives Canada Cataloguing in Publication

Grills, Barry, 1948-   , author
The Pack / Barry Grills

Cover Design: Jennifer Rouse Barbeau
Cover Photos: Max Ravier [Brown and White Siberian Husky · Free Stock Photo] and Harrison
Haines [Man Wearing Jacket Carrying A Gun · Free Stock Photo], modified with Pexels license
permission by Jennifer Rouse Barbeau
Author Photo: Liz Lott

ISBN:
978-1-7780612-2-6

THE PACK

Barry Grills

I will face my fear.
I will permit it to pass over me and through me.
And when it has gone past
I will turn the inner eye to see its path.

Where the fear has gone there will be nothing.
Only I will remain.

Frank Herbert,
Dune

Barry Grills

PROLOGUE

SARA DOES THE DRIVING. You like it when she drives. You can lean back against the door, your left leg crooked on the edge of the seat, watching her as she steers her BMW with only a finger or two, like she belongs to the car more than the car belongs to her. You slouch close to the open window and your hair blows in the gust of wind the car's speed contrives along the highway. You enjoy that Sara is so bold and vibrant, so capable when she's behind the wheel. You feel two connected sensations at times like these: a perfect freedom and a sense of being at home—not safe exactly, not permanently free, but complete and whole and careless. It's as if these moments when she is driving represent the conjunction for you of some kind of necessary definition inside an even larger, achievable goal, an even larger purpose. Not that you frequently think about purpose or goal, at least in a larger sense, but there are times when you are with Sara when you glimpse the notion that a quietly wondrous destination has been determined for you. You don't try to define this conclusion any further than a vague idea it exists. You simply wonder, inside your non-belief, if there is a chance that you can be happy.

"What are you grinning at?" Sara asks suddenly, aware that you have been watching her.

You feel caught and embarrassed by her question. Because life has taught you to lie so much, you nearly deny the smile on your lips. You don't want to respond at first. A ritual caution suggests you shouldn't confess that Sara might have a role in some deeper future purpose you are envisioning for yourself. Thinking it was love, she would hug it to herself, holding you while she was holding it.

"C'mon, Kovacs, what are you grinning at?"

"I like to watch you drive," you reply at last. "When you drive, it's a work of art."

You like that she calls you Kovacs most of the time. It's an easy intimacy between you, a casual endearment, the kind of affection you respect when you are together, when you're in between periods of making love. It's only slightly possessive. It doesn't smother you much. But she calls you Keith when you are fucking, when you speak in sex-befuddled cries or whispers. You like that she has one name for you during sex, another during all those other times that you move inexorably towards sex. You are wary, though, when she calls you Keith after the lovemaking is over, when she brings up the future, what should be done about it, what soon should be settled or arranged. You draw back fiercely when she brings up what lies ahead. "Call me Kovacs," you say sometimes when Sara wants to make plans. "It's all I can ever be."

This saddens her, you've noticed. Someday, you expect, Sara will slip away because the Kovacs you really are won't be enough for her. You love more comfortably, you know, within the certain inevitability of an affair's conclusion. While you now believe Sara is the best lover you've ever had, you know better than she does that the two of you are merely at play in a world too disingenuous for long-lasting love. Not your fault, you know. It's just what the world's become. Long-term partnerships are business; love is overwhelmed by strict definitions of function, by economic expectations, by obligation and responsibility. You ought to know. It's how you make your living. At some point, after you inevitably drift apart, Sara will blame you for giving up on her. She anticipates more in life. She would exchange more for what you've known all along is the more authentic less that love and romance must eventually become.

Sara still thinks you have more to offer her: permanence perhaps, a nest, maybe even a child or two. You sense she delicately waits. You sense she may be only months away from her inevitable disappointment.

Maybe the two of you should just keep driving. Nowhere in particular. Or everywhere. Sara at the wheel. No particular destination. Just keep driving to keep the affair alive, to defer the inevitability of its conclusion. Not practical, you know. As an investment advisor, you're having a good year. Despite nine-eleven, despite Iraq, despite Covid, despite the predilections of Donald Trump, you have never been unsuccessful. Or maybe because of them. Everyone says you're going to make a million this year. You want to. You've always wanted to. Because everyone says you can. You've believed for many years that you should make a million. Society knows what you must do. The word the social machine uses is should. But driving with Sara, without destination, just to keep love and sex going—you'd like that too. If you could clone yourself, you'd do both. One of you could make that million; the other could be happy as Sara's erotic passenger, the two of you spiriting the nation's highways like a lovelorn tumbleweed, enmeshed in the stylish body of Sara's precision-talented BMW.

You have thoughts like these more often than you want to admit. A man needs his secret thoughts. Because he can't live them. Because they're a little embarrassing. No, more precisely, it's emerging from them that's embarrassing. As if secret thoughts are conceived in a fetal state and, when you burst out of the womb where you think them, the first sensation in a cold and ruthless world is embarrassment. Embarrassment at being something other than what the world needs you to be. The slap on the bottom of your thoughts is only your first punishment in a world so narrowly defined. Eventually, to avoid any future penalty, you keep your thoughts to yourself. For long periods of time, you even labour never to think them again.

"C'mon, Kovacs," says Sara over the roar of her freeway cruising. "You're grinning again. Care to let me in on it?"

"Don't want to," you admit. "Just thinking about you and driving. Just thinking about the love we've made after someone's been behind the wheel."

"Shit," she says. "I wish you'd share."

"A man's thoughts are his own. Just like a woman's."

She glances at you a moment, then seems to accept what you have said.

No wonder you think these things when Sara is behind the wheel. You began what you've become together in this very car. It started the day she drove you to your office from her father's home where she was visiting one afternoon, to save you calling a cab— you don't drive in California the way you once drove back home in Kelowna. Sara wore a skirt that day. Shifted gears in it. Hit the brake. Pressed down on the accelerator. The skirt rode up her thighs a bit. You couldn't help but notice. You grew partially aroused.

"You have gorgeous legs," you said.

You didn't realize you'd spoken aloud. You believed you'd only thought your appreciation for her legs, tanned and long and slim. Until she glanced at you and you heard the echo of what you'd said, what might possibly be an inopportune remark.

"If you don't mind my saying so," you added hastily.

There was an awkward silence before she said, "That's okay."

You were already prepared to seize one of two opposing explanations, whichever one saved the day, whichever was most appropriate. You could make her believe that you'd meant it only as a compliment. No offense intended. Or, if she gave you some kind of sign that warranted it, you would make it clear that you were beginning to want her in some way.

It was a tense moment. You glanced out the window, your near-erection wilting. Part of you sought the remedy of a swift and safe topic change. But behind your Ray-Bans, your eyes kept returning to her legs and her right hand grasping the gear shift, delicately long fingers splashed at the ends with fingernails painted purple. In a perfectly sexual world, she would have hiked the skirt higher to celebrate something erotic with you. If she was offended, though, you knew she would tug it down as an ambassador from a more conventional world.

She did neither at this moment. Her inaction impaled you on her unexpected mystery, denied you whatever judgment was passing through her mind.

In the parking lot at your office you thanked her for

the lift. "I owe you one," you said because to say so would neither help nor hurt.

"Yes, you do," she replied. "You owe me dinner, Kovacs, for that remark about my legs."

And there it was for the first time, the car and her driving, the unexpected intimacy you felt at her use of your last name.

You know Sara is in love with you. Women being in love with you happens now and then. Usually you run away from their love as inevitably as you can. But, for now, you keep seeing Sara. The affair remains torrid. Her love hasn't yet transformed the passion into ritual. And Sara is your favourite; this much you can admit. When Sara decides to go, when she realizes she's had enough of your intransigence, you know the next woman in your life will be a disappointment, less appealing to you. For all you know, you may never again encounter a woman who heats up your feelings the way that Sara does.

Which is why, when you're driving and Sara's behind the wheel, you sometimes enjoy the enticing notion that you can drive forever through a cobweb world that otherwise sticks to your personal purpose so that it can hold you back. With Sara behind the wheel, you like to think you would break the web, if only because of the speed at which you're travelling.

Sara freely admits she didn't expect to fall in love with you. "I needed a toy," she has said. "I thought you might be it." This intended carelessness on Sara's part may be the reason, you suspect, you first made love in the front seat of her car, the same seat on which you now recline while Sara drives you north.

A crisp night, the car poking out of a litter-smudged lot overlooking the valley. Sara straddling your lap, both of you still dressed but all your clothing pushed aside to

keep it out of the way of your urgent sexual friction. The window steaming up. Neither one of you stifling your cries. Both of you coming in a soup of sexual juices and joyful, gasping invectives. Fortunately you had finished by the time the policeman's flashlight beam lit up your flushed faces through the condensation on the passenger window. The policeman, you like to think, seemed to understand. "Jesus Christ!" was all he said as he flicked the flashlight beam off and walked away towards the rear of the car.

"He's writing down the plate number," Sara reported from her vantage point on your lap, watching him through the back window.

"In case you decide to strangle me now that you've had your way with me?"

Sara chuckled at your remark.

Like so many of its kind, the affair began as only play. Now you tell each other you love one another, Sara because it's true, you because it follows naturally her more sincere exclamation. Your response is probably nothing more than the period at the end of her sentence. Telling her you love her contains a modicum of truth— it's way ahead of "one day we'll do lunch" but falls well short of the myth of permanent passion Sara now believes in and which you cannot accept.

Sara believes in many things inspired by what you've come to know is her version of hope. You, on the other hand, now realize you believe in very little. Knowing Sara, you now conclude most hope evaporated for you some time ago, unmissed in the kind of life fate chose for you to live. It's not that you question life's choices; it's just that lately you've felt rather passive and have begun to wonder why you are what you've become.

CARMEL-BY-THE-SEA, YOUR DESTINATION, is shrouded on this day by a gray and chilly mist, but Sara knows where she's going. You've been to Carmel together before. No one, she claims, especially her husband and her father, would think to find you together here. It's often crowded with visitors, with tourists and amateur historians. History and tourist wanderlust are preoccupations, Sara says, her father and her husband consider irrelevant.

Of these two men, Sara fears discovery of your affair by her father most. On nights when she is nervous, when she is with you in a crowd, she frets that someone who knows her father will catch you holding hands. "I'm sorry," Sara often says, despising her jumpiness. "My father," she murmurs then, not completing the sentence, letting it dangle between you in desperate nebulousness. You know he's the one with the grand plan for her life. He's the one, she maintains, who would have the most to lose if he knew she is in love with you. You believe her—not so much because she always tells the truth—but because you keep a secret of your own: the month and a half two years ago when you were screwing Sara's mother. Being with Sara now, you are ashamed of what happened then. Not your fault, but had you known that you would now be with Sara, that you would care for her as much as you do, you wouldn't have allowed the other affair to happen. In a way it was purely business, part of the cost you had to put into securing Marjorie Hamilton's investment portfolio. But you wish it hadn't happened now. You wish you could forget it. Sometimes, when you let yourself remember the other affair, it taints this finer one with Sara. It makes you shudder at how many dirty little alleys you have travelled to reach this shiny boulevard you explore these days with Sara.

As for J.D. Hamilton? You've bedded his wife and

daughter. In the past, no doubt, some men were killed for less. You smirk when you think this thought—it's a bad movie script after all—but hidden within the smirk is a glimmer of true apprehension.

Sara feels this delicate fear. She thinks her father loves her too much. One night she admitted she's shuddered at times during one of his embraces. "I don't know why," she said. "It's just something that I do. What makes us wish our fathers wouldn't hug us the way they do?"

You have no answer for this. Men puzzle you anyway, because you're a man yourself. You have no answers for Sara that will not offer up a slice of your secret soul, the one you try to keep hidden from her love.

She doesn't bring Tony Pirelli, her estranged husband, up as much. She maintains he'll come around as she moves towards divorce.

"It's my father who wants me to stay with Tony," Sara has said. "Tony, he keeps telling me, is the son he never had. What I can't figure out is why I have to be married to a man my father believes is a stand-in for a brother."

"You make it sound like incest," you replied. "It's just that people have their own values. J.D. wants everything to go on after he's passed away. He's told me so himself."

"Values?" Sara snorted. "Look around you, Kovacs. I don't see much in the way of values anywhere. I just see people fighting it out for control. The more they control the better. Amassing wealth isn't enough any longer. You've got to amass millions of human souls. You have to micromanage the entire species."

You're never certain what Sara actually means on those occasions when she is harping about what's wrong with the world. And she's the first to admit she doesn't explain it well.

"I just think we're all a little lost, Kovacs," she says. "Even you and me."

"I don't feel lost," you counter.

"That's the trouble with being lost, at least in the larger sense," Sara replies. "When you don't know you're lost, when you can't understand what's missing, all that shows you is how deeply lost you actually are."

But Sara's abstractions are too vague for you. Although you've never suggested this to her, you remain convinced what Sara needs to do is lower her expectations. She's not ready yet to embrace the harsh realities of a world that has discarded its illusions.

SARA HANDS YOU A LONG, NARROW BOX wrapped in silver paper after you've ordered dinner, passing it across the tiny restaurant table. "I bought something for you," she says, "because you're going away."

Sara often gives you things—you wear them on your body, find shelves or tables in your apartment to set them on. Watches, rings, shirts, jackets, bowls, statues, even paintings she finds occasionally on the beach, created by lost souls she forgives for being lost. You accept her gifts gratefully, although there was a time earlier in your affair when you felt inadequate, when you knew you couldn't compete with her on gifts because you lack the imagination. You said so at the time. "It isn't a matter of imagination," Sara argued. "When you feel the love, the imagination takes care of itself. It'll come, Kovacs, when you're ready."

You have grown grateful for her generous words. It's easier to bear feeling inadequate about what you seem unable to feel than it is to feel inadequate at your lack of generosity. So now you just feel grateful that Sara thinks of you so often and, when she does, she finds something beautiful to give you, reminding you how much she cares.

"I don't deserve you, Sara."

"I know," she replies this evening. "Just open the damn thing."

Nodding, you tear away the silver paper and take the lid from the box revealed underneath. You peel away some white tissue paper to uncover what is nestled incongruently inside it.

"Well?"

"It's beautiful," you say.

And it is.

It's a handmade hunting knife complete with a fine leather scabbard. The handle is made of bone; the rest of it is gleaming steel. There's a small whetstone tucked into a leather pouch sewn into the scabbard.

"Do you like it?"

"It's beautiful. A work of art."

"Aren't you going to take it out of the box?"

You glance around the crowded restaurant. This is America, forever on alert against terrorism, perpetually apprehensive. While it's just a hunting knife to be used in the near future, there are people all around you who might view it as a weapon you intend to use on them.

"Oh, c'mon," says Sara impatiently. "For a Canadian, you sure act American. I don't think anyone is going to confuse you with an enemy of the state."

You take the knife and scabbard out of the box. "Beautiful," you say. "What craftsmanship."

You take the knife out of the scabbard, casting one more quick glance around you to make certain what you're doing will not get you into trouble. But no one is looking in your direction. So you gently run your finger over the edge of the blade which has a hook in it.

"Don't cut yourself," warns Sara.

"Beautiful," you reply. "Does this mean you've changed your mind about me going on your father's hunting trip?"

"It means no such thing."

"Well, thank you, Sara. This means a lot to me."

She watches as you put the knife into the scabbard. She watches you place the works back into the box. You close the lid, setting the box on the edge of the table where the wrapping paper lies wrinkled.

"For all you know," you say, "you've just saved me from a grizzly bear."

Sara's expression grows stern. "Wrong thing to say, Kovacs, even in levity."

Sara has objected to this trip from the very beginning. You discussed it with her in bed in your penthouse the other night, naked and satiated, feeling important enough to one another to permit the infrequent afterglow of a minor argument. "Why would you fly way up to British Columbia to hunt big game? Why would you do it, Kovacs?"

"I was invited and I'm flattered. It's good for business. There'll be five of us. That's two more potential clients for a go-getter like me. Opportunities like these don't come along every day."

"But you don't hunt. You don't camp."

"I camped when I was a kid. I used to have the scouting badges to prove it."

"But with Tony and my father?"

"Why not?"

"Because it's dangerous."

"There'll be a guide."

"It's still dangerous."

You sighed. "They don't know about us. You've said so yourself."

"It's not that. It's not what's known about you and

me. It's just that you'll be with them. You'll be with Tony. Worse, you'll be with my father."

"Worse?"

"Yes! It's all too close, Kovacs. It's getting too close to people who are standing in our way."

You didn't know what to say to this last remark. She was right. It would be too close. In the end, though, she'd be wrong—when you and Sara parted, you knew it would be because of you. You could never be the permanent kind of man she wanted. Your proximity to two men who probably have always known what is best for her—on J.D. Hamilton's hunting vacation—wasn't going to make any difference in the end. This was business. You and Sara? Sara and Tony? J.D. and his legacy? All of these dynamic relationships would evolve in their appointed ways, hunting vacation or no hunting vacation. Life would transpire. Transpiring is what life does best. You wished, lying in the darkness, Sara would understand this as well as you did.

When she next spoke her voice had softened sadly. "Don't you feel awkward whenever you see Tony? Don't you feel a resentment?"

"I don't see Tony often."

"But when you do, don't you wish he didn't exist because of you and me?"

You grew cautious. "I guess so. But it's business, Sara. That's the part you don't understand."

"What about my father? You know he'll disown me, if he learns about us."

"Why would he do that?"

"Because you're not Tony. Because . . . I don't think I can explain it."

You said nothing to this. Family life is a little like incest, you thought. The rules of family life. You remembered this from your own past: family summits, the parameters that were established for you as a child back home in Kelowna, the way your parents determined the direction you must take to show your gratitude, your acquiescence, your sense of responsibility. These were your familial arrangements before the car crash that took their lives when you were eighteen, freeing you to choose the very direction in life they had already chosen for you. It is a little like incest, you decided, the family tree that is so knotted with each member's branches that, if one branch is weaving under a strain, all the others begin to shake in insecurity. In this way, the tree ends up so solidly unified people resist the impulse to take on life on their own terms, even after death has removed the obligation to give in.

"You still don't believe in us," Sara said, vacuuming up your silence with her doubts. "So Tony and my father aren't really in the way."

"It's early, Sara. We're new."

"You know something, Kovacs? I want to be a fly on a nearby wall the day you discover, the day you admit, how much you really love me. Because you do, Kovacs. You're just afraid to give in to it."

THE WAITER, AS HE MOVES YOUR GIFT ASIDE to make room for the dinners he carries in his other hand and precariously on his wrist, asks if it's your anniversary. Sara has gone to the bathroom and you must answer him on your own.

"Yes," you lie without thinking. "Five years ago today."

"Congratulations, Sir."

"Thank you."

"Will your wife be back soon?"

"We'd better wait and see."

"I'll take these back to keep them warm," the waiter says.

"Thank you," you say to his back as he whisks your

meals away.

You should put the box and the knife away somewhere because the table is very small, but Sara has taken her purse to the bathroom and the gift is too bulky for your jacket pocket. You've eaten in this restaurant before and you've mentioned the tables are rather small. But Sara likes the intimacy of this place and she likes the French cuisine. She likes the duck with peppercorns, ginger and apples that they serve here. You like the beef with mushrooms and white wine. The portions are as small as the table, but Sara, so slim and healthy, maintains Americans eat too much. Besides, here Sara nearly always pays. It's only fair she gets to make this choice for both of you when she's covering the tab.

When she returns from the bathroom, you ask her to put the knife in her purse. The waiter has been watching you from some station near the kitchen and he materializes a moment later with your meals.

"Congratulations, Madam," he says.

"Huh?"

"On your anniversary."

Sara glances at you a second, briefly dismayed. "Why thank you," she replies.

"He saw the box and the paper," you explain after the waiter has gone. "It seemed best to leave him with his conclusion."

Sara grins. "Wishful thinking on your part, Kovacs?"

"I guess so," you reply, not knowing what else to say.

SOMETIME DURING DINNER YOUR PASSION for one another builds the way it always has, displacing the awkwardness the impending hunting trip in British Columbia has created briefly between you. Your passion comes to life again as it so frequently does, in the urgent, provocative way you believe it should, your wanting of Sara, her wanting of you, between each of three glasses of red wine, the coffee and the dessert you shared with only one fork. You barely make it to your room before you are making love. While she is inserting the plastic key into the magnetic lock, you are pushing yourself against her from behind, your hands on her small breasts, your lips on her neck, your cock rubbing up against her buttocks.

Sara enjoys you when you want her this much and she laughs appreciatively at your sexual insistence. She manages the door handle despite your clutching and pushing at her, and you tumble into the room to fuck on the floor just inside the door. It's as wonderful as it always is. The grunting and compliments, the appreciative curses and groans. Making love this way, you are tempted to admit to your inner self that, yes, you love Sara Hamilton like crazy. You are even tempted to tell her so, to cross that line you've established for yourself about giving in on love. But your tongue is swollen from the sucking of her lips. The swelling makes it large enough to bite when you're tempted to say too much. In the end, as you always do, you remain silent. Perhaps another time, you tell yourself. Perhaps some other day you will tell her what, at this particular moment, seems to be the truth about love, and about her and love, the way Sara and love sometimes seem to be entities essential to one another.

IN YOUR DREAM THAT NIGHT, Sara is doing the driving on a dark country road somewhere else in time. Far away from the ocean, the Carmel fog nonetheless drifts in waves across the road, brought to this inland location far away from the sea by the creativity of your slumber. Here, the mist dances pagan rhythms inside the car's headlight beams. Even in the deep darkness inside her automobile, you admire how she drives. All it takes is the lights from the dash to show you what she can do when she's behind the wheel, even in the fog. It's all quite perfect in this dream. Sara drives. You watch and admire her, until you step out of the fog into her blazing headlights and you wake up with a grunt just before the BMW runs you down.

You are drenched with perspiration, although the hotel room is rather chilly. You are out of breath. You gasp into one clenched fist for a second or two to determine groggily whether you are still alive. Your heart pounds. You frantically inhale, trying desperately to breathe.

"Kovacs?" Sara's voice from the pillow a few inches from you sounds half asleep or half awake; you're not sure which. "Are you okay, Kovacs?"

Your throat is dry and sour. You can taste the remnants of wine and freewheeling sex inside your mouth. So your voice sounds cracked and hoarse when you whisper, "I'm okay."

She's silent for a long moment or two, as if she's gone back to sleep. You lie next to her, awash in perspiration.

Then.

"You'd better come back to me, Kovacs, after this stupid hunt."

"I will," you promise her.

"I love you, you sonofabitch."

"That helps me," you reply.

Sara soon goes back to sleep.

It's the delicate sound of her slumber, the gift that she's so near, that finally compels you to fall asleep as well. But you don't accomplish this until an hour or two have passed, until you have lain in the dark alone, twitching in the grasp of some gradually receding yet inexplicable fear.

THESIS

THE GRAY WOLF MOVES SOUTHWEST, downwards out of higher country. It is morning and the sun drifts over a horizon to the left rear of his shoulder, reaching him in tiny slivers refracted by distant Rocky Mountain peaks and stands of white and black spruce or jackpine. A few days ago, the wolf's large feet traversed miles of open alpine tundra where he caught and ate deer mice and jumping mice before lucking upon a marmot. This morning, though, his paws whisper over deep carpets of fallen coniferous needles now brown, rust or golden, as he works his way in a southerly direction.

He has begun his autumn molting and is scruffy in appearance. His thicker winter fur is coming in and the down he wore for the summer bursts out of his outer coat in white tufts light enough to float on the wind behind him, a delicate vapour trail catching on shrubs or tree branches in his wake. He is grey, black, white and brown, in patches or in combination. In a way, anachronistically, this concoction resembles the landscape of a beach rendered in miniature, someone's oil painting of a storm-tossed seashore—white breakers, gray sea, brown beach and black shadow. Strange to imagine this scene on the body of a wolf in this remote section of British Columbia many miles from the Pacific Ocean, strange but not difficult to manage.

His face is a blend of all these colours except for his muzzle where the greys and browns give way to a white snout and black nose with just a hint of beige etched across the top. Black lips cover his teeth, pink tongue dancing to the rhythm of his panting. His eyes—at times red, often brown, sometimes yellow or green in colour, depending on how the light hits them—are wary; although his eyesight is less than satisfactory, a flaw in his species. There are dark crevices originating in the corner of each eye as if he secretes an acid that burns a riverbed into the fur on his face as he weeps.

His sense of smell is keen, making up for what he tends to see in a blur. Scents arrive at his nostrils in currents and compounds, and he sorts them automatically. Earth scents, tree smells, the aroma of food in the air, the unsavory pungency of danger. Occasionally he stops at some other animal's stool to sort out details of its source, age or potential. He sniffs at mule deer or moose pellets, bear manure, sometimes even the less familiar droppings of a wood caribou or elk. At times he encounters the fur-twisted scat of his own kind, lying out in the open along a frequently travelled path. These deposits of animal waste tell him the story of when, what or why.

Smell is the wolf's morning newspaper; hearing is his radio bulletin. Sound and smell are utilitarian. They offer little delight or amusement, preferring to tell him only what he needs to know to survive. This morning, for instance, an early call by a killdeer implies all is as it should be. And he can smell no danger at this moment. Everything is satisfactory—there will be food further down the mountain and man, so potentially wicked most of the time, is out of range for the time being, some great mysterious distance away. He knows this because here in the woods he can detect sounds from four miles away. On the tundra, out in the open, it is ten miles.

This wolf is frequently alone and is therefore extremely practical. He is unchanged by ceremony or ritual, chooses to be aware only of what he needs to know to be ruggedly prepared, to continue to persist. A large wolf, more than one hundred and forty pounds, he is what humans call their practical survivors, "the strong and silent type."

Yet he has a genetic history in this remote section of the mountains in the northern interior of British Columbia. Relatives. Offspring: children, grandchildren, great-grandchildren and their mates. Sometimes, when he meets up with them, these other wolves remember his parenting and let him accompany them for a day or two of their wandering. In turn, he does not challenge them for a permanent place in their various packs, respecting their current hierarchy, content to be just a visitor. In human terms, he is like an uncle from a distant but neighboring town who drops by to share in the news and enjoy a meal or two while he's at it. Quiet and unobtrusive, he is the kind of uncle (if he was human) you'd find out on the porch in the twilight, smoking his pipe reflectively, responding to your remarks with affirmative nods or grunts, conveying that he has wisdom he is too shrewd to share—someone who makes you feel unexpectedly at peace, newly aware of things you haven't noticed recently even though they're always there. Or because they're always there.

This wolf descending from higher country mated

more than five years ago. For life. But his mate was shot by a poacher one day last year and he dimly recalls this event in continually dissolving fragments. His mate's sudden yip of pain, then her body rocketing up from the ground, twisting in the air, then falling twitching, shuddering and soon dead onto the forest floor. And he recalls the thunderclap of the shot, showing up a few seconds after the deadly bullet, late and breathless, a tragic afterthought.

Frightened by the roar of the echoing rifle shot, he darted into a wide crevice between some rocks, unknowingly unnoticed. Stealthily he fled down the side of the mountain, slipped into some trees, then evaporated into the deeper forest. Although there were no other shots and he never glimpsed the poachers, he didn't return to the body of his mate until well after dark, many hours later. And when he did return, he didn't get close. He discovered by smell, sniffing at the graphic currents of carnage, that the head and the tail were missing, removed by the poachers for bounty or trophy. Bits of other flesh had been eaten by coyotes, ravens, magpies and an assortment of other scavengers. He even detected the intrusion of one of his enemies, a wolverine, not just hungry, he suspected, but likely bent on some kind of glutinous revenge, a grudge as old as the Earth itself.

Ever since the day of his mate's death, he's been alone, evolving into a powerful, resourceful loner. Allies or friends, if he had any, would consider him noble, martyred, and wronged. But he doesn't have any friends, and nobility and martyrdom have no place in his consciousness. Most of the time he is alone, even among the packs he helped to sire, an unusual circumstance in the society of wolves.

He doesn't see many men in this rugged part of the

country. Highways are hundreds of miles away and he keeps to his territory here. Still, he crossed trails with some men one afternoon earlier this year, members of the Omenica Wildlife Patrol, although he didn't know who they were. As such, they didn't shoot at him. Instead, patrolling against poachers, one of them waved his hand. But the wolf didn't understand the greeting. Unnerved by the blurred suddenness of the gesture, he faded into some trees. Too aloof to bolt, he headed towards a place a few miles deeper inside his territory.

Territory is important in this section of the mountains; it is key to his survival. Here, where the wilderness is so much more remote than most areas of modern Canada, wildlife remains prolific—grizzly, black bear, wolf, coyote, wolverine, marten, beaver, muskrat, otter, lynx, mountain goats, cougar, infrequent wood caribou or elk, and, in places not far away, errant pockets of wild sheep clinging like the roots of desperate evergreens to the cold, ungiving rock.

Last night a cougar screamed in the distance and the wolf, realizing he had inadvertently encroached on the territory of a dangerous enemy, abruptly departed, jogging along for more than two hours to vacate the cougar's domain. He's heard the scream of a cougar often enough to recognize its phlegmy chorus of outrage. Big cats are frequently ill-tempered, their anger naturally built in. Their rage is so innate they do not need to nurse it. It goes with them everywhere.

The wolf was headed down to lower country anyway last night, vaguely aware of the need to be looking for beavers building lodges for the coming winter, in stream and pond capillaries draining down from a glacier heart now many miles away. He's seen the glacier only from a distance because he doesn't move up that high. But it's there just the same, large and craggy, melting in tints of light blue, pinned between the mountain peaks at a cold, secretive elevation he does not wish to visit.

This wolf has a stronger preference for beavers than most of his peers. Beavers are practical prey for a wolf who hunts on his own. Not as welcome as small deer or the rare baby moose he can take, they're so much more accessible, at least until winter comes. Although this wolf is rugged and strong, he must be an opportunist, eating the occasional red squirrel, pouncing on whatever he happens upon, caching for later what he doesn't need at the time of the kill. A few days ago, the heavens sullen with clouds, a small and tattered snowshoe hare fell like a gift to him, dropped by a gyrfalcon as it was climbing back into its medium overhead. He was on this unexpected boon quickly after it struck the earth. The gyrfalcon kept going despite its size, not challenging him for the prize, resigned to accepting this loss.

On the way down to where the beaver are, the wolf will even fish for trout if he happens on a shallow stream. As a fisher, this wolf is proud. He likes the way fishing tests his mettle and the speed of his head and jaws. When he was a yearling, half the joy in catching fish was in the skill that it required. His mother and father showed him how back then. Their lessons were seasoned with urgent warnings about those other dangerous fishermen, the unpredictable grizzly bears they encountered a couple of times, giants of the mountains who stumble so noisily and ferociously through the cracking, protesting woods.

This morning the wolf moves out of the trees into a rocky clearing. The sun, now positioned a little higher, parts a deeper cleft in the rocks and penetrates a stand of spruce to wash brightly along his body. The wolf has seen many other mountain mornings like this one and he appreciates their value. If he knew about death as a contrast to life, that someday he will surely die, he would feel glad to be alive on a morning such as this. Instead, some primeval instinct, some historic wisdom imbedded in his genes, merely tells him this morning isn't insane and he should be relieved. His days aren't marked by life or death. In human terms, they're defined by insane or not insane. Not insane is the easy relief that comes from living preciously; insanity is finding some desperate inevitability in dispensing or embracing death for some reason other than survival. He doesn't think about these things but he's aware of them just the same, instinctively cognizant of how dangerous insanity can actually be.

In other species he encounters, he feels such insanity rippling towards him like a pool. Rutting stags, quarrelling men. Even on a morning like this one by times, he feels its approach, a greedy, larger neurosis he can never comprehend, intruding, encroaching, pushing, taking, clutching. As it comes for him he knows he must retreat from it or eventually give in. He knows this even on a morning like this one, sun-drenched and breeze-caressed, filled with the comforting scents and sounds of his private wilderness life.

ELSEWHERE ABOUT THIS SAME TIME OF YEAR, three men at the edge of a small town several hundred miles away slip clumsily through the darkness towards Leo McKendrick's dog pen located twenty yards from his house. It is late, around four a.m., and the men hide inside the darkness which, having no density, falls away from itself like thinning mist. Potbellied, beard-stubbled and sweat-smelly, a fraternity of self-abuse, they are drunk, occupying a giddy, confused utopia between silly prank and booze-benumbed belligerence.

Although it's still summer, the night sighs with mountain chill. The men wear plaid flannel jackets and old ball caps so faded that the monikers etched on the front of them—slogans (Kill the Gun Registry), advertisements (Bud Light), calls to arms (No Fear)—evaporate in the weakened darkness, forgotten philosophy. Here, even so late or so early, the long, northern twilight is well known to all of them as merely dusk becoming dawn or dawn becoming dusk. They have lived all of their lives this far north. They are used to long days of stubborn light and long nights of unforgiving darkness, depending on the season.

Not far from McKendrick's place now, the men creep down a rutted gravel roadway, stumbling at times over unrepaired erosion, trying to remember to stay close to a long row of nearby poplars they can duck behind, in case someone with influence comes along and wants to know what they're doing, what it is they intend. Sometimes, nearly losing their grip on the plan they conceived of two hours ago, they come to a halt in the middle of the road, puzzled to be where they are, coughing or farting, lighting a cigarette and talking, drifting back and forth on an ocean of aimless giggle and conversation, not committed to much of anything, let alone the plan they can barely remember contriving even this close to their destination and the deed itself.

They pass a mickey of rye back and forth whenever they come to a halt in the middle of the road, wiping their mouths afterwards with their sleeves. Then they teeter there, listening to the clumsy sound of the bottle's owner rescrewing the cap.

"What're we doin' again?" the one with the bottle asks suddenly, peering at the gravel beneath his feet, then spitting at what he sees.

"Jeezus, George, you got shit for brains?"

They fall to chortling after this remark, George along with them—picking on George is a familiar practise—until one of them brings it to an end with loud shushing sounds that make them want to laugh even more.

"I just can't remember what we said," complains George hoarsely. "I don't know what the fuck we're doing." He holds the fragile mickey out from his body as he talks, tenderly, distantly aware that it contains the hopeful menace of some kind of genie.

"Leo's dogs. We're gonna set Leo's dogs loose."

"Why?"

"Jesus H. Christ! Because we said that's what we're gonna do, that's why."

"But how come? I forget."

For the moment, no one answers him. One of the men, the largest of the three, moves off a couple of yards and is soon heard pissing into the ditch, his legs spread very wide to help him keep his balance. He urinates so powerfully his stream cascades against the dirt on the other side, silencing the other men, filling them with a vague awe they've occasionally discussed whenever the conversation has turned reverently to the topic of pissing. The pissing champion's name is Norm and the other men look up to him—he's married and big and stubborn, and neither one of them can piss with even half as much force.

"Because he's a fucking prick, George," Norm says eventually as he turns and zips up the front of his jeans. "You remember that much. And you remember what he said, don't you?"

"I guess so," George replies, unscrewing the cap on his bottle again.

The jug goes around once more and is drained.

George tosses it into the ditch and, to their astonishment, it explodes on a rock.

"Sssh," says the big man shortly, after he has recovered from his dismay. "Jesus, George."

"Maybe we should just go home. You know?"

But they remain where they are in a careless triangle at the side of the road, weaving and chuckling about what a bastard Leo can be even though sometimes he's their friend.

Hours ago, an eternity now, he sat with them at their table in The Belmont Tavern, drinking beer. He was in one of his moods and, at some point before last call, he told all three of them they were assholes—like he was bringing down a judgment after reviewing evidence. They can't remember why. That said, he abruptly left to go home and sleep it off. Later, after closing time, about the time they got to drinking the new mickey they'd found in George's glove compartment, they began to feel bruised about being called assholes by someone like Leo McKendrick and they decided to free Leo's dogs just to teach him a lesson, even knowing, as George calmly pointed out, that they'd probably only end up helping Leo round them up again.

"Maybe we will and maybe we won't," said Norm, the man behind the scheme who, while he was thinking of it, felt an unpleasant guilt about the wife waiting for him to come home, which only made him as irritable as Leo had been at The Belmont.

"We probably will, you know," George says now, out of the blue, dizzy and leaning easterly in the middle of the road.

"What? We'll do what?"

"We'll probably end up helping Leo find his fucking dogs."

"C'mon," says Norm. "Let's go. A deal is a deal."

"Yeah, c'mon," echoes Jack, Norm's cousin. "It'll be dawn before you know it."

They begin to stumble down the road again, now not far away from Leo's cabin.

When they get there the cabin is dark, turned gray in its twilight valley setting, like the wilderness around it is sucking it home, drawing it back into the woods where it must have initially been conceived. One of Leo's dogs, his only hound, attempts to sound an alarm but its hiccoughy barks are more like a pleasant yodel than a snarl of menace; shortly, as if embarrassed by its own mournful song, it falls silent. Most of the other dogs are huskies watered down by casual parenting with various other breeds. None of these are watchdogs and they whine and wag their tails, not knowing what else to do. Besides, the men stumbling towards them aren't strangers. If the dogs feel any apprehension, it's only because the three men, weaving, whispering and shushing one another, are drunk and unpredictable.

"Jesus, Leo," Norm whispers as they draw close to the dogs.

And he's right. The stench of dog shit from the large pen is nearly overpowering.

"Fucking Christ!"

Gasping and holding their breath, cursing at the smell, Norm and Jack open the pen, slipping two catches at the top and the bottom of the gate. A hinge squeaks as the gate swivels in their direction.

"Sssh," rasps George nervously.

The dogs don't move, perplexed by the darkness, the strange mood of the men and the unexpected riddle of the open door. Instead they fidget inside the pen, gazing at the intruders, tails wagging cautiously, some of them yawning nervously.

"Jesus," says Norm, squinting at the dogs, shaking his

head in disgust. "Just like Leo. Dumber 'n' a bag of rocks."

His friends stifle their mirth. They've heard this metaphor before but they still laugh whenever Norm retrieves it from his repertoire of sayings.

"Whadda we do now?" asks George when no one moves for a time.

But as usual no one answers him. The long ceremony of motionlessness between the men and dogs stretches out like a woebegone wake.

"It smells like shit 'round here," George remarks at last just so something is said.

"It is shit, you asshole."

Without explanation, Norm stumbles inside the pen, startling one of the huskies that then begins to growl. Annoyed, Norm picks him out of the group, concluding it's the dog Leo sometimes brags about because he's convinced it has wolf in its blood. Leo shoots wolves whenever he can, Norm knows, yet brags about the one dog in his possession he believes could have wolf nestled somewhere in its genealogy.

"Asshole," mutters Norm, moving deeper inside the pen with the dogs.

The growling dog snaps at him ambivalently, but Norm just kicks it in the ass. Its snarl, more for show than anything else, gives way instantly to an injured yelp.

Losing interest in this escapade, indeed in this entire night, Norm turns away and exits the pen. He's sure he's stepped in dog shit by now and this has annoyed him further, especially since the stench here is so overpowering he cannot tell for sure.

"C'mon," he says, "let's go. The dogs 're too dumb to bolt."

They decide to leave the gate open, however, to make their expedition worthwhile: Norm's idea. "I'm all pissed off," he says by way of explanation.

"How come Leo keeps so many dogs?" George asks

later, as they stumble down the road towards town and the spot on its outskirts where Norm has parked his truck. "I've always wondered about that."

"Fucked if I know. Maybe he's not originally from these parts. Maybe he eats the fucking things."

This sets them to laughing again, although their glee grows melancholy with fatigue and impatience. Their mirth owns a drifting quality—like the rest of this ordinary night, moving the way it does in the general direction of dawn.

Back at Leo McKendrick's place, however, now that the men have gone, some of the dogs slip cautiously out of the pen. Eventually they wander in twos or threes across an adjacent meadow and through a patch of woods towards town.

A HEAVY RAIN BEGINS TO FALL later that morning, squeezed from a group of insolent clouds caught like cotton batten on the summits of some nearby mountains. The rain will persist for much of the day, the falling temperatures concocting a lazy mist along the ground before gradually rising to become a cold fog. When Leo McKendrick steps out on his cabin porch to take his first look at the day this morning, his ragged breaths take momentary shape like fragile, white, cartoon balloons inside the damp chill in front of his face.

Shortly, when he goes to feed his dogs, he discovers only three of them remain, curled up on mud or shit-splattered rugs scattered around the pen, their wet fur adding to the stench he knows he should soon clean up. Leo sets down the pail of Purina and utters a vicious invective when he notices the open gate. He stands there for several minutes, the steel pail on the ground beside him, gazing in each direction, ignoring the whines of the remaining dogs hungry for their breakfast. But he sees nothing in the distance except a soaring golden eagle that glides so quickly out of the mist it looks for a moment like an approaching dragon. Mesmerized, he doesn't bother to whistle for his missing dogs until the eagle soars into the clouds again, vanishing inside the gray milk of the day. He whistles then through his teeth so that the sound is needle sharp. But it's a futile exercise. He can only hope some of the dogs will return of their own accord. It's too much for him to expect all of them will come back.

He refastens the gate after he has fed his dogs, then climbs into his pickup truck to head for town to report the incident to the RCMP.

"Kids, I expect," he tells the tall corporal at the counter.

"Yeah, probably."

"Fuckers need their asses tanned."

"No doubt about it," admits the corporal, so fair and clean-shaven he looks to Leo like a child himself.

There isn't much the Mountie can do except have Leo fill out a report. He mentions, though, that he'll alert the other officers in his detachment. He suggests, it being Sunday and Leo isn't working, that Leo take a drive around town to see how many he can find himself.

"And when you get them back? Buy a padlock," suggests the corporal, remembering to squint down at the other man from some great respectable height it is important he maintain.

McKendrick swears under his breath again. "I shouldn't have to, you know. If people would just leave other people be . . . ."

By the time he reaches home, three of his dogs have returned in the rain. He puts them in the pen and locks both catches with two padlocks he's grudgingly purchased while in town. He enters his cabin and eats lunch, some cold stew he spoons out of a heavy steel pot he takes directly out of the refrigerator. Then, in a foul mood, the stew trapped in a tender nook at the top of his belly, he climbs back into his truck to begin searching for his dogs.

Later that afternoon, during an intermission in the rain, he notices George Sackienkawicz on the main street, not far from the barber shop, so he pulls over and leaps out of the cab to say hello to him.

"Jesus, George, you look like shit," he remarks by way of greeting.

George, sometimes nicknamed The Sack, won't look him in the eye, certain he's done something to wrong this man, but too hung over and bleak for the moment to remember what it is.

"What time did you get home last night?"

"I don't know," George manages to reply.

No longer interested in whatever's ailing George, Leo spits on the sidewalk. "Someone opened my dog pen last night. Most of my dogs are gone."

George gapes at him, nearly stumbling with the force of his recollection as most of last night's shenanigans surge into his memory. Right away he's tempted to confess because he feels so stupid and vulnerable, so needful of punishment, so angry that he took part in the whims of his accomplices. Norm and Jack, fucking assholes. Some people shouldn't drink. Why, he wonders now, does he listen to those bastards?

"Kids, I guess," offers Leo, aborting George's confession. "I've locked the fucker up. I see anyone around that pen and they'll get a butt full of buckshot."

Solemnly George nods, fully aware that last night the buckshot might have found him or Norm or Jack.

"Wanna help me drive around and pick up some of my dogs?"

"Yeah, uh, sure."

"Might clear your head."

"Yeah, it might," concedes George, although somehow he doubts it.

They only find three dogs by dinner time. There are nine still unaccounted for. Leo's in such a temper by the time he drops George off in the vicinity of his truck, George is deeply relieved to escape the afternoon unscathed.

THREE OF THE MISSING NINE DOGS, hungry and tired, find their way home before midnight's twilight falls. The others remain at large. Leo's favourite has assumed command. In truth, there's not much wolf in him—the little bit there is is four or five generations removed—but he's strong and punitive and finds something sporting in his need to be briefly wild and free. By the end of the day, he's nipped, bitten and bullied the remaining dogs into following him anywhere. The collection of followers is less a pack than a gang, something obsequious and stupid that believes in nothing but everything.

Still later that night, under the cover of darkness, the lead dog guides them to an inadequate homemade dumpster at the end of the driveway behind Ben's Burgers. It's overflowing again with french fries and rancid meat, with half-eaten hot-dogs and moldy rolls. The dogs feed themselves on what has fallen to the ground, beating area skunks, wood rats or bears to the banquet, quarrelling and arguing as they eat, gradually bullying one another into a structural hierarchy that makes them feel secure. After they've eaten all they can find, they follow their new leader on a haphazard course out of town, heading north towards the mountains, some of the most remote in the Omenica range.

Before they enter the forest, they encounter a

female Collie-German Shepherd mix out on her own lark. She's strayed from a neighbouring, soil-starved farm after managing to slip her collar. A nasty fight takes place between the bitch and the husky leader. Blood is drawn from cuts on the Collie's neck and belly and from a minor abrasion on the husky's nose. But the quarrel is soon over and, as far as the other dogs are concerned, has established the rules and framework for their new feral pack. The dogs are roughly structured by size and the smaller ones in the pack are grateful that they have an alpha male and female to guide them into their imminent future.

Now the ragtag pack departs for the forest and the distant, formidable mountains where they can set about their business of becoming desperate, hateful and mean—all they can really be in view of their previous domesticity. Soon they begin to grow truly hungry. By the time the next day's morning light sneaks through the wilderness mountain peaks, burping out of an eastern sky of gathering clouds, the town where the pack was born lies several miles behind them. Lost, the dogs travel in ever-widening circles in the deep and rugged wilderness. In time, the wilderness will be disrupted and appalled by the violation of their intrusion.

THOUSANDS OF MILES FURTHER SOUTH, two men keep an appointment in a restaurant in a metropolis someone once believed should be called the City of Angels. Before the smog and clutter, before the myths and disappointments, before the bath of human congestion transformed it into L.A.

The younger of the two men, Eddy Knox, stands up politely as a balding headwaiter escorts his associate towards the table. The older man, John Hamilton, dismisses the waiter with an impatient wave of his arm when he is still a few feet away. Knox offers his hand for a handshake.

Hamilton hesitates for a second before grudgingly accepting it. Nothing against Knox actually, just an assortment of other complaints—the stench of downtown outside, the noise of the restaurant, an ache in his belly and some vague notion, considering the nature of their business, that shaking hands is inappropriate. Hamilton is sure, once their arrangement is successfully concluded, they won't want to admit ever knowing one another. They will someday pass each other by without acknowledgment on the street, relieved and gratified their brief association is over.

But Knox needs to shake hands, is even adamant about it. If someone is watching them at this moment, even with only idle curiosity, they'll remember the two men shaking hands and forget to speculate about whom they might otherwise have been or what they might otherwise have been up to. Knox finds normalcy useful, drawing it like a drape across his window. Ordinariness is discreet, a device he hides behind. He works at blending into life, at being invisible. He prefers when no one remembers him or whether he was actually there or not. Knox isn't mostly professional. No, he's always professional.

"Nice to see you again, John," he says as the two men take their seats.

"Nice to see you too," Hamilton replies, not knowing what else to say, not as accomplished as Knox at all this obtuse choreography.

Knox smiles. He knows about the various components of intrigue that Hamilton does not and why it would be pointless to explain them. The handshake, businessman to businessman, a meeting in a restaurant, two men making a deal. The ceremony and accolade in entrepreneurship is to appear as unquestionable and forgettable as the common cold or the planet's ability to spin. The conservative suits they wear, made to measure, their silk ties, their snake skins of success, all of these are to paint a stereotypical portrait. Hamilton doesn't know he lives inside these small clichés, but Knox does. Knox uses and manipulates them inside a larger stereotype, the one he has learned defines modern life. As a professional, Knox has worked with ideologues for his entire career. As a professional, he serves their needs. He feels superior embracing ideology but knowing it for what it is. He knows what Hamilton will never know, that ideology means never having to think too much or too deeply. Knox is an unusual man because even knowing ideology for what it is, he feels no need to rebel against it.

"Come by limo, John?" he asks now that they are seated.

Solemnly the older man nods. "I don't like downtown. It stinks. Each time I see it again, I realize it's only getting worse."

"You have higher expectations, John."

"Yeah, maybe I do. If you ask me, some day we'll have to come in here and bulldoze most of it flat. Maybe we can start over again, hanging onto what we build. No bending the rules this time. No letting things slide. Know what I mean?"

Knox nods. "Technology's the answer, John. The things that used to get away from us, well, we can control them now. This time, when we start fresh, we'll be able to manage the result."

"Trouble is, at my age, I'll never live to see it."

"I wouldn't be too sure about that, John. We've come pretty far in a short time. Technology these days has enough power to make you dizzy."

Vaguely Hamilton nods. He glances a few tables

away to where a man in a business suit much like his own contemplates a laptop on his table, reaching over his meal with dancing fingers to tap out some apparently urgent business. Technology in this setting isn't something Hamilton can respect. Here it's just fodder for his deep, unending distaste.

In the silence, Knox fingers a laminated menu on the table in front of him. He decided before Hamilton arrived what he was going to eat and his dark, decisive eyes carefully appraise his companion. It's mostly an exercise. He already knows so much. But his eyes are trained to observe and motivate, to compel or demand respect. In a few moments, when he glances at a waiter for service, the waiter will respond quickly without knowing why he must, feeling a vague fear perhaps or an urge to surrender to the cold imperative of Knox's eyes. Caught in Knox's authoritative gaze, he will feel a comfortable familiarity in being under someone's control again. Used to manipulation. Used to everything required by modern convention.

Knox's air of authority is part training and part gift. Pushing forty, he is now experienced at utilizing unusual skills. Only five-foot-eight, for instance, by the time he leaves this restaurant anyone remembering him will have decided that he was tall. It's a trick he's employed for years. There are people with whom he works, he's heard, who refer to him as The Chameleon. Although Knox is essentially egoless, he's still flattered somewhat by the nickname.

For his part, still glancing around the premises, Hamilton doesn't bother to conceal his disdain. The restaurant is pretentious and noisy, imitation European with white stucco walls divided here and there by slats of dark varnished wood. The tablecloths, white and too large for the tables, bunch up at times as they catch at people's knees. The flowers, collected in tinted vases in the centres of the tables are gaudy, even by California standards, so real and odorless they could be made of plastic. There's a print of the Last Supper on a wall in the distance and, to Hamilton, it's vaguely tasteless in this setting, sacrilegious, although he's a man with no serious religious affiliation or interest. Bronze plates, bowls and platters decorate precarious wooden shelves in, shadowy nooks. The restaurant is overdone, shallow, noisy and cluttered, ultimately banal.

This is West 7th Street not far from where it intersects with Wilshire Boulevard. Hamilton isn't sure how far away it is from the sector of deep decay, perpetual violence or hopeless human reproduction he believes downtown has become, but no matter how far it is, he's sure it's much too close. Spics, Blacks, Asians and half-breeds, what's happened to his city? It's like looking through a window you haven't maintained in years, only to discover it smeared with so much fly-shit you might never get it clean. Easier to avoid downtown altogether, skirting the helpless rage and deep disappointment he feels here and, in a politically correct sense, can't explain to anyone.

Still, he understands Knox's reasoning in meeting him in this place—the tables are well-spaced, a good distance from one another, and the clatter of dishes and rumble of voices is loud and indecipherable, so loud that even a brown carpet beneath his feet, decorated with fraying beige diamonds, cannot buffer it. What he and Knox discuss will not be heard; it will dissolve inside the restaurant's cacophony of noise.

"I was in the mood for Italian," Knox has been saying. "And being as you're paying . . ." He smiles enigmatically as a waiter approaches them.

Hamilton merely grunts. Everything has a price,

especially the things that he needs done, and dinner in a restaurant like this is chicken feed. He'll be out of here eventually for only a few hundred dollars, a pittance for a man of his astounding wealth.

The waiter's accent is Latino rather than Italian and his report on available wines is so earnestly performed it's comical. Hamilton despises superficiality. Everything wrong with this restaurant is what's wrong with America. Too many average people not knowing they're average, not even conceiving of the possibility. Enough money to eat in this dive and they think they've had a night out, not noticing the shabby Mexican waiter in a pretentious Italian restaurant on the fringes of a decayed downtown. Hamilton hates the middle class, believing it is too large. No one knows their place any longer. No one knows the fucking Difference between what is and isn't real, what can and can't be changed. The Difference has disappeared and the race is on to reach the bottom. America was built on initiative, he believes, the kind of initiative only a select few actually possess. In recent years, the talentless have forgotten that those with talent are Different from them. No wonder Difference continues to die. And, for God's sake, there has to be a Difference.

"John?"

"Sorry. What'd you say?"

"I asked if you wanted Red. Good for the cholesterol."

"Red's fine, but it has to be American, okay?"

"American it is," Knox says, turning to the waiter. "The Coppola then," he says. "And I think we're ready to order."

Hamilton remembers to open his menu. The glare of its lamination virtually explodes and he squints. In the background he hears Knox order Insalata di Calamara and Filetta Napolitano in respectable Italian. "Rare," adds Knox in American before the waiter can pose the question.

"The artichoke palm salad," Hamilton says gruffly as soon as the waiter turns to him. He'll have to push the radishes it comes with off to the side, knowing they'll be too hot in the already smouldering volcano his stomach has become.

"Your entrée, Sir?"

"The salmon. Bring me the salmon."

"Salmone Peperonata. Very good, Sir."

Hamilton watches the waiter depart, hating the little bastard for trying to be something he's not, whatever the hell it is.

KNOX STUDIES HAMILTON AS HE SULKS across the table from him. The wealthy industrialist is twenty years older than he is but is the taller man. Knox notes his jowly cheeks and jaw, wondering if Hamilton is too old, too out of shape for what he himself has proposed. Although he reported at their first meeting that he works out two or three times a week in a gym in his house, Knox has noticed a bit of a paunch in the older man that he should be concerned about. Then again, nearly sixty, Hamilton's belly could just be age winning out over exercise the way time wins out over life itself. Knox has considered the irony it would represent if Hamilton did not possess the stamina to take part in his own scheme. Then again, there's the factor of his hatred. Hamilton may feel it deeply enough to survive his proposed adventure despite his lack of physical conditioning.

"I know what you're thinking," says Hamilton with a gentle flush. "You're wondering if I can pass muster."

"The least of our problems, John, on a project like this."

"Well, if it was easy, it probably wouldn't be worth it."

Knox ignores the other man's painfully facile conclusion. "I took a look at your dossier, John," he remarks instead.

"My dossier? Of course."

Dossier is one of those words Hamilton hears in a worshipful echo. It makes him feel important; he can dance to its hissing syllables.

"You don't seem surprised that you have a dossier."

"Of course not," Hamilton snaps. "The Pentagon, NASA, they're my primary customers. I manufacture sophisticated components. I'd be appalled if there wasn't a dossier. This is my country, Knox. I can afford to be in a dossier if it furthers America's interests."

Knox nods, believing him.

"Look," says Hamilton then with clumsy directness. "There's only one thing I want to know: are you going to do it?"

For the moment, Knox ignores the question. "The point is, the high tech stuff you make—most of it is classified. Which makes you an important man. You've come a long way, John, building a company like this from the ground up."

Hamilton frowns impatiently.

"I only mention this with respect to your immunity. I just want you to know it's there, up to a point, at any rate."

"That's a good thing, isn't it?"

"Of course. But immunity isn't license. Immunity has its limitations."

"No doubt," says Hamilton wearily. "But I have a life to lead. What else does a man have to uphold, if not his personal principles? I get to take matters into my own hands when it's unavoidable, don't I? Life, liberty and the pursuit of satisfaction. It's only protecting what's mine in the end, isn't it?"

"As long as you remember to use your head."

"What about your immunity, Knox?"

"I have some," the other man replies. "But in many

ways this whole escapade is more dangerous for me than it is for you."

Hamilton considers this a moment, succumbing to a trace of curiosity. "This kind of thing is moonlighting for you, isn't it?"

"I suppose you could look at it that way."

"What's your day job? CIA? NSA? Seals?"

Knox doesn't answer him, knowing he doesn't have to.

"It doesn't matter," Hamilton says. "The less I know the better. Ignorance is bliss."

Knox nods his head.

Privately, Hamilton would bet the farm on military. It's Knox's crewcut, dark brown but peppered with premature gray, and something else about the way he carries himself, rigid, upright, parade-ground straight. But you never know with Knox. What is real? What's performance? Knox is the consummate actor and could be playing a part right now. Cryptically cryptic, Knox is less a man than a book of shifting codes. You can't get to the core of him. The codes just change into something else and you end up lost again.

"The people you work for, they don't mind, do they? They don't object if you freelance, do they?"

"Not really," replies Knox. "It keeps our skills sharp. And they know it satisfies our entrepreneurial needs. Usually the services we dispatch are focused on people no one will miss. It's a crowded planet. Globalization. You'd be amazed how many people in this world are simply in the way."

"I suppose," admits Hamilton vaguely.

"Now," adds Knox, "if I were to take on your project and fail, I'm sure my superiors would mind. As long as I work within the rules and I don't fail. . ."

"How can it fail?"

". . . then everything will be fine."

They fall silent as the waiter brings their wine and fills their glasses. Both of them watch him depart until he's out of earshot. Neither man reaches for his goblet: neither proposes even an insignificant toast.

"YOU HAVEN'T ANSWERED MY QUESTION," Hamilton says shortly.

"What question?"

"I asked you if you're going to do it. That's what I want to know. That's why we're having dinner in this crappy restaurant."

"I know," replies Knox. "I was coming to that." He takes his first sip of wine. "I have a number of concerns, of course."

"Okay, I'm listening. Concerns are good. Better to deal with them now."

"This guy, Kovacs, for instance."

"What about him?"

"Well Jesus, John, he isn't important. He's nobody. I mean, as nobodies go, he's even further down the food chain than most. He doesn't seem worth sanctioning at all." Knox shrugs. "Notwithstanding your personal feelings, of course."

"The fact he's nobody is an advantage, as far as I'm concerned."

"Yeah, maybe. But I keep coming back to him being a Canadian."

"Living in America by our good graces," barks Hamilton.

"My point is, you want to do this thing in Canada, don't you?"

"It's the perfect place."

"Canada's a sovereign country. It complicates things."

"Christ!" says Hamilton then, his hands fidgeting on the table, his wine still untouched. "Don't worry about

Canada. We own those fuckers now. Immunity here is immunity there."

"I know, I know," Knox says, although he isn't entirely convinced.

"Money talks. It always has," Hamilton adds.

But Knox holds up his hand, partly to avoid the possibility of a victory speech and partly because the waiter is on his way towards them, carrying their first course.

Hamilton grunts, not liking to be silenced.

"Artichoke Heart of Palm Salad," the Mexican recites with an exaggerated flourish, setting the plate in front of Hamilton. "Insalata di Calamara," he adds as he serves Knox. "Enjoy your appetizers, gentlemen."

Hamilton sighs. He feels a bitter acid in the pit of his stomach as he slowly reaches for his fork. God, maybe he should see a doctor, except he hates doctors. They intrude on his privacy in a way he cannot tolerate. Knox is hungry, he notices. Knox doesn't have stomach problems. He isn't that kind of man. Inhuman bastard, he concludes.

They eat in silence for a moment or two while Hamilton suffers—the black olives too salty, the radishes, as he expected, unpalatable. It occurs to him that he should have had the squid, like Knox. Abruptly he pushes his plate away.

"What else about Kovacs?" he asks impatiently as the other man continues to eat.

"British Columbia, where you want to do this thing. It's his home turf, John."

"Maybe technically. But he's no mountain man. City slicker. Weakling. Whaddyuh call that place he's from?"

"The Okanagan Valley. Kelowna," Knox replies, dabbing at his lips with his napkin.

"Well there you go. If he knows anything about the wilderness, it's from standing on a street corner and seeing it in the distance. Christ, they grow grapes there. Just about burned down a couple of years ago. Forest fires. But it's civilized."

Knox merely nods.

"And don't forget he has no family. His parents are dead, no brothers or sisters."

"I know. No next of kin."

"Look, just for the record, Knox, I know why you're going over all this crap again. I know what you're trying to do. You don't want to leave anything to chance. I respect that. I approve. I wouldn't have it any other way."

"Well," says Knox. "Under the circumstances. I'd rather he was Jane than Tarzan. That's what I'm driving at."

"He's no fucking Tarzan, that's for sure."

Knox attacks his squid in silence.

"I've given this a lot more thought than you think I have, you know," Hamilton reminds him.

"I'm sure you have, John."

The waiter arrives to take their plates. "How were your appetizers, gentlemen?" he asks.

"Fine," replies Knox.

Hamilton merely grunts at the man's intrusion.

For his part, Knox finds himself hoping the waiter won't remember them through the conduit of Hamilton's rudeness.

The waiter soon returns, presenting them with their entrees with an even more exaggerated flourish— Salmone Peperonata and Filetta Napolitano.

Hamilton scowls, gazing unhappily at his plate while Knox regards him carefully, weighing several significant pros and cons.

"PERHAPS IT'S STILL A MATTER OF MOTIVE," says Knox eventually.

"It you mean mine, my motive, I've explained all

that to you."

"Well you're going to have to tell me again," the other man says, cutting a medallion of filet mignon in half with the delicacy of a surgeon. "I mean, it's not like he ran off with a couple of your many hundreds of millions, John."

Hamilton detests glibness, especially from a professional like Knox. He glares at the man across from him before he considers how to reply.

"If it was only a matter of money, it would be so much simpler." This observation emerges quietly philosophical, not flat exactly, but softly, like the beginning of a forty-five minute session with a psychiatrist. Hamilton sighs. "It's much worse than money, which is the point for me. You see?"

Knox gazes at him in silence. Vaguely he is aware he should feel compassion for the other man, yet it doesn't bother him that he is incapable of the feeling.

Sadness makes Hamilton angry. Hardly is he done moping about the injustice that has been done to him when his rage—familiar, expected, yet somehow still a bit of a surprise—flares up again. It takes but a second to achieve its maximum intensity and passion. Much of this anger is felt because he knows he cannot make Knox understand him, that Knox cannot comprehend why he hates you the way he does. Hamilton believes his emotions and frustrations exist beyond any need for justification; his familiarity with these feelings has made them sacrosanct. But he needs Knox to work for him, to bring the pain to an end. To convince Knox to do so, Hamilton swallows his pride and begins to explain the history again.

"Marjorie met him," he explains. "He sells funds and investments, a glorified life insurance salesman. Like I told you before."

Knox nods.

"Always has his nose up someone's ass, looking for a sale. You know the type. Kovacs is one of those. I first met him at one of Marjorie's parties. I realized right away what kind of man he is."

"Marjorie's your wife."

"Yes, my wife. I don't imagine she was still sleeping with Kovacs at the time. Maybe that was over by then. I don't know. Frankly, it doesn't matter. Marjorie's not the point."

A cell phone at the table nearest them rings loudly and both men turn to it, briefly mesmerized by the sound, as if perhaps one of them should answer it. But a woman in a tailored suit reaches into her purse and extracts the device, hunching her shoulders as she responds, seeking privacy. Hamilton, uncomfortable with some of the things he has been preparing to confess, glares at her briefly. Her telephone has made her seem more real, more relevant somehow than he can ever be. It's just a feeling of ghostliness—it isn't real—but he hates it anyway. Sometimes, when he is tired and worried, he becomes suspicious that he's only imagined himself, that something about his life makes him feel self-invented. Knox inspires this feeling sometimes. How can an underling convey that he's more real than the man who wants to purchase him?

"Go on," says Knox coldly, as if he's been reading Hamilton's mind. "Tell me about Marjorie."

"What about her?"

"You're saying she had an affair with Kovacs?"

"Yes. But I also said it's not the point. It has nothing to do with anything. You see, Marjorie and I have an understanding in our marriage. It's evolved, you see. We take an open approach to sex outside the marriage. We've never talked about it, but we both accept it. It's just the boredom a lot of people won't admit defines their marriage." Hamilton reflects on this a moment. "She was young when we met, about thirty years ago. She got pregnant. I married her. I think marriage is just being mesmerized by tits and ass, Knox, if I'm not being too blunt. It happens to a lot of men. It's just another system people put in place, you know? Hard to know if we really fall in love or just have romantic relationships because we're supposed to."

Knox nods, but only to placate the other man.

"Marjorie's well-preserved, still has some glamour left. She sleeps around. I let her. Kovacs was one of her flings. Right now I think it's her golf pro. She likes them young. Me? I don't give a fuck."

"Okay."

"But Sara? Sara's another matter. Sara's been special to me since the day she was born. From the beginning I've thought of her as the only true accomplishment I've ever achieved. Don't ask me why. I could never explain it. As bad as it sounds, I think of her as mine. She's my only child, my only daughter, and she's the key to my future, my immortality, I suppose. I won't apologize for loving my daughter, Knox. I'm not sorry I see her as the most important person in my life."

Now breathless, Hamilton takes a moment to scrutinize the man across from him. "Do you have kids, Knox?"

The other man shakes his head.

"Married?"

"No."

"So you've never loved someone so much you'd do anything to keep her happy, to protect her?"

"No."

It's a blunt response and Hamilton feels betrayed by it. He wishes Knox could share this common ground with him. As mutually emotional territory, it would form a pleasant basis for their agreement, a foundation on which to build the deal they're trying to make. But Knox seems not to possess the necessary feelings. It's a bitter disappointment.

"Are you telling me you've never loved a woman?"

"No time for it. Apparently not enough need either. I don't think I care for the mythology of it, John. As you said, is love actually felt or do we only suppose we should feel it?"

"I see," says Hamilton.

"My job is to explore the viability in your proposal," Knox explains carefully. "We don't have to understand or interpret the value of each other's life experiences."

"I suppose not."

"And just for the record," adds Knox, "I'm not queer, if that's what you were thinking."

Hamilton hasn't had time to consider Knox's sexual preferences. "No," he says, "I was just thinking I might envy you. No wasted feelings. No time wasted on people who let you down."

Knox ignores Hamilton's remark. He's never needed anyone's envy. Envy is a hollow egg. "Keep talking," he says.

The older man nods. "As long as I'm clear. Marjorie isn't a factor in this. Marjorie's discreet. She knows what butters her bread. Bottom line, all of this is about Sara."

HAMILTON FEELS LIKE HE IS CHOKING, like the hands of life itself have clutched him around the throat. He gasps for air, knowing it's the intensity of his rage. He can feel his hatred for you devouring him. He puts down his knife and fork, then pushes his plate away. He cannot eat, his belly will not let him.

Calmly Knox waits for him to recover. He's never endured this kind of pain himself. He eats in silence, savouring every bite, measuring out his enjoyment, controlling it, making it last. Perhaps this, he reflects, is what Hamilton should envy, the more commonplace pleasures a man can enjoy when he rises above any larger appetite that might ultimately destroy him.

Shortly the industrialist resumes his story. "Nearly fifteen years ago, I hired this wop kid straight out of MIT. Tony Pirelli. I liked his stuff. I liked him and his stuff. Gradually, over the years, he's become the son I never had. When he and Sara began to see one another six or seven years ago, I was delighted. Their relationship seemed predestined, like fate was anointing everything I'd done with my life. I was convinced Tony and Sara would continue on with what I've created for myself. I anticipated grandchildren. It was going to be perfect. You know what I mean?"

"A dynasty," suggests Knox.

"A dynasty and a family," modifies Hamilton. "Every piece in place. Something for me to leave behind, my mark on history."

"Okay."

"I remember the day they got married, Knox, like it was only last week. I sent them to Europe on their honeymoon. Everything first class." He would describe his happiness further—how Tony went home to Italy, to the place he'd left when he was three, how he'd been disappointed and then relieved that the connection with his roots no longer mattered much, how he came back an American once and for all, pleased to be who he was, any illusions about his heritage well behind him now, settled at last—but he feels a bolt of pain knowing none of this matters to Knox, beyond filing it away to maintain his professional advantage. "Nine months ago," he says with a sigh, "Sara left him, moved out. I couldn't believe it. Tony couldn't believe it either. Neither of us had seen it coming. She said she wasn't sure she loved him any longer, that she needed time to sort things out.

I pressed her about what kinds of things she meant, but she couldn't, or wouldn't, explain them to me. I was furious with her. It made no sense to me."

"Had she met Kovacs yet?"

"I don't know. It's possible. But I don't think so. You'd have to know Sara. Sara's not the kind to see another man while she was married. She's not the kind to have an extramarital affair."

"What makes you so sure?"

"I know my daughter, Knox. She wouldn't do that to me."

"Okay. I just wondered."

"Since then, Tony's been trying to win Sara back, of course. I've done everything I can to help him. I even hired someone at one point to keep an eye on her, to keep me fully informed."

"A firm?" asks Knox, his eyes narrowing.

"No. I brought in an old friend. He used to work for me in security before he retired out east."

"Where is he now?"

"Back in New Jersey."

Knox nods, mollified.

"I trust this man completely," Hamilton reassures him, "if that's what you're worried about."

"Okay."

"Anyway," continues Hamilton, "at some point during the separation, she began to see Kovacs and she was smart enough to hide the fact from me. She knows how I feel about Tony, what their marriage meant to me. She and Kovacs have been meeting on the sly ever since."

"Is she in love with him?"

"Only in her own mind," Hamilton snaps, resenting a cruelty he perceives in Knox's question. "Sara has a romantic streak. God help me, I used to encourage it. We make mistakes, Knox." Resisting the intervention of some painful emotional memories he doesn't want to recount, Hamilton scurries on. "Sara's naive. She hasn't always understood what's good for her. I suppose it makes her perfect prey for a man like Kovacs. I don't think she'd necessarily recognize that he's a loser, but she's too good for him. I have to make it clear to Sara. I have to look out for her best interests before it's too late."

"You haven't confronted her about Kovacs, have you?"

"No," says Hamilton with a vehement shake of his head. "I thought about confronting her but my instincts were to remain patient. I suppose I was already considering a more permanent solution to the problem."

"And you're absolutely sure she doesn't know you know about her and Kovacs? This is important, John. She has no idea?"

"None."

"What about Kovacs?"

"Not a chance. I still have him in my house occasionally. Business as usual."

"Do you think Kovacs is serious about her?"

Hamilton's eyes widen with horror then explode in fury. "Are you kiddin' me? Kovacs is a greedy little opportunist, a womanizing bastard. In love with Sara? Not a fucking chance. He's just found a way to claw his way inside everything I've built. He's just using her to push to the front of the line."

"Why haven't you bought him off then?" Knox dabs at his face with his napkin, his plate empty. He pauses. "Here comes the waiter. You want dessert, coffee?"

"Coffee," replies Hamilton miserably.

His belly continues to scream. His rage comes over him in waves, in spasms. He can't get used to it. For months now he's thought of little else, his disappointment in Sara and his hatred for the man she's sleeping with, you, a financial advisor, one of Marjorie's lousy castoffs. Hamilton feels it as humiliation. He feels like a giant nearly felled by the bite of a flea. It's not just that the flea is small, but that it has the temerity not to know it is small.

The waiter departs with his instructions, carrying away their plates, most of Hamilton's salmon, Knox's few surviving crumbs.

"I was asking why you haven't just bought him off."

"I considered it," admits Hamilton. "In the end I decided it was too uncertain. Scum like Kovacs? How could I be sure he wouldn't come back again, wanting more money? That's the thing about blackmail. Sometimes it never ends."

"What about setting him up? You know, another woman, a videotape showing him in a compromising position? Wouldn't this tell Sara what he really is?"

"It's the same problem. What if it doesn't work? What if he doesn't stay away? What if Sara forgives him? What if he doesn't take the bait? What if she resents that I took the liberty? Too many ifs. A man like me has to set aside his fundamental decency, sink to Kovacs' level to come up with the right solution."

"But setting him up could work, if Kovacs is what you say he is. He doesn't sound like the kind of man who turns down an opportunity, sexual or otherwise."

Hamilton sighs in exasperation, wondering if Knox is being spiteful, making a religion out of covering all the bases. He hates being tested this way. It just adds to his pain and fury.

"Look," he says at last. "As far as I'm concerned, Kovacs is a cancer, a tumor on my life. I mean, who the fuck does he think he is, seducing my daughter, tarnishing everything I've worked for? What do you do with an abscess like that? You lance it. Permanently. People like me, people with value, people who matter, with an important role to play, with so much to look forward to—what was it you said, people with immunity?—well, we have to take care of the weasels who sneak into our chicken coop." His voice drops to a hoarse whisper. "To put it bluntly, we have the right to kill them, don't we? Isn't that what freedom is? Isn't that liberty? The right to kill the cancer you discover destroying your life?"

THEIR COFFEE ARRIVES. They wait for the waiter to leave. Hamilton feels exhausted. Somehow he never expected he'd have to defend the rightness of his feelings, the basic rightness he believes has always embroidered his life.

"You're a proud man, John," Knox remarks.

"And pride's a bad thing?"

"That depends. It can be. Sometimes it makes us careless."

"C'mon, Knox, lots of people think the way I do. Is it pride to stand up for yourself? Is it pride to defend what's yours, everything you've worked for? Don't we have the right to apply our personal standards to our own lives, to determine what has value, what doesn't have value? Isn't that the true essence of liberty?"

Knox cannot answer this. He's heard a thousand renditions of the same old argument. In the end it's just passion, place and purgatory, the same old human dance of envy and contempt. It's recognizing the dance for what it is and not caring to dance himself that makes Knox the unusual man he is. Sometimes Knox imagines life as a large and classy bar. His function is to serve as its bouncer when trouble breaks out among the patrons.

"You know, John," he suggests. "You could just have him hit, cleanly, professionally."

"What about Sara? What if she suspected I was behind it?"

"It could be made to look like an accident."

Hamilton sighs again. "But it doesn't guarantee she'd go back to Tony. What if another Kovacs shows up? Sara's a beautiful woman, you know. Then I'd be back at square one. But if Kovacs disappears, without explanation, like he's simply abandoned her, then I think Tony will appeal to her again. Sara will learn from the experience. And all I have to do is express my own disappointment in Kovacs, my own surprise. I think she'll turn to me about this. I'll be able to explain why she's better off with Tony."

Knox makes a steeple of his fingers. The professional process of his thoughts is almost audible, a whisper of flawlessly meshing gears. He's trying to find a courteous way to tell Hamilton what he has just said is nothing but a crock of shit. He knows Hamilton is lying. Why doesn't the industrialist realize lying is just a waste of time?

The industrialist waits, wondering what more he can say. Sara doesn't matter to Knox and he shouldn't be surprised by this. But he feels like he is in court, like he's on trial only to assuage Knox's devil's advocacy. The humiliation of this state of affairs gnaws at his fragile belly. When did it happen that he had to explain himself so much? He's never liked it and he doesn't like it now. Yet, to achieve his ends, it's clear he must make the professional across the table from him understand the urgency in what he needs.

"What I'm thinking, John," says Knox finally, knowing his words will corner the other man, "is you could have Kovacs disappear without bothering with all this business up in Canada. Sara would still be abandoned and there'd be a lot less risk. I think you know this as well as I do." Knox lifts his cup, calmly sips his coffee black.

"Okay," says Hamilton with a tired exhalation of breath. "I'll be honest with you." He leans across the table towards the other man. "I need more satisfaction than that."

"More satisfaction than knowing Kovacs has been removed for good?"

"Yes. I want that dirty little fucker to know he's going to die, why he's going to die. I want to hear him recant his sins, beg me to change my mind, plead with me, shit his pants, feel a pain in the pit of his belly like the one he makes me feel. I want him to know he's going to die before it ever happens. You understand what I'm saying, Knox?"

"I figured as much. But it doesn't make your plan very credible, does it? Revenge isn't smart, John. It leaves things to chance. You've identified a practical need to get Kovacs out of the way, but you're shopping for a crime of passion."

"So what?" counters Hamilton. "Sometimes a risky investment gets you what you want out of life."

"But a hunt? Jesus, John. Neither one of us is the kind of man to leave things to chance. What would happen if he gave us the slip? If he survived?"

"All four of us? And you a professional?"

Knox nods. "But consider what happens if he gets away."

Hamilton raises his left hand, begins counting on his fingers. "One: who's going to take his word over ours? He'd look nuts. Two: even if he gives us the slip up there in the mountains, how's he going to survive being exposed to the elements? Three: you don't really think he's going to get away from us, do you? Four: our immunity. We're important in this world; he's not. 'Expendable' was the word you used. Law or no law, no one's going to care when Kovacs dies."

"But there's a chance, John. It's incredibly slim, but,

professionally speaking, you have to consider it. Imagine what happens if something goes wrong with the plan, that Kovacs is believed, that our immunity fails us somehow."

Hamilton leans back in his chair, idly tapping his coffee mug. "I don't care," he mutters.

"You don't care?" Knox is stunned by the other man's petulance.

"Look, Knox, I've been candid with you. I've already paid you research money. Your research is supposed to all but eliminate the risk, even of a hunt. That was our agreement. I've been straightforward with you, explaining the satisfaction I require. I want that sonofabitch to know he's going to die because of what he's done to me. I'm trying to hire you, for Christ's sake. All of these stipulations represent my terms. It's how it's got to be done."

"The hunt was Ernie Fieldler's idea, wasn't it?" says Knox, undaunted by Hamilton's remarks.

Hamilton pauses, caught by surprise, then shrugs. "Of course. Fieldler's a hunter. He's hunted everything in this world there is to hunt. He's been to Africa, for Christ's sake. It didn't take much to figure that out. Ernie's hunted everything."

"Except a man, of course."

"That's right," says Hamilton. "I'm sure he finds the notion appealing. It's not rocket science. Notwithstanding his friendship with me, I think Fieldler wants to hunt Kovacs for his own reasons."

"Fieldler's motive is boredom."

"C'mon, Knox, what difference does that make? With his skill and your professional experience, Kovacs won't have a chance. Throw in me and Tony, and Kovacs has no hope. Two professionals and two of us with respectable motives, Kovacs is done."

Knox milks the ensuing silence for all it is worth. Then, "Okay, John, I'll be candid with you. I don't like it. It's not professional. I know you want Kovacs to suffer. I see what you're saying there, but that's the part of the plan that could backfire in the end. It unnecessarily increases the risks. In my view, the risks are unacceptable."

Hamilton's eyes blaze. His stomach burns with frustration. "Recommend someone else then. Give me the name of someone—another mercenary—who can take your place."

But for the moment Knox does not reply.

"LOOK," HAMILTON SAYS AT LAST. "Let's cut to the chase here. All of this hesitation on your part is just negotiation. The risks are a negotiable part of your fee. We both know that. I believe you're the right man for the job. If I didn't think so I wouldn't be going through this process with you. Right?"

Knox merely gazes at him, his eyes narrow and cold.

"You see," Hamilton adds, "you and I aren't as different as you think. Oh, you've never loved a woman the way I have. You don't understand about Sara and me. But you and I both know about the lure of money. It's a religious experience, isn't it, Knox. It's evangelical. Big money like this? Like kissing God, right? You suspect that's true about money and I know it's true."

Still, Knox remains silent.

"Now," Hamilton says, pressing a perceived advantage. "I gave you fifty thousand in research money last time we met. What have you found out for my money, Knox? The key to this thing succeeding is you. Where it happens. How it happens. You're the man responsible for nothing going wrong. You, Knox, are the man who's can make it happen."

"Fifty thousand is peanuts, John. My services on a project like this, with a vengeance factor like this, it'll cost you a fortune. It's a matter of upping the ante, my insurance against greater risk."

"How much?"

"Enough that I can disappear if it all goes for one big shit."

"How much, Knox?"

"Ten million."

"Done," says Hamilton, making sure he doesn't blink, overriding the dagger of pain that pierces his agonized stomach. He thought maybe five million. But ten? Jesus!

"Plus expenses."

"Expenses?"

"Renting an airplane, the equipment we need, for example."

"Done."

"Half now, half when the job is complete."

"Done."

Both men are surprised to find that they are suddenly breathless. The restaurant has become vague and distant. They are conscious only of themselves and of each other. The sensation is harsh and euphoric, like being born directly into ruthless adulthood. They are twins. who have discovered and will exploit the exotica of their shared Truth.

SHORTLY KNOX SIGNALS FOR MORE COFFEE. The waiter appears, pours, departs.

Knox stares into his coffee cup. Ten cool million. He takes a deep breath, trying to let the news of it and what it might mean truly sink in. Ten cool million. It isn't what he'll spend it on. It's just having it. It's just knowing it will be there. That's freedom, he supposes. A concubine all his own. Ten million dollars; now that's a perfect lover. It only gives and asks nothing in return. In this Hamilton is right. Knox has begun to feel like he is kissing something resembling God.

"Knox?"

"Yes?"

"I asked if your research was successful."

Knox nods. "There's a large and extremely remote wedge of mountain terrain up there in Canada, more or less between the Stewart-Cassiar Highway and the Alaska Highway. It's called the Omenica range. I'm talking rugged, John. It'll be rough and dangerous, a challenge even for me and Fieldler, I expect. The only way in is by floatplane. It's such wild country I can almost guarantee that it would be impossible for an unarmed man on foot. Kovacs wouldn't have a chance. Even if he gave us the slip, the elements would eventually get him."

Hamilton wants to grin like a spoiled child. He freezes his face to hide it, to give less of himself away.

"Hundreds of miles to either highway. No towns. Nothing." Knox sips smugly at his coffee. "People hunt there. There'll be hunters and guides. We go in at the end of hunting season, the last weekend. Then, when everyone else goes home, we stay behind and finish the job."

"Can you get a plane?"

"Yes. I can rent one out of place called Smithers. A Beech 18, rebuilt and ready to go. Twin-engine, carries nine people or about eighteen hundred pounds. Lots of space for us and our gear. It being a floatplane, I just land it in a lake."

"Have you picked a spot?"

"Not yet. I'll go up there and do a run-through."

"Okay. You've flown this kind of plane before?"

Knox nods. "They stopped manufacturing them in '69 but they're a good plane. I can fly just about anything. Another reason I'm expensive."

"What about guns? I mean Fieldler will have his own, but . . . ."

"No, he won't!" Knox leans forward to convey his urgency, cups his hands around his coffee cup. "Fieldler does what I tell him to do. I need to establish that right now."

"Okay," says Hamilton.

"I mean it, John. This isn't Fieldler's expedition. It's yours and mine."

"Okay, Knox. You've made yourself clear."

"I don't want to sanction anyone but Kovacs. Okay?"

Hamilton blanches at Knox's words but slowly nods.

"I supply the guns. I can get some Remingtons, big game rifles that will do the trick. These are special, though. Nothing traceable. Fieldler leaves his hardware at home. Am I clear on that?"

"You don't like Fieldler being in on this, do you?" Hamilton says then.

"I don't like Ernie Fieldler at all. I've looked into Ernie Fieldler. Too many exotic appetites makes him dangerous."

"Care to be more specific?"

"No," replies Knox. "That's as much as you need to know. We're not here to gossip about vices."

"What difference will it make in the mountains, for Christ's sake? Fieldler's appetites, I mean, whatever they are."

"Simply this—I don't trust people who can't control their proclivities."

"And you can?"

Knox nearly grins. "The best way to control an appetite is to have no appetite at all."

"Okay," grants Hamilton, wondering briefly how a man accomplishes this.

"I'll be watching Fieldler carefully; that's all."

"Fair enough," concedes Hamilton. "If that's what it takes."

"Which brings us to your heir apparent, Tony Pirelli. Frankly, he makes me nervous too. I see him as the weakest link here."

"Tony? A weak link?"

Soberly Knox nods. "John, I have to trust you on this one. Do we know he's absolutely committed to this thing, that he won't lose his nerve out there?"

"Tony hates Kovacs as much as I do. You can take my word for it."

"I hope your word's enough. We don't want someone having a change of heart. You know what that would mean, don't you?"

Hamilton nods slowly as the threat in Knox's words dawns on him.

"So I'm going to assume your assessment of Pirelli is accurate."

"Of course it is," Hamilton says indignantly. "To Tony, hunting Kovacs will be like shooting a skunk that's been getting into your garbage. He's said as much himself."

"Bravado maybe," murmurs Knox.

"No, it's more than that. This business with Kovacs is war. There's a rightness about it that makes it necessary. It's a holy war. That's the way Tony looks at it. Besides, Tony's got the most to lose. Sara, his future with me and my business, ultimately his whole life."

"He understands that it's business."

"Yes, but more than that—to Tony and me it's a crusade, the meting out of justice."

"This won't be like any crusade you've ever seen," Knox remarks, lifting his arm to signal the waiter for the check.

HAMILTON'S LARGE, LUXURIOUS HOME in Beverly Hills sprawls inside its large acreage in visible gluttony. It's both empty and full, cluttered yet spacious. Everything he needs resides inside its walls, yet everything, or at least something, seems to be missing. It has no odour, no scent. It's air-conditioned and purified. It's like living inside a cloud made of plaster and wood. It has edges, doorways and spangly chandeliers, but one passes through these artifacts with such a sense of distance they all but disappear. Even the home's sounds are strictly mechanical, a clunky concerto of new millenium tin or aluminum. It ticks with clocks and delicately blinking lights, evidence of a discreet but complex alarm system on duty in almost every room. The system seems alive sometimes, when Hamilton remembers to notice it. He respects the way it listens and watches, waiting for intruders, recording each passing moment of his day or night, collecting and cataloguing, he knows, even his most mundane word, breath or burp. It makes him feel safe—not just from intruders—but because it verifies he lives here as it records his every move. It writes his history for him. Hamilton wants to be historic. He wants people to know he passed importantly through this life.

Back home from his meeting with Knox, Hamilton slips through the various watchful rooms like a wraith. Marjorie is out again. His mood has soured since he enjoyed the surprisingly expensive triumph of coming to terms with Knox. In the aftermath of their accord, everything emotional in him feels sucked away. He showered and masturbated half an hour ago, a vague kind of release having less to do with Sara or you or the revenge on you he's going to achieve than some kind of disappointment he recognized in the tedium of success. Now he just feels tired, blaming a growing anxiety over the ordeal a few weeks ahead of him for his fatigue. These aren't second thoughts. No, they feel more like the vacuum in the wake of a declaration of war, the period of patient preparation for battle, as necessary and inevitable as the declaration of war itself.

He pours himself some bourbon, his ritual nightcap, shaking the glass gently in his fingertips to hear the ice cubes tinkle. The sound is attractive to him. He finds comfort in minutiae, as if it proves he has successfully returned to a state of essential reality.

But he groans after he takes his first swallow. The liquor arrives in his belly with a painful scream, altogether too real, too familiar. He gasps, curses and places a helpless hand over his stomach until the pain subsides. He blames you for the reality of his pain. When he disposes of you, he anticipates his agony will gradually disappear.

Stubbornly, as if to make some private point about the threshold of his pain, he takes the drink with him to his study. There he turns on a lamp at the edge of his desk, positions his glass on a blotter and picks up a phone. He punches in the familiar digits and sits impatiently through a couple of rings at the other end.

"Tony? It's me. Just wanted to tell you it's on, that it's a go."

Pirelli breathes. It's the only sound he makes.

"Tony?"

"Sorry, J.D. I'm fine. Just taking in the news. I'm committed to this thing. You know that."

"Yes, I know it."

"Funny thing, J.D. It seems like we've been talking about it for years."

"I know."

Pirelli's voice is higher in pitch than a man's voice should be. To Hamilton, it's his only flaw. The phone exaggerates this fact, transforming his son-in-law's voice into an annoyance.

"It's gonna cost ten million, Tony," Hamilton announces.

Pirelli whistles. "The sonofabitch!"

"It's the risk, he says. He needs insurance."

"Jesus. Do you think he's worth it?"

Hamilton has already considered this. "Probably," he replies. "The man doesn't have any feelings. He's just a machine in a human body. Considering what we want to do, I think this robot aspect is an advantage. Knox won't make mistakes. He'll make sure nothing goes wrong."

"Well, you always know best, J.D."

Hamilton's heard this statement before. It doesn't mean anything to him. He's always known what was best, for himself and for others. At this stage in his life, knowing what is best is virtually meaningless. "Anyway, Tony," he says, "I just wanted you to know. We'll talk tomorrow, okay?"

"Okay."

After his son-in-law has hung up, Hamilton turns in his swivel chair towards a large portrait of Sara on the wall to his right. He's aware he veers in the portrait's direction with a certain inevitability but he forgives himself for this, drawn to it more and more as she has troubled him increasingly over the past few months.

It's a painting he commissioned more than a decade ago. He loves it deeply. Sara, only nineteen, is perched on a swing in the back garden, wearing a leather miniskirt, her long, perfect legs tucked under the seat in a modesty so innocent it cannot help but fail. Her blonde hair is in ringlets to her shoulders, the way she wore it then, tousled by a breeze the artist cleverly captured in oils. He loves the disarray the picture conveys, her hair, the wind, her tentative, nearly lopsided smile. Hamilton enjoys most the innocence in her expression, not in its own right, but because innocence, by its very nature, is enigmatically terminal. It's an innocence he knows must inevitably give itself up to the verdict of wanton justice. Sensuality lingers just outside her naivete in this portrait like some shadow she casts. He believes sensuality, especially in Sara's case, is only the gradual withdrawing of innocence, the way cold, absolute zero, has always been the inevitable surrendering of heat. And he believes he's permitted to feel this way—Sara is his daughter and she belongs to him. This fact is so fundamental to him, he now believes the various messages and promises he sees in this rendering of Sara can be decoded only by him. In this way, the painting is more than a portrait of his daughter. It inspires him sometimes as the perfect reply to all his unanswered questions. It verifies for him, in a way he could never explain, everything he has ever believed or felt.

Sara maintains she doesn't like the painting. She says it embarrasses her. He wonders if this is because she cannot yet except what it says about her or what he knows about his daughter better than she knows it in herself.

Hamilton gazes at the painting for several minutes longer, feeling a ritual, delicate longing. Then, remembering the glass in his hand, he gulps the last of his bourbon, futilely steeling himself against the shriek it unleashes in his stomach.

IN BRITISH COLUMBIA LEO MCKENDRICK'S DOGS gradually climb higher into the mountains, intruding on deep forest broken in places by craggy gullies and dizzying cliffs. Now nearly a week further way from the pen in which they once were housed, they are a pack of animals transformed. A gradually diminishing state of ineptitude and an endless tryst with happenstance to made them mean. The dogs have discovered whimsy has a price. To keep paying this fee irritates them and, as much as they are capable of it, they suffer a nasty regret about the risk in their state of freedom. They refuse to acknowledge they are lost, although they suspect they are.

Soon, as they forget a little more each day about the place they once called home, their exchange of then for now will replace their sense of lostness with an innate conclusion that they have found themselves. In a human this conclusion would be idealistic. In a dog it is instinctive. Even so, their memory of their previous home continues to dissolve inside the intense immediacy of this newer world they inhabit. Here, in this endless expanse of elusive plenty, of woods, streams and wildlife, the pack of dogs is conflicted— they sensibly need to survive yet are tempted to senselessly destroy. Even now, after a week in the wilderness, they endure the sense that they have been swallowed whole by this world of endless survival. Hunger inspires periods of desperation, often revealing to them their clumsy strangeness, reminding them that they were better at the limited existence they've lost than they are at this new adventure they've found.

They now number six, one less than when their escapade began. One of the smaller pack members, a mongrel with a bent left ear that gave it a quizzical look, its husky genes several distant generations behind it, is dead, a victim of its own incautious behaviour. It lost its life one afternoon after the pack encountered and then attacked a large male elk. The dogs are not yet wild enough to employ the canny, propitious judgment of wolves, and the elk was too much for them. The mongrel with the bent ear came in too close during the pack's hapless attack, drunk with stupid bravado and brainless ferocity. Its quarry caught the dog on its impressive antlers, tossing it against a rock, breaking one of its legs and a couple of ribs, shattering its spine.

All of the dogs wear bruises or abrasions from the kicking rear hooves of the elk, from encounters with its sharp antlers. Even the collie has a cut on the side of its muzzle. And the Husky alpha male continues to limp from a bruise caused by a glancing kick to its right shoulder.

Startled by the skill in the elk's self-defense, the dogs fell back to regroup and their quarry used this opportunity to dash deeper into the trees. By the time the dogs contemplated giving chase, the elk was gone. Even though they were hungry, the pack didn't bother to go after it. Instead the dogs stood there in a dazed, bedraggled group, bemused by and whimpering over the elk's astonishing skill in battle.

Eventually, one by one, following the lead of their now bruised leader, the dogs approached the fallen mongrel broken against the rocks. It whined sadly, trying feebly to get to its feet again, the damage too severe to permit it. For a few moments everything seemed locked in a state of stupor: the dogs, the silence following their attack on the elk, even the dying breeze in the trees surrounding them. This strange and wild setting was as puzzling as their fate. The woods encroached, quiet and dazed, holding its breath, apparently still unwilling to explain itself.

Shortly, though, as casually as an afterthought, the Husky leader limped closer to the mongrel, sniffed its privates for a moment, confirming the scent of blood, then lunged at its throat to finish killing it. Soon, as hungry as they'd ever been in their lives, the dogs tore the mongrel to pieces, growling at one another as they devoured what they could of its warm flesh.

Since then, Leo Mckendrick's dogs have learned

more about survival. Not as efficient as wolves, not as polished at hunting just to survive, they have learned in awkward fashion to kill small game for food, briefly staving off hunger while they work their way north towards their provocative role in an even more provocative providence. A hare, some squirrels, some carrion they stole from a group of dissenting ravens: these are the bits and pieces helping them fend off starvation.

As they move deeper into the wilderness, they grow more and more desperate because their need to eat is rarely satisfied. Each day brings with it the need to hunt again, the ache of relentless hunger. They are trapped in a canine version of blue collar existence; they are never free of the reminder of the living they must make. These are domestic dogs lost in a feral world. Gradually, as they suffer from the strangeness in their surroundings, they fall more deeply into madness and increasing savagery. So hungry so constantly, they lose any notion that there is somewhere they belong. They do not belong here in the woods, in the wilderness or the mountains where they have become a cruel and uncontrollable virus. But neither can they return to Leo McKendrick's dog pen. The pen is too far behind them. It no longer makes sense to them. So they head north in desperation because they cannot conceive of anywhere else to go.

A GREAT DISTANCE FROM THE PACK OF DOGS many miles away, the gray wolf has dug himself a small, temporary den where he wolf-naps away the afternoon not far from the bank of a stream. He lies here on a bed of sand, digesting a meal of beaver he killed for himself that morning. He naps, wakes, then naps again, too cautious to ever be deeply asleep, yet gradually approaching a state in which he will feel refreshed.

The forest sounds healthy to him and smells exactly as it should. Blue jays call and screech. Above him, squirrels fidget in the trees, their claws scrabbling on the bark as they scurry from limb to limb to bough in this large density of trees. Now and then they natter at one another, sometimes in play, sometimes quarrelling. Winter is coming, and they feel a deep urgency to be industrious. There are preparations they must make. Procrastination would be unwise.

But the wolf enjoys more flexibility. He has come down from higher country to seek his share of plenty. When the plenty here is no longer plentiful, he will move upwards again. In this way, he will continue back and forth between higher up and lower down, regardless of the season, living from week to week, meeting his practical needs like a night watchman patrolling the property he is responsible for yet never considers he could possess.

The calm of this day, its smooth fabric of predictability. Despite the lack of danger, the wolf feels a growing anxiety at the fringes of his caution. He senses the coming of something mysterious—even though it is not yet imminent—something erratic or deformed. He dreams of this advent clearly during his naps, though the dreams become vague and unreliable the moment he fully wakes. When he is alert, he finds himself gazing along the curve of the nearby stream bank towards the edge of the descending mountain in anticipation of a danger he cannot yet articulate. The wolf is confused by the nebulousness of his trepidation. The little he sees, the little he smells, the little he hears that might be different from what he has learned to expect is not strong enough to be clearly defined. But when he sleeps, he sees it more sharply, the threat of something moving in his direction, that peculiar insanity he has briefly glimpsed on previous occasions when senseless killing has invaded his territory. He dozes fretfully, not knowing what it is or if it will catch up to him, but absolutely certain what is coming is probably dangerous and he should be wary of its destructive force.

SOME MORNINGS JOE LEONARD PATROLS the relatively small parcel of land he borrows from the Earth just to appreciate it before he embarks on his daily labours. Not every morning, but perhaps once a week when the mood hits him, his life feels euphorically perfect. It verifies for him that he has achieved a state of authenticity he has needed for so long. This is his home, the fruits of his decision, his life, the gift from Mother Earth that he has arranged to gratefully live inside. This morning he has awakened conspicuously conscious of the wondrous peace around him he otherwise takes for granted. These mornings are never ritual; but on days like these they are an unexpected blessing.

He climbs gently out of bed, leaving Allison to sleep, her head tucked into the crevice between her pillow and his. He dresses in front of a curtainless window. Joe Leonard has no need for insincere modesty. This is the wilderness, deep and distant from homes or communities requiring windows with drapes. No, in this way, Joe Leonard isn't modest. There's nothing to be modest about because there's nothing he needs to explain or rationalize. Modesty, he knows, would shame the way he has chosen to live.

He goes to the woodstove and replenishes its smouldering fire. He puts the coffee pot Allison prepared last night on top of the stove. Then he slips silently onto the porch of his two-room cabin to appreciate the budding of what promises to be a reasonably warm and sunny autumn day. Standing there on the porch, he takes tobacco and papers out of his shirt pocket and rolls a cigarette. He lights it with the last match in a beaten-up box he's been carrying around for more than a week. He blows the match out with a gust from the right side of his pursed lips then drops it into a nearby coffee can that is stationed on the floor near the door, placed there for this purpose. Allison likes coffee more than he does. He doesn't have the same taste for it. In fact, he doesn't even smoke very much, just this one in the morning before he starts his day, one after each meal and the one that glows in front of his face in the darkness on this porch before he goes to bed.

Two mule deer at the edge of the woods a couple of hundred yards away gaze at him briefly before resuming their grazing. Joe gazes back at them, enjoying his cigarette. He's completed all the hunting he needs to accomplish this year and these deer come here each morning more or less as timid colleagues or relieved survivors. They gaze at him in forgiveness, he likes to think. He gazes back at them in unapologetic gratitude.

Joe selected this piece of land seven years ago, when he was barely twenty-five. He and Allison had come a long way north to be here, searching along the way for a place to build a life. Then they found this gentle valley. "We'll start a new Senaki nation," he said, standing not far from this very spot, his arm around her waist. "You and me, Allison." She was as committed as he was, two years younger than he is but knowing her own mind.

When they came to this location, they knew it was their place. It slopes down towards a stream that runs cold and clear and fast regardless of the season. And the soil, while not rich, is deep enough and possesses enough nutritional affluence for a large and viable garden. This location is sheltered by some ridges not steep enough for winter avalanches but high enough to represent the stubble of a surrounding beard of higher mountains. This land is less than a day away from abundant fishing; and there is game enough to trap. And Joe Leonard is a skillful hunter, certainly better skilled than most. They get by with what he sells for gasoline for his ATV and other supplies and equipment he must purchase three days away on the reserve where he was raised. There they purchase, nontraditional clothing and other necessities they cannot improvise on their own. There has always been enough food derived by growing, foraging or hunting it. They pay no rent. They pay no taxes. They manage everything themselves. The world they've left behind barely knows they are here.

Eventually, after finishing his cigarette, Joe moves down to the stream, disturbing the dew on the slim grasses through which he strolls. The dew splashes the legs of his faded denim jeans but, although it makes him wet, he is only vaguely aware of it. Dew is part of what lives with him here in the morning, like rain and snow, like sunshine. The weather will always visit him here with various expressions of certainty. He crouches at the edge of the stream, cups his hands in it, lifting them two or three times to his mouth to drink. The water is cold enough to inspire a delicate ache in his calloused fingers. But even this is the way it should be among all the other of life's sensations he has come to know and expect.

He stands up again and squints in the direction of their garden. It accepts the morning sun, opening its arms to the light, which, at this angle, silhouettes the harvesting he and Alison will accomplish today. Allison is waking. Joe senses this. They have come so far together they are always at least a little in touch with one another, even when they are apart. Joe used to know people back on the reserve who were unable to be connected in this way. This inability to connect was true for him too, until he found himself connected to Allison. Now he finds it easy to be aware of where Allison is. It's a matter, he maintains, of paying attention, of living in a world simplified enough to let you pay attention.

He wasn't certain Allison would stick it out back in the early days. When winter came that first year, more than twenty feet of snow fell. Even though the cabin had been built and was secure against the elements, even though there was enough food to see them safely into spring, he feared she felt threatened by the isolation he more readily preferred. She has forgiven him for this brief lack of faith in her. They visit family once a year, usually in the spring, but no one visits them here, although friends and family claim to respect Joe and Allison's courage and independence. These sentiments could be true. They might be false. Joe and Allison don't fret about it much. It's enough to know Joe is never angry here the way he was back on the lands the white man had arbitrarily set aside for him.

Both of them keep journals of their lives here in this valley. Someday Joe intends to write a book based on the accumulation of their days of peace on this bit of land. Joe maintains there are other people who will be glad to know a man and woman can live this way. The usual contrasts and comparisons created by "civilized" living de-authenticate lives, he believes. Allison doubts they can change how other people think. She keeps her journal more or less for her own purposes, as a personal memoir. She does not share Joe's need to journal in a way that suggests another way of being, that recommends a better way.

Joe heads back to the cabin, taking a shortcut through the garden he and Allison will spend much of the day harvesting. He smells the coffee being brewed in the cabin and knows Allison is now in the rocking chair he made for her a few years ago, drinking her first early cup black and hot. He sketches her sometimes in a thick pad he carries with him most of the time. Some have said he's a talented artist. He has one picture in his dozen or so finished sketches that captures her in this chair with the steaming mug in her hands.

When they have children here, Joe intends to sketch his children's lives. Maybe the sketches will find a place in the book he wants to write. He and Allison are ready to have children, to have them born in this place. They have everything they need to handle the birth themselves. They have the knowledge, they have the skill, they have the faith and ingenuity. They even have the sense of what is a long tradition for their people. When Allison gets pregnant, if things are difficult for some reason, he has arranged to move her temporarily to where there's more appropriate medical help.

So far Allison hasn't managed to get pregnant but they both believe she will when the time is right. It will happen when it's supposed to, when this valley commune and communion has decided it has the space. They offend no spirits in this place. It is probable that he and Allison will have many children here.

THAT AFTERNOON WHILE JOE AND ALLISON are working in their garden, an airplane passes overhead. They both straighten up in the sunshine to watch it fly over the ridge, feeling a similar twinge in the smalls of their backs, from bending over so much. Joe knows his northern airplanes and recognizes the craft as a Beech 18.

"Going north," he says to Allison in their traditional

tongue.

She merely nods at him.

In the mornings they practise the language of their people to keep it alive on their tongues. By mid-afternoon, they switch to English so they don't forget how to speak English too.

Joe watches the plane until it vanishes, vaguely dismayed that it's flying north. Hunting season is over in just a couple of days; most people are going south, leaving this territory with whatever trophies they have earned. It's unusual at this time of year for an airplane to be flying north, unless the plane is on some other business not related to a hunt. Deciding this must be the case, Joe bends again to the task of harvesting the fruits of his and Allison's labours. The plane is soon forgotten here in Joe Leonard's valley. The valley and its garden—and the man and woman who traditionally manage it—resume their method of existing without blemish. In a matter of moments, the silence the plane has interrupted embraces them again. This place Joe and Allison have borrowed to live out their only lives is once again at peace.

ANTITHESIS

YOU STAND IN THE CIRCULAR NO-MAN'S LAND around which your tents have been set up, trying to make conversation with Tony Pirelli and Ernie Fieldler. It's grown chilly and overcast, and your breath is a cloud in front of your face. You brought gloves on this trip but these remain inside your pack in the tent. So you stand there with your hands in your parka pockets, trying to warm your fingers, fighting back the unmanly urge to shiver. It's been years since you felt this kind of northern chill. It's going to take an adjustment to get used to it again.

Fieldler, you've decided, is going to be difficult to get to know. During the flight up here, he talked in gallon bursts then fell as silent as an empty beaker between two detailed stories about trophies he'd brought down on previous hunting trips. Both stories were about Africa, one about an elephant he shot many years ago, the other about a buffalo. The buffalo, he said, was the more dangerous animal of the two, which seemed to surprise everyone on the plane. You know the stories are true. Fieldler doesn't strike you as a man who exaggerates. White-haired now and in his early sixties, he is tall and lean. You can imagine him in the gym on a rowing machine, crossing imaginary oceans tirelessly, his face lined with single-minded purpose. With a beard as white as the thick hair on his head, he reminds you somehow of photographs you've seen of an aging Papa Hemingway, but thinner. Regardless of his slender build, he owns a kind of Hemingwayesque intensity. Fieldler's not a man for nonsense: this much is clear. And for this reason, you find him vaguely disturbing. Certainly he believes killing animals represents some kind of fundamental right. In a war, you speculate, if he was ever your enemy, it would be dangerous surrendering to him; there's at least an even chance he would execute you anyway, regardless of the rules of warfare. You enjoyed listening to his stories, though. At times they mesmerized you. When you commented at one point to fill the gap, he only grunted to acknowledge your remarks. And when he looked at you, you realized he disapproves of you for some reason. He gazed at you a moment like a quietly furious tailor about to take your measurements for a made-to-measure suit.

You remember thinking you'll have to earn this man's respect over the next few days if you want to talk business with him. Until then, discussing investments with Fieldler will be nearly impossible. It's going to be a challenge making a portfolio of rising stocks look interesting to a man so at home in this wilderness. He has brought a strictly defined love of hunting here to the exclusion of any other interests he might enjoy. His was the first tent up and locked in place on the shores of this lake. He was the one who gathered firewood while everyone else was still setting up. He was the one who dug a small pit for the cooking fire this evening. Fieldler is obviously a dedicated hunter. Standing here beside his chill and distance you are reminded clearly of the reasons you are not a hunter. These reasons aren't profound. You've never been to war and you've never shot even the most innocuous wild game. You suppose some combination of circumstance and aptitude has allowed you to develop your motto of live and let live.

So you don't care whether you take a trophy on this expedition or not. You've come here to do business most of all. You doubt you'll be participating in the atmosphere of competition you feel pervading the group. It's so palpable already—this sense of needing to succeed, to better your comrades—you've come to the conclusion you might have to fake interest in even goodhearted rivalry. Men gathered in a group in this deep wilderness run better than even odds of being drunk with testosterone. Whatever game is ultimately brought down, you know, will reflect someone's winning or losing. Already you're making adjustments to your behaviour, paring down the moments when you are tempted to be gregarious. It's been clear out here so far that none of these men are going to be won over by your charm or sense of humour. When you asked Fieldler and Pirelli a few moments ago if they were satisfied with their accommodation, Pirelli said it was fine, not getting the joke, gazing off instead across the lake in the direction of some steep cliffs in the foreground. Gently slighted, you glanced across the lake too and beyond at a bank of dense white spruce stretching up into the distance towards some snowcapped peaks where autumn snow has already begun to accumulate. Fieldler didn't even answer your well-intentioned accommodation question. Instead, with an utilitarian abruptness, he strolled a few yards away and pissed into a moss-covered crevice between some rocks.

Pirelli's different here too. His face displays new furrows, as if he's aged since the last time you saw him. He's still handsome in that dark, Italian way, swarthy with a smile as shiny as a saint, but there are flecks of gray in the nest of his dark curls. You sense he wants to impress everyone here before the hunt is over and all of you go home. He's tense and distracted. You can detect the emanations of his intense resolve. His determination is a second skin he's sewn around himself. He's more of a stranger here in the mountains than you anticipated he would be.

But then, a moment later, he turns to you as if forcing himself to remember you stand beside him here. "Smells different," he says. "Like we're in a vacuum. It's nearly odourless."

Actually you don't agree with him. You can smell the jack pine and the lake, the moisture in the air. But you are a man who doesn't argue with your customers' observations. So you say, "Yeah. When we get back to LA., the urban stench will knock us down."

"But you're a city slicker just like me, aren't you?"

"You bet. The city's the place to be if you want to make your fortune."

"The woods are a good place to visit but you wouldn't want to live or die here. That's what I'm hearing, right?"

"That's what you're hearing," you reply, disturbed by the notion of your death in a place like this.

A strange thing for Pirelli to say, you reflect with a shudder. If Sara were here she would nudge you in the ribs at a remark such as this.

Behind you, finished relieving himself, Fieldler does

not return to this impromptu meeting near his fire pit. Instead, he goes to his tent. The zipper screams in the wilderness silence and you turn in time to see him vanish inside.

Knox and Hamilton are down on the shore where they have been talking for several minutes. You would join them but they too seem intense about their conversation, and you sense it would be best not to intrude on them at this moment. Besides, you know how demanding J.D. Hamilton can be when he's hired someone's services. The hoops he sometimes devises in his professional arrangements are put in place only to make you jump through them to earn your fees.

You ask Pirelli if he knows where you are.

"No," he replies. "Apparently all will be revealed tomorrow morning at breakfast. Knox is going to brief us on our whereabouts."

"What are we hunting, Tony? No one's mentioned it."

"Like I said, all will be revealed around tomorrow's morning campfire."

You nod, satisfied with this, and glance at your watch. You hope the hunt will not be too demanding, that whatever game you will be stalking isn't dangerous in some way.

"It's hard to tell because it's gotten overcast, but I think we're quite far north," you remark. "I'm trying to remember when it gets dark in the northern interior this time of year."

"Shit, Kovacs, I already figured out we're way up north. That was a helluva long flight, don't you think?"

"And bumpy sometimes too," you murmur, just for something to say.

Pirelli can behave this way—you've encountered his churlishness before. He doesn't have much patience and, when it runs out, he can be snippy. His attitude pisses you off at this moment and conjures Sara in your mind. Just for one insane and spiteful moment, you want to find a way to tell Pirelli his estranged wife is one great fuck. But of course you can't and don't. Besides, immediately afterwards, with Sara in your thoughts, you feel ashamed of yourself. Up here in British Columbia where you thought you once belonged a couple of decades ago, thinking of Sara makes it clear to you that she is a good deal more than someone you take to bed. Up here it seems more obvious Pirelli could never be the kind of man Sara would ultimately need. In your mind, he exudes a kind of counter sexuality. Sara has mentioned this. Her own sensuality represented nothing more than a short-term diversion for him, she's said. In the end he convicted her of needing too much attention. Remembering her words comforts you a moment; men are rivals, after all. Immediately afterwards, though, you just feel shocked to be shivering in the woods so far from home with Sara's estranged husband standing nearby as you contemplate with unexpected new wisdom why their marriage could not work, like the three of you are involved in some tragically masochistic ménage a trois, error on error on error, all of you the butt of some perfidious, sexual joke.

"Whaddyuh think of Knox?" you muse aloud to drive Sara—and wanting her—from your thoughts.

"A consummate professional, Kovacs. That's what I see." Awkwardly Pirelli clasps your shoulder, perhaps in subtle apology for his frostiness a few moments ago. "Knox is going to be the key to our success."

"Our success?"

"Well, I'm not leaving here until I've got my trophy."

Vaguely you nod in agreement.

"Anyway, I don't know about you, Kovacs, but I've got some gear to unpack and sort."

"Yeah, me too, I guess."

Pirelli walks away and disappears inside his tent.

As for you, you stand rooted to this tiny spot among the tents, not knowing what to make of Knox. He seemed to be half a dozen men with different personalities while he was piloting the airplane north. Robotic at times. You sensed disingenuousness as well. Normally disingenuousness doesn't bother you—you must frequently employ it yourself—but Knox was so unreadable your instinct to know him failed you completely. Like Fieldler, you can't imagine selling him anything. It's early yet but you feel disappointed. What was J.D. talking about when he suggested Knox and Fieldler would be good clients for you to know?

But it's not this that troubles you most, not really. You've locked your assessment of Knox into one brief, disturbing moment inside the airplane. You keep thinking about it, the moment his right pant leg eased itself up along his leg, revealing an inch or two of holstered revolver strapped to his calf. An instant later, as if he sensed you might have seen it, he tugged his pant leg down to cover it again. Instinctively, you don't know why, you glanced away quickly, peripherally aware that he turned to you to see if you had noticed the gun. You kept your eyes averted, pretending to be engrossed by what was revealed through the airplane window, apprehensive about the notion you had glimpsed some kind of secret you shouldn't know about. Even now you wonder why he wears the revolver when his profession is hunter and guide. Pistols are not for hunting big game; everyone knows that. Revolvers such as the one you saw strapped to Knox's leg are used for killing people, if the need should ever arise. Up here in British Columbia's northern interior, the gun concealed under his trousers would serve no other useful purpose.

Up here there is no practical reason to strap a weapon to your leg. You've kept silent about what you've seen. You feel alone with your knowledge. You don't ask a virtual stranger why he wears a gun designed to kill people instead of game. And you don't ask the other men either, when none of them is prepared to be a close friend to you.

"SO FAR SO GOOD," SAYS HAMILTON to his hired assassin, where they stand on the shore of the lake. "Do you think he suspects anything?"

Knox glances up in your direction then turns to Hamilton and slowly shakes his head.

"When does it happen, Knox?"

"Tomorrow morning, first thing. When you verify this with the others, be cautious about it."

"I will. It's probably the best time."

"Yes. No point in losing him in the darkness the first night."

"What do you think of his chances?"

"Lousy," replies Knox.

"Good. I can't wait to see his face tomorrow morning, the fucking sonofabitch."

Knox still doesn't care about Hamilton's need for revenge. "The first five million is in my account, I see," he says, diverting Hamilton from his unending anger, himself from its inherent risk.

"Of course."

"And the rest of it?"

"Two weeks from today."

"Okay."

"Jesus, Knox," says Hamilton about the man's remorseless, professional chill. "Don't you feel anything?"

"I want to fly out of here tomorrow afternoon,

everything done and completed, everything all cleaned up," Knox says, ignoring him.

"I know."

"Morning after tomorrow at the latest."

"Okay."

Hamilton muses on this a moment then remembers his other two accomplices. "What about Tony and Ernie? What do you think now that you've met them?"

"They're fine," replies Knox.

"Pirelli too?"

Knox nods. "As near as I can tell."

"Good. Tony's one of those guys who rises to the occasion. When you think he's in over his head, he ends up coming through in spades."

"Yeah? Well I'm hoping it's over so fast it won't make any difference."

"I know," says Hamilton, still disappointed that Knox has no interest in the justice of their mission.

"And until tomorrow morning," Knox says then, "I'm watching Kovacs like a hawk."

"Our weapons, Knox?"

"Tomorrow morning. Kovacs might notice we're one rifle short. And I don't know who to trust here, who might let something slip. I'm going to be very cautious. Just leave everything to me."

YOU WAKE UP WITH A START just before dawn, your only way of escaping a second coming of the insidious dream you suffered through the other night in Carmel. It's the one in the fog with Sara driving in the darkness, the dashboard lights as bright as a carnival, the car whispering along some narrow road through a wilderness much like this one where you now recline inside your tent. This time, though, you already know the dream has split you in two: that you are two men, one sitting happily beside Sara in the passenger seat and another one who will soon dart into the illumination of her headlight beams from some mysterious place along the side of the road.

So you wake up remembering the last time you had this dream. You wake up before the dream splits you in two. You wake up before one of your selves is run down by her car while the other one watches in terrified dismay.

Waking up isn't so bad this time, not like a couple of nights ago in the hotel room bed with Sara. This time you wake up apprehensive but your heart doesn't pound. And you don't perspire; it's much too cold to sweat. The stupid, fucking dream! You don't normally endure nightmares like this one, certainly never more than once. Awake now, in a different sense you are a man divided. One half of you wants to believe the nightmare is important prophecy. The other half is convinced the notion of prophecy is patently ridiculous.

It's cold, even in your sleeping bag. It was cold last night too and you clambered into your bed in shirt and jeans. At one point, you woke up because your ass was numb where you'd been sleeping on your wallet. Tempted to take it out of your pocket, you merely moved the bulge out of the way and went back to sleep again. You care deeply about money. Even here in the deepest of wildernesses, you are comforted to know your wallet still resides in your pocket.

There's an oppressive silence here in your tent. You listen hard, picking through the quiet as you would through the wreckage after a fire. Some small bird chirps laryngitically. Someone snores gently in one of the other tents. These are the only sounds you hear in a silence that, itself, seems to be somehow alive. Like a vibration. Like a heartbeat. It's attempting to be dawn outside, a day that struggles to determine which personality to assume. You can make out the morning's milky grayness through the fabric wall of your tent. You feel somehow that you should lie here until the day makes some kind of decision.

You won't go back to sleep now. That fucking fucking dream has left you with a cluster of fidgeting butterflies fluttering in your stomach. And you're hungry. Knox cooked up some chili last night he must have prepared in advance. It wasn't spicy but you didn't like it much; it seemed sour and incomplete, like some important ingredient had been left out. You ate sparingly, aware that the other men seemed tired and anxious. There was a tension around the campfire. Poor Knox. No one seemed to like his chili.

"Jesus, boys," the guide remarked at one point. "You're on vacation. You're supposed to be enjoying yourselves. I'm beginning to think I'm letting you down." He gazed at all of you one by one as if seeking some kind of consensus. Although he intended to be light about his observation, something in his demeanor hinted at urgency. There was some chortling at his remarks but even this sounded forced and fraudulent.

"It's been a long day," you remarked then. "I think we need to get some rest."

Everyone grunted in assent.

It wasn't long afterwards that everyone went to bed. You fell asleep wondering why no one had brought anything to drink. A nightcap might have helped all of you coalesce. Then again, liquor would be heavy to carry. Who knew? Knox struck you as the kind of man who sets stringent rules—maybe he forbids alcohol on this kind of hunt.

So now you lie here in your tent, wishing you could eat. Even Knox's lousy chili appeals to you at this moment. Worse yet, you've got an intensifying urge to have a shit. This means you're going to have to find the will to get up, climb out of this sleeping bag, find a reasonable route up the hill away from the lake and remember how to crap in the woods without getting it on your pants. You recall Sara's question several weeks ago. Why would you fly way up to British Columbia to hunt big game? At this moment—with Fieldler and Knox showing little or no potential as clients—you want to modify the answer you gave then. Now you want to admit you have no idea.

Certainly it's not homesickness that attracted you to this hunt. You've lived in California for more than fifteen years. In all that time, you have never returned to British Columbia, not even for a visit. Your divorce from this place, from Canada, bears only one outstanding incongruity—you have remained a Canadian citizen. You suspect this decision reflects nothing more than laziness on your part. You haven't gotten around to becoming officially the American you now believe you are. And yesterday when you flew over the rugged British Columbia landscape, looking down on a quilt of white, gray, blue and green, you felt no tug of familiarity, no sense at all that you were coming home. Yet, this morning, lying chilled inside your tent, you feel a trace of subtle experience in being in this wilderness, like you understand it better than you once thought you did. Then again, perhaps you are only here to reaffirm the reasons you moved south to California a decade and a half ago: to make yourself the kind of financial success you believed you could never be at home.

Okay. You count to ten because the day is cold and forbidding. Then, quietly, because the others are probably still sleeping, you ease yourself out of the warmth of the sleeping bag and shiver where you kneel on the hard ground separated from your knees only by the flimsy floor of your tent. You bear the pressure on your knees for a time, trying to figure out what to take with you just to go for a crap. It's still half dark and you don't feel safe. You have a roll of toilet paper in your small pack and half a dozen Power Bars. And a leather-sheathed hatchet dangles from a loop in its lightweight nylon. And Sara's knife. This you remove and slip onto the belt holding up your jeans, knowing Sara would approve of you taking it along with you. What was it you said to her in Carmel after you opened her gift? *For all you know, you've just saved me from a grizzly bear?* All right. The pack goes with you to have a shit. A grizzly encountering you with your trousers bunched around your ankles isn't an impossibility. Besides, taking your wilderness gear with you just to have a shit somehow counters the vague message in your dream that Sara's BMW intends to run you down.

You slip into your down-filled parka and climb quietly out of your tent. You shrug into your pack and squint into the murk of developing dawn. It's so quiet this early in the morning all you hear as you depart the sleeping campsite is the gentle creak of your hiking boots on the coniferous-needled ground.

FOR LITTLE MORE REASON than wanting to put off the chilly and vaguely humiliating act of having a crap without benefit of even a box, you walk a fair distance up the occasionally steep incline away from the lake. It grows consistently more misty as you climb. The ground is rough and slick in places, rocks and moss wet under your boots. As the mist intensifies, you find it gradually more difficult to see very far in front of you. It's so silent at this moment, it almost seems the mist is sucking sound out of the forest, plugging the entire morning with a thick gauze of insulation.

Gradually you realize how similar this thickening mist is to the fog portrayed in your dream. For a second you even imagine walking into the path of Sara's careening BMW. "Shit!" you mutter under your breath, perturbed by your apprehension. What's with you, Kovacs? you wonder. What the hell is going on?

You keep climbing, remembering from your youth to make sure you walk in a straight line. Knox and the boys would be pissed, you know, if you got lost on the first day of the hunt because you strayed too far from camp, merely seeking enough privacy to defecate. Still, you keep climbing, despite the pressure from your bowels. You want to climb high enough from camp to cure yourself of the uneasiness you feel in the wake of your dream. And you're not ready yet to face the other men who will be entirely preoccupied by the hunt.

One fact is inescapable now. Coming on this expedition was probably a mistake. The circumstances are cold and primitive. By the end of the week, a meal in a restaurant and a hot shower are going to seem like the holy grail to you. It might have been worth it, had Fieldler and Knox been different kind of men. But Fieldler and Knox are no more going to let you handle their financial investments than fly to the fucking moon. So here you are for dubious reasons—cold, tired and apprehensive, and in need of a rewarding shit. And you must wonder why J.D. Hamilton believed his big game hunter friend and his revolver-toting guide had potential as clients for you.

You stop to rest a moment in the mist and suddenly remember the revolver you saw strapped to Knox's leg. You do not know why this memory continues to trouble you, why it preoccupies you so much. Americans are enamored of guns—you're used to the fact—but Knox's hidden weapon is a nagging worry your thoughts cannot dismiss.

Your stomach rumbles. Your bowels are out of patience and you must give in to them. When you were a Scout so many years ago, the Scout master ritually brought a supply of prunes and other dried fruit into the wilderness as part of the troop's supplies, to combat constipation in young men who were shy about their bodily functions in the wild. No need for that this trip. No need for prunes at all.

You find a spot and go, setting down your pack so that it faces the straight line you've been careful to maintain in your climb away from camp. You use toilet paper then, using the toe of your boot, cover everything up with dirt and coniferous needles. Satisfied that your clothing is clean, you refasten your jeans. Cold now, you search your pack for your nylon trousers. It's hard to tell in the mist, but there's always a possibility it will rain, and you want to be prepared. After you've donned your pants, pulling them over your jeans, you take out a Power Bar and tear away part of the wrapping. You eat the bar voraciously to combat your morning hunger. Who knows when Knox or someone else will get up to cook breakfast?

Looking into the mist shrouding the way you've come, you stand here a long time, not wanting to return to camp. Even after depositing the wrapper from breakfast into your pack, without considering the ritual environmental reasons from your past that compelled you to do so, you stand there in the mist, hesitant to return. Even after you shrug into the pack, you remain exactly where you are, nearly frozen to this spot, still aware of a growing uneasiness.

Your stomach fidgets from butterflies and you begin to consider the possibility this nervousness may be based on fear. And the source of your fear? An amalgam of factors, you realize. The fucking dream, for one thing. Knox's secret revolver for another. The strange chemistry between the other men, their palpable intensity. You feel yourself to be on the outside of their preoccupation with this hunt, with the apparent intensity they share with one another. Different personalities perhaps, except they all emit an urgency that you, at least, wouldn't normally share with them. In fact, it's possible your urgency exists only because you feel yourself to be on the outside of theirs. And last night around the fire, while all of you nibbled at Knox's lousy chili, any mood of relaxed celebration that the hunt was underway was entirely absent. Even Knox noticed it. No wonder Knox expressed his disappointment, you reflect at this moment, reminding all of you that this was no way to behave. And did you not notice that none of your companions met your gaze in the flicker of the campfire flames? It was almost as if they wanted you to feel unwelcome on this expedition.

And so it is that you hesitate this morning to return quickly to the tents. The other men make you nervous, as if, as a collective, they have become antagonistic to you. Where's the wilderness camaraderie you expected? No wonder you continue to stand alone here on the slope of the hill, apprehensive in the mist. No wonder you are deeply ambivalent about going back. Something here is making you uncomfortable. You wish they'd all decide to go back home.

And one more thing, this from the mouth of beautiful Sara. But with Tony and my father?

Why not? you said.

Because it's dangerous, she replied.

And standing where you are several hundred yards away from the camp, the first distressing "what if" questions burst through the walls of your thoughts. What if Pirelli knows you're sleeping with the woman he still believes should be his wife? What if J.D. Hamilton knows? Would they want to confront you here where you are entirely alone? Would they want to shame you in some way? Would they perhaps enjoy the prospect of killing you? What if they have come here together to kill you? What if the revolver strapped to Knox's calf is the weapon that will do it?

What was that strange statement, that question Pirelli asked you yesterday? The woods are a good place to visit but you wouldn't want to live or die here. Die here? What the fuck did he mean by that? "I'm not going home without my trophy," he also said. What trophy, Tony? The man who's been banging your wife?

"Jesus," you murmur aloud, still standing rigid in the mist. What is it, Kovacs? you ask yourself. What inspires dark fantasies such as these? Overactive imagination? A fear of the wilderness? Or just some incredibly creative guilt? Okay, door number three, you decide. Creative guilt, powerful and persistent. That increasingly nagging suspicion that you should be somehow ashamed of yourself, the way you make a living, the way you take Sara's love for you for granted. These are the insidious doubts, you know, that would explain the apparent message in your dream of Sara driving head on at you.

You glance at the place on your wrist where your watch should be, discovering you've left it in your tent, exposed on the plastic floor near your sleeping bag. This, in itself, is enough of a reason to return to camp. Sara gave you that watch. It's engraved with her initials. Unlikely anyone would conclude S.H. would apply to her but, in your state of uneasiness, any bad thing seems possible.

With an audible sigh designed to establish you've

gotten hold of yourself, you begin to descend towards camp. But you do so gingerly, still preoccupied by a powerful sense of caution and fear. Your stomach is tied up in knots. Circumstantial or not, you continue to believe you have reason to feel some kind of persistent fear. You move as quietly as you can, aware of the gentle swish of your nylon pants, retracing your steps, barely blinking, staring into the slowly receding mist until your eyes ache.

THE MEN IN THE CAMP GET UP within minutes of one another. Fieldler is first, then, a few seconds later, Knox follows. Pirelli and Hamilton join them shortly afterwards. The men gravitate towards the centre of the campsite bordered by the ring of dew-damp tents.

"Should we build a fire?" Pirelli asks, his voice barely a whisper.

Knox shakes his head. Then, still wordlessly, he gestures for Fieldler to follow him. Carefully they pick their way down to the lake where the airplane dances delicately on its pontoons on the misty, morning mirror of the lake.

"I don't like the fog," remarks Fieldler as Knox opens up the cargo door and reaches inside for the first of the rifles.

"We have to live with it until a wind comes up," is Knox's reply.

Fieldler lowers his voice. "He may not run. He may stay with us, trying to change our minds. Do you think he'll run?"

"Wouldn't you?"

"I'm not Kovacs. What if he doesn't run? What if he refuses to run?"

"Makes my job easier."

Fieldler nods and frowns.

Knox gazes at the aging hunter a moment, knowing the other man is disappointed by the prospect of such an easy kill.

"So what did you bring?" Fieldler wants to know.

"Remington Composites."

"Scopes?"

"Yes. If we down him at some distance, it looks more accidental. Just in case."

"Ammo?"

"Enough. It's a hunt. I wouldn't want it to look like we're going to war."

"Travelling light is better."

"That's right," says Knox.

He shuts the airplane door, then bends to pick up two of the cases holding the rifles.

In a moment, Fieldler helps him.

"Already loaded?"

Knox nods.

Fieldler takes one of the rifles, removes its case, then points it out over the lake, squinting into the scope. "Okay," he says when he is done. "Light."

"Seven and a half pounds before the scope."

Quietly they lug the four rifles up to the campsite. There, Hamilton and Pirelli step forward to claim a rifle. Zippers on cases are undone, the sound a choir of seductive whispers.

"Okay?" says Knox.

Fieldler nods but Pirelli and Hamilton are as stiff as mannequins.

Knox must ask again. "Ready?" he whispers. "Tony? John?"

At last, as if emerging from a daze, the other two men begin to nod.

Hamilton's expression is so gleeful he looks like a child. Noticing this, Knox feels a provocative impatience.

He is reminded his tolerance for his employer can run thin at times. Ten million dollars. His fee. He is convinced at this moment that he would never have accepted this mission for anything less. Five million in the bank, with five million more on the way. Okay, for that kind of money, he'll try to maintain his patience.

He turns in the direction of your tent. "Kovacs! You getting up? We want to get started here." His voice carries here, in this location not far from the water's edge.

But there is no reply.

"Jesus, Kovacs," Knox says, approaching your tent, chuckling convincingly. He glances at the other men before he adds, "You going to sleep all day?" He bends and unzips the opening of your tent. The zipper wails in the morning silence. "You with us, Kovacs? Are you awake?"

Knox peers inside your empty tent, squinting in the dim light. Then he stands erect again, turning towards the others. "He's not here," he announces without inflection.

"What the fuck?" cries Pirelli.

"Relax," says Knox.

"Relax?" This from Hamilton. "The sonofabitch knows. He's smelled it out."

Knox doubts this but he doesn't say so for the moment.

Hamilton's breathing comes in gasps. All the men can hear it. It's the disappointment he feels that you have escaped this place somehow. He flushes angrily, unable to find any words to express his frustration. Your fear, more than a successful hunt, was what was to give him satisfaction. He is enraged that he will not get to see the necessary manifestation of the terror he has imagined etched upon your face.

Noticing some of this, Fieldler touches Hamilton on the arm, eventually clasping his shoulder. "Don't assume so much," he suggests gently.

But Hamilton is nearly frantic. "What gave it away,

Knox?"

For the moment Knox merely stares at him, as if in resignation.

"Knox?"

"Jesus, John, he probably went for a walk," the professional says at last.

"A walk? Where are we? Acapulco? Central Park? Atlantic City? Whaddyuh mean he probably went for a walk?"

"Get a grip," says Knox in his most menacing tone. He lowers his voice. "If he comes back in a few minutes and hears you, the game will really be up. So let's just keep our voices down, okay?"

Shaking his head, Hamilton turns away, already beginning to hope that Knox is right.

Knox moves to your tent again, opens the flap, crouches and this time crawls inside. The other men wait in silence until he emerges again.

"His pack's gone," Knox reports, getting to his feet.

"Jesus," curses Hamilton.

"It still doesn't mean anything," Knox remarks.

Pirelli has been aiming his rifle up the hill away from the other men, squinting into the scope, wondering how to adjust its focus. Now he lowers the gun to address his father-in-law. "He's right, J.D. I can't see Kovacs striking out on his own because for some reason or other he's become suspicious. What would make him that suspicious? What would make him run into the deep woods on speculation? Besides, we haven't done anything yet. Even if he found a cop or a forest ranger way out here, who'd believe him?"

Still flushed with anger, Hamilton forces himself to nod. Although he would never admit it, he's aware at this moment that he doesn't care if he and his colleagues are safe. He doesn't actually care if your death is the perfect crime. He's here to kill you, to see you frightened and debased. Saving his own skin isn't the issue here. He can worry about his own fate later. Don't the others understand how important you actually are to him, how much he needs you to die?

"He's right, John," says Knox, endorsing Pirelli's view, "notwithstanding that none of you guys are going to win any acting awards. Last night around the fire, you could slice the tension with a knife."

"Maybe this morning was too late," Hamilton counters. "Maybe yesterday afternoon would have been better."

"We would have lost him in the dark," says Knox.

"Lost is lost," cries Hamilton. "We don't even know how long Kovacs has been gone."

Pirelli has been trying to sight through the scope on his rifle again. As you draw nervously closer in your descent towards the camp, he catches a brief glimpse of your movement in the mist, not really knowing it is you still two hundred yards away. But he flinches. To his surprise, he discovers his finger has been resting against the trigger. The rifle fires. The Remington recoils, the barrel jerks upwards. His shot whistles into the trees about a foot from your right shoulder, its sound echoing like a cannon shot in the mysterious silence of the morning mist.

INSTINCT. IT'S A POWERFUL COMPULSION. The bullet has already hissed through the trees a yard or two from you when you dive to the ground. The sound of the gunshot is departing too, in rippling echoes along the ridge. You feel a bolt of pain along your forearm after you strike the exposed root of a jack pine on your way down to the ground. You smell moss and rock and earth. You breathe in desperate gasps.

For the moment you do not move. Then cautiously you lift your head. You can make out the mist-shrouded shape of the camp and the shadow-bodies of the other four men standing among the tents. In the distance they seem entirely immobile, cardboard cutout characters without true life or function. Knox is the first one to move in the silence. Roughly he forces the barrel of Pirelli's rifle down towards the ground. Was the errant bullet in your direction possibly an accident? For a second, you swim towards the life raft of this conclusion as desperately as a drowning man.

I'm not going back without my trophy, Pirelli said.

You wouldn't want to die here, he also said.

And remembering these words again, you believe—or think you believe—why you've been invited on this hunt. Could it be you are here to serve as an unsuspecting victim?

The question makes you break into a cold sweat. You lie where you are on the ground, paralyzed with fear. What if you were to charge screeching down the rest of the hill and into the camp? Angrily and defiantly? Or maybe just to receive your just desserts? Get it over with—the punishment you deserve. What if you did that? It's a strange but powerful motivation at this moment. Although you don't know why, something habituative in you craves being guilty and accused. You even want to get your punishment over with. You want to be sorry enough to accept even some notion of forgiveness, as truly unjust as this sentence of death seems to be. Or maybe you're just in shock because, most of all, you want the fear gurgling in your belly to come to an end.

Your insanity passes. You lie where you are, not moving. This motionlessness, this playing dead is all you can think of to do.

"Kovacs?"

You recognize Knox's voice. "Are you ok?"

"Kovacs, you fucking bastard!" This time it's J.D. Hamilton's voice. "You scared, Kovacs, you fucking sonofabitch?"

And your terror begins anew. You realize you had convinced yourself the gunshot in your direction was only an accident. Now there is no question Hamilton— What makes us wish our fathers wouldn't hug us the way they do? Sara mused—is the man who wants to see you dead. You try grappling with this fact, a man torn in two. One half of you is convinced the hunters are here to kill you. The other half wants to maintain you've made some kind of mistake.

"One hour, Kovacs," Hamilton calls out now. "One hour to run and shit your pants before we come and blow your brains out."

Carefully you glance down into the camp, into the delicately drifting mist. You can see Sara's father standing in front of the other men. He's holding his rifle under his arm, his hand cradling it there with the barrel pointed to the ground, looking strangely unthreatening except for the menace in his words.

"You scared, Kovacs, you fucking sonofabitch?"

And, yes, you are terrified. In a moment you will want to dash in terror into the trees. But for the moment, you feel an overwhelming urge to cry, to whimper, to come awake in the dark of this new, nocturnal nightmare, and find someone to comfort you. But you're not dreaming this. The bruise on your forearm is enough to make this fact clear to you. Soon you can not resist the urge to prepare to run. You glance down at your hunters again. None of them has moved. Their rifles are aimed at the ground. "One hour," Hamilton said. Are men who wish to kill you also men of their word?

The trees are thicker on your left. Instinctively you

begin to crawl in their direction, gradually rising to hands and knees, then finally to your feet. You duck into a nearby stand of pine. Feeling safer inside the trees, you begin to climb the hill again. You run several feet, then turn and stop, feeling a mild relief when you notice the mist has swallowed up your hunters. It is likely, then, in reverse, the mist now hides you inside its cloak.

Hamilton's voice, growing hoarse and weak, sounds disembodied inside this shroud of mist, as he continues to shout at you. He's barely coherent at this point; hate has such a limited vocabulary. Shortly, you don't even discern what he is saying, it's so garbled with invective.

You begin to run. And you run some more. You climb. You climb towards higher ground. No reason behind this need to seek the heights, just instinct, hot and frantic. And you are the only sound you hear inside this deep wilderness morning, your breathing and your feet, the whisper of your nylon trousers swishing together, your thoughts terrified, an astonished jumble, your dismayed body running hard and breathing savagely as you embark on this passionate mission to save your life.

AT LAST HAMILTON SHUTS UP, his voice ragged and sore from the insults he has shouted.

Knox and the others wait inside the ensuing vacuum of his silence, hoping Hamilton remains quiet, hoping he embarrasses them no further. Sometimes they think they hear the sound of your flight over rocks and through trees and bushes, but the silence all around them possesses a devious quality and they cannot be certain of the true nature of sound as a deeper quiet closes around this morning like an infant fist around a finger.

"Thirty minutes," says Knox to the others.

Hamilton turns around in surprise. "I said an hour."

"In this mist? It's thirty minutes now. That's all he gets."

Hamilton moves towards him to argue, but Knox holds up his hand. "We've fucked things up enough for one morning. Between Pirelli's itchy trigger finger and you're big mouth, John, he has all the advantage that he needs. We're not going to sit here for an hour based on some tenuous principle of fair play versus revenge. Do you want him dead or not?"

"Wait a minute, Knox."

"No. You wait a minute, John. As far as I can tell, he didn't know the score until you opened your big mouth."

"You work for me, Knox."

"Yeah. And I'm going to complete the job to your satisfaction. But you've just made things more difficult for us and you're going to have to accept the adjustments we have to make."

Hamilton wants to debate the issue longer, but he flinches instead, reaching up to place his hand over his belly, the victim of a fresh bolt of stomach distress, his first in days. He nods abruptly and turns away. He supposes Knox is right. He wants to explain, though, why the moment with you up on the hill got away from him, so the others understand, as a way to make amends, perhaps to ease the agony of the pain in his stomach. He needs the other men to realize how justified his hated for you is. "I wanted him to be afraid, that's all. What's the point, if he's not scared?" he says at last.

But Knox, the wrong man for this question, merely ignores him.

"You see what I'm saying?" Hamilton asks the others. "What's the point if he's not scared?"

"I know, J.D.," says Pirelli. "I'm with you on that. I agree with you."

Fieldler nods too, though somewhat halfheartedly. Then he bends into his tent to retrieve his pack. He slips it easily into position, the wide straps married to his shoulders, his sleeping bag already fastened securely to its bottom.

"John, Tony, get your packs," instructs Knox. "We should be ready."

"How long?" asks Hamilton. "How many minutes?"

Knox glances at his watch. "Twenty-eight minutes."

The men use ten minutes more to ready their equipment. With Knox's and Fieldler's help, they adjust the sights on their scopes, conduct a detailed review of what should be in their packs, rolling up their sleeping bags and tying them to their packs. Knox divvies up some food between them, the same Power Bars you carry in your pack, a couple of apples, a few oranges, some dehydrated meals Knox hopes they will not need.

"Okay," says Knox when they are done. "John, you're with Ernie. Pirelli, you're with me. The mist is lifting. You'll see tracks some times, broken tree branches along his route. We'll crisscross in pairs every one hundred yards or so in the general direction that he went, until it's clear which way he's going. Now, here's the important part. You don't have to get in close. These rifles have scopes. If you see him in the distance and you have a clear shot, you take him out. That way, if we have to explain it to anyone, it looks like a hunting accident. Okay?"

"What do we tell Sara?" Hamilton wants to know at this point. "I don't want her to think it was a hunting accident. I need her to think he left her behind, that he vanished at the end of the hunt. What do I say to Sara, Knox, if it looks like an accident?"

Knox glares at him angrily. "Tell her whatever the fuck you want. We've got lots of time to figure that out, for Chrissakes."

Hamilton falls silent. Pirelli and Fieldler too. All of them know what Sara must be told isn't the issue now.

There's an awkward moment among the other men as they begin to realize, with varying degrees of tolerance, that Hamilton's preoccupation with his daughter is deeper than they once suspected.

"So you shoot him from a distance if you can," says Knox. "Am I absolutely clear on this?"

Pirelli and Fieldler nod like twins.

Knox shifts his gaze to Hamilton. "I mean it, John. It's too risky to get in close just to see him sweat. Don't fuck this up. It's your plan. Don't fuck it up."

At last Hamilton nods.

But Knox wants to be absolutely sure. "John?"

"Yes, for fuck's sake, yes! You want it in blood?"

"Fifteen minutes," says Knox, not entirely convinced. "That's all he's got left. One more thing. If you need to have a crap, now's the time to get it over with."

But the men all stand like statues in the centre of the campsite. It grows into the longest fifteen minutes most of them have ever known.

TOO SOON, YOU RUN OUT OF BREATH. Gasping and wheezing, you must stop to rest for a couple of valuable moments. You argue with yourself. Your fear doesn't want you to stop but your ill-conditioned body is temporarily out of stamina—you can go no further.

You have begun to doubt reality and this too saps your strength. You keep wondering if you've made a mistake, if you've somehow misunderstood, if you've taken far too seriously what might be nothing more than a complicated practical joke. It would be one thing for J.D. Hamilton to want to frighten you, quite another to take the step of having you murdered. You keep coming back to your need to know your universe is in safe and predictable alignment. The universe you're used to doesn't permit a hunt like this, doesn't allow murder, won't tolerate the transformation of someone like you into unarmed, human game. It's a violation of normalcy, a rape of chaste, predictable destiny. In your universe, when someone dies, they're someone else, some stranger, some unnoticed cardboard cutout you're relieved you didn't know.

So far in life you have had no real relationship with death. Not like this. Death has always been someone else's reality, not yours. You have little experience with unexpected death. Even the night your mother and father died when you were just a young man, that night of disbelief and shock, there was a quality to your caring that gradually allowed you to succeed in distancing yourself from death. You felt relief that death had made its selection and its selection wasn't you! Your parents were real, their death was real, you wished they were still alive, but at the edges of your dismay you felt a guilty relief. Because it wasn't you! When your parents died so suddenly they became strangers. Because the people who die in your structured universe were and are always separate from you. You realize at this moment, gasping for breath, that you are walled inside a fortified world where it is easy, even necessary to believe you will not die. The evidence of death is by necessity outside yourself, residing in the misfortune of some unknown, luckless stranger whose prevailing characteristic is that he's never you.

No wonder you believe you've made some kind of mistake, that Hamilton was just kidding when he threatened you. Because if Hamilton wasn't kidding, if he actually meant what he said, then the world has tipped on its axis. If you have been selected for imminent death, then you are the cardboard prop and everything you've done until today has been lifeless— the lawn you cut for your father when you were twelve years old, the homework you did for school, the investment you sold last week to fulfill someone's retirement dream. Dying now means you've wasted time somehow, frittered life away. If Hamilton's ravings aren't an elaborate hoax, if he and death have actually selected you for disaster, then somehow everything you have done so far in life has dwindled to a pointless waste of time.

It's a hard habit to break, the notion that death (your death in particular) is a work of fiction. If you turn around right now and go back to laugh along with the other men at the success of Hamilton's practical joke, your world will right itself. Your safe, unchanging orbit will resume its timeless voyage. You will be immortal again. You will have time to kill, to waste, to squander on conventional distractions. Again.

But standing in the trees, gradually regaining your breath, you pinch yourself awake and know instinctively what is happening this morning is no mistake. The other men have brought you here for the satisfaction of hunting you down. As a joke, it's already gone too far. As a joke, the silence all around you would have concluded by now, replaced by a joviality over how you've been successfully duped. Better to be terrified. At least the terror you feel underscores that you are still alive. Inspired again, nearly blindly, you begin to run once more, your pack slapping you on the back, its hatchet dangling from its loop, swatting you on the hip.

You climb and run and flee. With each step, you pray. You beg God a thousand times to save your life. You ask Him to forgive the various misdeeds in your life that now seem to be collecting for review, like mosquitoes on the screen of your selfish past. You offer to exchange all of these sins, and all those that might have otherwise occurred in the future, for a new opportunity to remain miraculously alive.

THE MEN EASILY FIND EVIDENCE OF YOUR PASSAGE, easily determine which way you are going. In places, they can see the impression of your boots in the mud or where your running feet have smudged the carpet of needles littering the ground. At one point they even discover a hand print in the mud where you have slipped and fallen. In the trees they find a broken branch or two where you have tried to run through a narrow gap. They lose you at times on the rocks but find evidence of your passing when your footprints are located a few feet away on the forest floor.

"He's still climbing," Knox tells the others.

"Straight up," adds Fieldler.

"He's running. He's not saving anything up. He'll be out of juice soon."

"Scared?" Hamilton wants to know again. "Terrified?"

Knox's confidence has been renewed and he feels more kindly disposed towards the other man. He will give him the satisfaction that he needs. "You bet he's scared. It's panic. We're seeing evidence of his panic here."

"You're telling me he's frightened to death? Scared shitless?"

"Yeah," Knox replies. "Scared shitless."

Hamilton nods. Tears seem to form in his eyes. The other men turn away out of embarrassment.

The hunters have spread out in a single line, gazing one by one up the hill. They speak in hoarse whispers. When they begin to move again, they walk as quickly as they can but they do not run. There is no need. Shortly you will tire and they will gain on you steadily.

"When he reaches the top, he'll have to go down the other side," muses Knox aloud. "Then we'll have him. One of us will see him. A clear shot and it'll all be over."

They hike on, inspired by Knox's prognosis.

"But we have to keep our eyes open. We have to see if he veers right or left. We need to know if he decides to go around the hill."

All the men but Fieldler acknowledge this remark. Fieldler has hunted so many times, he's already sorted through the various scenarios of what you might do. For his money, you'll keep climbing because you're so afraid. He knows, in your panic, you'll want to reach the summit to look down on everything, in case something in the distance will be able to rescue you. It's what he would do, he realizes, even though he's never known the deep and terrible panic he knows you must be feeling now.

YOU DO NOT STOP TO REST AGAIN until you reach the summit of the long rocky hill you have been climbing. You turn to glance down towards the lake but the mist obscures your view. Like liquid it has filled each crevice in the crowded panorama below you. There is a jagged cluster of boulders a few yards away in front of another thick stand of jackpine occupying the plateau you have now reached. Gasping greedily for air, your throat aching from such prolonged heavy breathing, you force yourself to scurry towards these rocks, where you can skirt them and lean against their shelter, hidden from view. Here, trying not to consider what a bullet must feel like tearing through flesh and bone, you steal a few precious moments to still your heaving chest.

The mist has begun to dissipate, a development you interpret as betrayal. A sickly sun somewhere on the other side of the gray clouds tries desperately to emerge. All of these changes in the day make you feel more exposed. Your belly is a knot of terror and exhaustion. You know the other men are coming for you, that they have rifles and you do not. In the throes of a passive fatigue, you've begun to accept that it is likely they will kill you before this day is done. The notion that what is happening to you is merely some idiotic mistake has begun to wane. All that remains of this optimistic conclusion is a childish fringe at the edge of your more rational thoughts. You consider the personalities of the men who are your hunters and you conclude each one of them is more than capable of a hunt such as this one. Out of motive, out of boredom, out of disregard for human life. Only a fool would continue to deny these men have reason to be dangerous.

Even so you cling to an hallucinogenic hope. Fleeing from your pursuers, you have conjured a fantasy in which Sara somehow realizes what has befallen you. Magically aware of your risky circumstances, she has called the police. Even now, you decide, they are on their way to rescue you. Never mind that she doesn't know exactly where you are, in the same way that you don't know. Your hope is unreasonable. You are compelled to believe help is on the way. You are not ready to be killed. Help must be headed in your direction, if only to verify your decision to remain alive. You cannot accept this nonsensical error. The world should have no actual interest in stealing your life from you.

None of your conclusions are rational. Sara clairvoyantly realizing you are in trouble is entirely unlikely. But the idea gives you strength and you cling to it.

You count to one hundred, then nervously leave the shelter of the boulders at your back. You race across the small distance dividing you from a thick stand of trees a few yards away on this plateau. When you gain this stand of jackpine, you break into a measured trot. Each time you are tempted to succumb to exhaustion, you force yourself to continue on. You run through a virtual vacuum. All you can hear is the wheeze of your own breathing, drowning out any other sound. When you begin to descend the other side of the plateau, the descent, you're relieved to notice, is quite gradual.

For the longest time, you travel only inside the repetitious sound of your own flight. A breaking twig, your ragged breathing, the whisper of your clothing in motion. Eventually, though, you begin to hear the murmur of something else. You can't make out what it is at first, but it grows gradually louder as you make your way through the trees, doggedly descending the plateau. Running water? Too soon to tell. You are a man more used to urban traffic, vehicle engines, human cries, wailing sirens. Out here, sounds are much too pure, as if they're too clear to be identified.

You break out of the woods with a surprising abruptness. The trees are thick all around you, in front of you too, then suddenly they are gone like a drape that's been pulled away from a window. Feeling exposed and frightened, you turn quickly to enter the trees again. Then, at this moment, you hear the steady mutter of running water. There is a river just ahead of you. You can hear its rapids somewhere off to your right. You abandon your plan to scurry deeper into the trees. Instead, hurrying, feeling frightened at exposing yourself, you break into a sprint and head towards the river you believe lies just ahead somewhere below the precipice.

You manage to come to a halt before you nearly run over the cliff. Acrophobia punches you in the stomach and you step back a few feet, retreating from the sensation. Dizzy, you bring a hand to your sweaty forehead. You stand there a moment, getting a grip on your senses. Teetering a little as if in a sudden gust of wind, you glance over the brink.

The river there is narrow but it flows relatively quickly through a cleft in the rocks, in a direction you cannot identify. You suddenly realize you do not have a compass and sadly begin to wish for one. It is gloomy. South, north, east, west? The sun? What time is it? Your wristwatch is back in the tent. Not only do you not know where the river is going, you don't know when it goes. Your disorientation is complete. But the stream flows in front of you, not only blocking your way but offering some kind of promise of ill-defined salvation.

Yes, there's something hopeful about this river. It, at least, knows where it's going. It's as gray as the sky except where patches of white water reveal themselves upstream to your right. Immediately below you, it washes against the wall of rock on which you stand. How far down? You're not certain. Fifty feet? One hundred feet? One hundred and fifty? How deep is the river? You tiptoe closer to the edge and peer down, battling another cruel nudge of fear. Deep enough maybe. Then again, maybe not.

You turn and glance back towards the trees from which you emerged a few minutes ago. No option in that direction. Back there, you know, your hunters are coming for you. You stand on the rocks, trying to decide what is best for you to do. Run along the edge of the river until it leads you somewhere safe? If so, right or left?

You stand there too long, tortured by indecision. You turn again and gaze back towards the trees. It strikes you with overdue clarity that you are leaving tracks and clues for your hunters to follow. You can see and remember evidence of some of the damage you've done before and since you emerged from this stand of trees. Human boot prints in the earth. Broken branches, flattened grasses. You feel sick with despair. You've telegraphed your passing.

You gaze down into the river again. The river must go somewhere. It must take a route eventually through some kind of civilization. And what if you jumped? Would Knox and Hamilton and the others refuse to believe you would actually risk your life this way to escape their clutches? Would jumping from this cliff fool them into believing you've gone somewhere else?

You count five paces backwards. You stand there for a couple of minutes, trying not to lose your nerve. You are frightened by the prospect of breaking apart on the rocks below. It's reason enough to justify changing your mind.

But this river must go somewhere.

You clamp your mouth shut so that you don't cry out. Before you can change your mind, you race towards the edge of the cliff and throw yourself into space. You linger a moment at the apex of your leap, just long enough to wonder if gravity has ceased to exist, just long enough to toy with the conclusion that you've made a terrible mistake, that this leap into the gray sky actually represents suicide. Then you feel that strange, unique, deep ache in your legs that tells you you are falling. A rush of air. The rising gray river waters. The grunt you emit despite clamping your mouth shut. The river as hard as cement. Then the splash, the shock in the immediate chill, the thin omnipresence of the churning water, the touch of your feet on the river bottom, a sudden, intense fear that you will not be able to float, that you will not have the strength to swim back up to find air. But at last you claw your way to the surface, gasping in rich relief when you begin to float. The water is very cold. It is careless to assume you will not drown. You feel yourself in new danger. You begin to swim with the river's current like the devil is after you.

THE GRAY WOLF, even at a relatively great distance of six or seven miles, hears your desperate body cleave the river's surface. He rises immediately from his crouch, calmly alert, ears cocked, nostrils sorting through the various aromatic reports offered up in the gentle breeze of this wilderness morning. He smells nothing for a few seconds, then focuses on the sound you make when you break the water's surface. He hears nearly as clearly as you do the grunt you make as you gasp for air, as if distance is only a canvas on which perspective can be painted.

The wolf is downstream from you. He stands ten yards from the river bank, just inside the trees at the edge of a small clearing at the water's edge. The sound vibration created by your flight into the river has unleashed a new silence on the day. This silence now radiates in circular ripples further and further from the epicentre of your panicky swim in the river. Like the eyes of a group of hurricanes these circles of silence, pierce the ritual sound of the morning until they reach the wolf in his immediate location. The ripples pass further into the wilderness. Each step of the way, bird sounds cease. Squirrels interrupt their labours and squabbles because of the growing tidal wave of silence reaching them. Then, as they wait quietly, these animals too become part of the stillness, part of the ripple of silence moving outward from the storm where you struggle on the surface of the cold, gray river.

In a moment or two, when you make no further significant sound, the wilderness near the wolf gradually resumes normalcy. But the wolf isn't fooled by this return to something typical. He has identified your intrusion as human and he thinks he can hear you struggling in the river. As a wolf, he is torn between a deep and characteristic curiosity and a fear that you, being human, have come here to harm him in some way. The wolf listens and considers. He now knows you are moving in his direction, riding the river current towards him. So he decides quickly to act. He turns away from you and slips deeper into the trees, heading in the opposite direction from you, moving further downstream, discretion having won the inner debate with his curiosity.

He does not run but breaks into the comfortable lupine trot that enables him to cover so much distance in such a short period of time. He is getting hungry again and intends to find something to eat. Food is one of his two preoccupations at this moment. The other one is you, because you are human and probably dangerous. The wolf wants to be well away from you when he must turn his attention to his hunt for food.

YOUR BODY ACHES BECAUSE THE WATER IS COLD. Then, shortly, with a speed you did not expect, you go numb. You become aware of the tremendous weight of your clothing and your pack, and you want to give in to the insistent persuasion of the river that it would make more sense than struggling at this point to simply sink and drown. But the current is strong and this is helpful. As you try at times to swim, to accomplish more than merely treading water, the current helps the cause of your fragile buoyancy. Even so, you feel exhausted. This is true exhaustion of a kind you've never known before. To describe exhaustion in any other context—working two or three long days at the office or not going home until after midnight—seems ridiculous. You remember clearly telling Sara you were exhausted the last time you were compelled to work long hours. Hyperbole, you conclude, struggling now in this exhausting present on the verge of drowning. Long hours in the office? Just fatigue, you decide. Wanting to just give up, wanting to fall asleep, wanting to permit the clutching fingers of this cold, heartless river to tug you inside its embrace where at last you can fall asleep, where at last you can find rest or peace; these are the tempting faces of true exhaustion.

No more panic, no more fear, no more caring pointlessly about destination or purpose, about some idiotic resolution to the ordinary dilemmas of life, wondering what everyone thinks of you, what anything means. No more catching a glimpse of the possible absurdity that may be life's true skeleton. No more preoccupation with the flesh and sinew of life's apparently empty promise that it has meaning beyond the number of dollars you amass. You feel yourself in possession of the heartless truth at this moment of near drowning, that everything you do hasn't meant very much in the end.

Except . . .

. . . Sara, perhaps. You can see her so clearly in your mind's eye. You can imagine her coming to find you here in these deep woods—delirium, really—but she is here to rescue you from the men she has suspected all along, the sexual cannibals intent not only on devouring her spirit, but now on taking your life as a kind of meting out of moral justice. As much as you can—because you are not Sara, because you are only a moment or two away from drowning in this enticing, peace-promising river—you absorb some of her outrage, some of her hatred for your hunters. You ride the current of this river and the current of a new understanding, navigating your shock and dismay, kicking hard in fantastic fury towards the shore on your left.

So tired. But so furious and appalled. Hamilton, Pirelli, Fieldler, Knox: fucking arrogant bastards. Their assumption that they enjoy a fundamental right to determine what is just. Having decided you are guilty, they have made a game out of your execution. Never mind their guilt. At the edge of your death you welcome the revelation that guilt and hypocrisy are kin. You feel wise and thoughtful now that you live a few moments from death. Life is giving up philosophical secrets to you now that you cannot share them with anyone else.

Gradually the cliff walls at the edge of the river begin to shrink away. You see broken tree trunks, rocks and boulders strewn along the shore some hazy distance away. You float, half-submerged, occasionally swallowing water, kicking in the direction of a gap along the shore where the cliff is interrupted by an opening in the rocks, like a cleft in a great, pale chin. Foundering, gasping, counting kicks of your feet, three or four or five, you force yourself towards the cleft in the rock face, trying not to think that you are out of strength. Then more kicks, two, three, four, the current helping you along. Your will battles fiercely with a shadowy, smarmy notion that trying to survive in this way reflects an embarrassing idealism.

Your feet graze the river's bottom. You half swim, half stumble along in the current, counting your steps, trying at the boundary of unconsciousness to remember what number follows thirty-nine. The number of desperate kicks that has brought you to the tip of salvation near this rocky shore.

At some point on the threshold of death by drowning, you reach the shallows near the a group of boulders reshaping the riverbank. Your knee strikes a submerged rock and the cold water embellishes your pain. You cry out brokenly, spitting water and gasping for air. You open your eyes. You hear the sound of the river again, now aware that while it was seducing you towards death, its entreaties were halfhearted. Finding yourself here in the shallows transforms into a sensory explosion. Sight, sound, the cold of your flesh inside your sodden clothing, the pain of your bruised kneecap, the ability of your voice to moan in agony, all of these enticements cry out that you've survived. Your sensations return to tell you you are alive. You stagger, stumble and crawl out of the river's cold grasp. You didn't realize you had lost your senses to the merciless cold of the river, but now that they are found again, it strikes you with a nearly psychedelic amazement that, for the moment, you have cheated death.

Dizzy, you stumble away from the water's edge, tripping over a final rock, pitching forward onto a wide patch of needled ground at the edge of another stand of trees. You lie there on your side, your pack so wet and heavy it literally pins you to the ground. You cough up a drop or two of river. Your breath is a cackle of phlegm and fatigue. Your eyes close. It seems for a moment that you will fall asleep, but the notion of slumber terrifies you. Its enticement is too reminiscent of the death you've just narrowly escaped. You force your eyes open. You call once again upon your furious will.

You are but five yards from the trees, a busy, culturally diverse mixture of pine, spruce and poplar. Still drunk with fatigue, you clamber, half walking and half falling, into the trees. Here, leaning sideways against a spruce, you permit yourself a few moments rest.

It seems strange to you a few minutes later, as the sun battles its way out of the fabric of the clouds and the mist gives way to its heat, that you begin to shiver. The shivering is innocuous at first but soon the tremors intensify, breeding prolifically, until you are racked by a violent shaking. You feel betrayed. As the sun exposes itself and the temperature climbs, you are badly shaken by cold. The sunshine comes too late. Everything is soaked, your clothing, your pack. Your coat and nylon trousers are waterproof but only from rainfall. Swimming has soaked them through.

Your teeth chatter. You cannot control your trembling. New fears terrify you. What if, after all you've been through so far, you die of hypothermia? And your hunters? What if they're still coming for you? What if they track you to this new location where you are too exhausted to move? What if they are only minutes away from discovering you here, shaking and trembling and afraid? Thinking these things in a confusing hodgepodge, you endure a new wave of panic. Your uncontrollable shivering, this fierce state of trembling, is as overwhelming as a seizure. Your body heaves and shakes violently. You are so overcome by this solitary physical violence, you fall to weeping. "Oh God," you cry aloud. "I don't want to die. I don't want to die like this."

Your trembling and your entreaties last for several minutes. Then, as if you realize it was merely a malevolent initiation, you struggle to get hold of yourself. Spitefully you slap your face, once, twice, three times. Think! You have to think!

Finally you shrug out of your sodden pack, leaving it on the ground. Then, hurrying as if you can outdistance the exhausted resistance in your body, you slip out of your coat. Piece by piece, despite the wild trembling of your fingers, you remove your soaked clothing, piling it on the ground beside you. You even remove your socks and boots. Naked, you move into a narrow strip of sunlight on the shore, rubbing your flesh with your hands, warming it with friction. The sun is at an angle to your right. It can't yet be noon, although you're not really certain. Still, it's probably safe to assume this particular river flows in a southwesterly direction. Your conclusion is based purely on faith; you don't really have any idea. Pondering this theory of the river's direction, mostly for the distraction it provides, you continue to rub your flesh in the sunlight. Soon, gradually, the violent trembling in your body subsides.

Hurrying now, you pick up each item of clothing and wring it as dry as you can. Socks, underwear, jeans, shirt. All of these you wring out and then force into your pack. You have to get going. You have to get moving again. You must leave this place. Your hunters may be close to tracking you to the precipice from which you leapt. You take time to glance up the river, but the cliff walls obscure your view and what you see doesn't tell you anything. You may have floated only half a mile or the distance may have been much greater; there's no way to know for sure. The eternity in the river may have lasted only moments. Not knowing how far you drifted, you have no idea how far behind your hunters are.

Still naked, you slip into your nylon pants. You shudder at their cold dampness. You put on your boots which respond with a wheeze of clammy water. You lace them up anyway. Your coat is sodden, but you slip into it, tugging up the zipper now stubborn because it is wet. New chills, new trembling results. But you have to be going. You slip the pack over your shoulders, wincing at its waterlogged weight.

The cold and wetness are painful on your flesh. Perhaps, as you would your hunters, you can outrun the wet and cold. Thinking this, you strike off into the trees, setting a course in the same direction employed by the natural wisdom of the river. This river has to go somewhere. You move through the trees, keeping the river in view on your right while clinging to the flimsy protection the trees afford you. You walk for several minutes, then, more or less to warm your flesh, you break into a jog. To control your panic, you count each step you take. For now, if you do not do this, do not count your steps, do not measure out some kind of progress, cold and terrified, you believe you will lose your mind. Without numbers to keep you going and shape some kind of reason, you fear death will find you raving like a lunatic.

KNOX DOES NOT SUFFER FROM FEAR OF HEIGHTS. In fact, Knox barely remembers fear at all. He has been trained to control his human phobias. Fear as a phobia has been removed from his being. Like love. Like compassion. Like empathy. All have been removed. These are the phobias—quaint and economically worthless—that impede success. Their absence allows him to thrive in the modern world in which he is an assassin.

Having no fear of heights, he is the one who moves to the edge of the cliff to gaze thoughtfully over the edge. He feels deeply in control of the hunt now. He knows this is so because he has been, in his mind, a professional from birth. He has never failed. Here too, on J.D. Hamilton's hunt, he will not fail. As he scans the distance from this precipice, his rifle slung over his shoulder, he searches each square of a meticulous grid beneath him, an invention of his mathematical mind, looking for clues that will tell him whether you have fallen over this cliff or not. It is clear to him and to Fieldler that you have emerged from the trees at this point. Now Knox looks for traces of your clothing, for a glimpse of your body, in case you have made it easy for him by falling to your death or drowning in the river or by breaking apart on the rocks immediately beneath this location on the summit.

When at last he concludes there is nothing to see, he

moves away from the edge and joins the other men waiting in anticipation nearby.

"Well?" says Hamilton impatiently. "Which way did he go? Right or left?"

"Which way would you go, John?"

Exasperated, Hamilton sighs. "You're the professional. You tell me."

"Pirelli?"

"I dunno. In the same direction as the river, I guess."

"Bull's eye."

"So you think he went left," Hamilton says.

"Yeah. Fieldler?"

"Left."

"We're all agreed then," says Knox. "Unless, of course, he wants us to think so."

In the silence that this observation inspires, a raven passes overhead, *hronking* intermittently. All the men look up at it. Then, after the raven fades into the trees, they stand there aimlessly once more, restless to get going.

"Do you think Kovacs is that smart at this point?" Hamilton remarks at last.

"No," replies Knox, "I don't. But we have to make sure. Ernie, I think you and Tony should go right. Cover a mile or two just to make sure. If you don't see any sign that he went that way, work your way back until you catch up to John and me."

Fieldler has moved to the edge of the cliff to peer down into the river. But now he turns and nods.

And Knox can see him thinking. Knox can read him thinking.

"Ernie?"

"It's fast water," the big game hunter says. "I think he could have jumped."

"Would you jump?"

"I might."

"Jesus," murmurs Pirelli. "The fall would kill him if he jumped. Wouldn't it?"

No one answers him. It's high but not that high. A desperate man could do it without risk of death.

"We should get started," says Knox after a moment. "Maybe he did jump. Maybe we'll find his body along the shore. Maybe not." Knox turns away. "C'mon, John," he says over his shoulder.

The men split up, moving in opposite directions along the cliff.

"You don't think Kovacs jumped, do you?" Hamilton asks when he and Knox are alone.

"Nah. I doubt a man like Kovacs would have the balls."

Hamilton likes Knox's answer; it satisfies his hatred for you, his hatred for his quarry.

YOU HAVE FOUND A RHYTHM IN YOUR FLIGHT, a cruising speed, a regimen. You run two hundred and fifty paces, counting them out along the way; then you stop to rest. While you rest, you count one hundred steamboats, then jog two hundred and fifty paces more. You make sure the river is always in view on your right, using it to keep your bearings. It is more than just a body of restless water; it is becoming the focus of your hope. This river has to go somewhere. But you wish it would hurry up and get there, whatever its destination. You wish it would hurry up and release you from your nightmare.

This rhythm of flight you have adopted occurred to you only after you collapsed in the woods and fell to silent weeping an hour or so ago. Just the terror getting hold of you, the frantic fear of dying when you're not finished living yet. This was what made you weep: the need to be alive, to avoid being senselessly killed. There was no guilt or shame attached to your fear, no sense of having to make amends. No, your fear was entirely logical. You feared the loss of freedom that death takes away from each of us. You didn't push your terror away and you didn't try to strangle it before it was done accosting you. You gave in to it. You let it finish its rant, its need for tearful expression. Then, when it was out of complaints, you let your terror slip away. You got to your feet, cleansed by the honesty in your fear, and decided to run for two hundred and fifty paces, then count to one hundred steamboats while you rested. You felt a better man for this, for conceiving of a system that might bring you closer to a necessary courage.

You even drank at the edge of the river, using your hands as a cup, wondering briefly—the way bottled water urbanites have been trained to wonder—if the river might be polluted. But you concluded, with so many devilish evils intent on taking your life, quenching your thirst seemed the most innocuous of all these dangers. You thought for a time about the fluidity of danger, the fluidity of what is perceived to be dangerous. In California, you drink only bottled water because it is supposed to be safest: the healthiest alternative. But here perspective has changed dramatically. With four men chasing you, intent on killing you, the safety surrounding the water you drink, the vitamins you swallow, and the dark slums you would never enter are no longer worth consideration. These fears seem foolish, even childish now. This is how it seems to you now, with your life reduced to survival. Those various fears you were trained to recognize in California are now a glittering mosaic of tokens contrived by an inauthentic world to distract you from a simpler, more truthful reality. And that reality? Life and death and your necessary affair with Mother Nature, you suppose. A return, perhaps, to a more basic authenticity.

In this way, you feel different now and, should you survive, you know you will be different long into the future. Your reaction to caution and fear has been stripped of its complexity. The economic propaganda was, only days ago, at the root of all your prudence. The pervasive fear dozens of skillful marketers have taunted you into feeling in life—the war against bacteria, against untreatable disease, against theft or inconvenience—these have been altered for you, a byproduct of your flight. You feel so different now, like you've danced with an epiphany. You feel as if your past has died, replaced by this clear present and the extraordinary danger your future holds. The world and civilization as you know it have been blown to smithereens. This moment is nuclear war or some natural calamity that has left you virtually alone in a dangerous universe unlike the one you used to know. It's simpler here, the danger clearer. The world you used to know, filled as it was with superficial worries and precautions, has paled by comparison with your circumstances now.

Running two hundred and fifty yards and counting one hundred steamboats, you find it laughable what you once feared. It doesn't matter any longer if someone important seemed to dislike you, or if you've failed to exert a lucrative influence. It doesn't matter now that you were unable to hide the intensity of your terror, that you wept brokenly a time ago because you desperately don't want to die. You are a naked man, reduced to prey. You need not be or hide behind anything else. There is only one important necessity now: your escape from your deadly hunters. The nagging worries of your past are now irrelevant, even difficult to recall. That they were once so important now embarrasses you.

You have thought these conclusions through during your regimented flight of running yards and counted seconds. Not rationally, not in a sequential process, but in tiny bits and pieces, in exploding mirror shards of gradual enlightenment. The result is true and complete. For the time being, you exist to keep existing. Everything else in life falls short of this naked, feral purpose.

You've eaten two more Power Bars, barely half an hour apart. The first one didn't satisfy your hunger. Instead it unleashed a salivating that demanded you eat another. Now, you have only two left. If you make it safely into the night, you'll need to eat them then to fight the pain of hunger. And tomorrow, you've already decided, you're going to have to find another way to feed yourself. You're going to have to take precious moments from your flight to scavenge for food.

Two hundred and fifty jogging paces, your wet pack thumping against your back. One hundred counted seconds of rest. You maintain this rhythm. You maintain a straightforward purpose. And death? Death won't be so terrible, just a pre-operative anesthesia that never wears off or ends. But no longer being alive to see Sara one more time or to see how some undefined future moment comes to a satisfactory conclusion, missing these will be hell, whether you will be aware of the missing or not. You are desperate to not be dead. It's not the size of the void or the endless darkness of death that drives you panic-stricken into the woods. No, it's arriving at the void's inevitable embrace prematurely—with a thousand necessary deeds still undone—that keeps you fleeing through the woods. Death's imminence inspires a stubborn strength in you. As far as you know, in other circumstances, your resolve should have depleted itself by now. Before today, before two hundred and fifty strides and one hundred breathless steamboats, you would have collapsed in terror, a capitulation by the lost other person you used to be.

FIELDLER AND PIRELLI CATCH UP to the others at the spot where you have come ashore. Knox has found a piece of Power Bar wrapper that slipped out of your pack when you were stashing your wet clothes inside.

"He jumped," Knox tells Fieldler and Pirelli when they join him and Hamilton at the water's edge.

"Jumped? You mean back there at the cliff?" Pirelli can't believe it.

Knox nods. "Like you suspected, Ernie."

Fieldler says nothing, accepting this small wafer of accolade as his due.

"This is where he came ashore. The trail starts up over there in the woods."

"At least he didn't drown," murmurs Hamilton, more or less to himself.

"I think we've underestimated our quarry," Knox tells the others, an expression of mild concern visible on his face. His eyes have narrowed to slits, an indication he is suppressing some kind of anger.

"Do you think we'll catch up to him before it gets dark?" Pirelli's question is less a matter of curiosity than an attempt to understand Knox's trepidation. He needs a perspective with which to deal with the assassin's visible disappointment.

"We'd better," says Knox. "If he travels during the night when we can't, he could get away from us."

"C'mon, Knox," says Hamilton. "He won't have the stamina to keep going after dark. You know that as well as I do."

"He shouldn't have gotten as far as he has."

Pirelli, discomfited by the antagonism between Knox and his father-in-law, asks, "How long until dark?"

"Seven, eight hours," replies Knox, glancing at his watch. "Mountains, the terrain, shadows could make it a lot less."

"We'll have him by then," says Hamilton. "Right, Ernie?"

"Maybe," says Fieldler. He gazes at Knox. "I think we should get going."

Knox isn't sure whether or not there's a rebuke in this suggestion, but he stares down the other man for a moment just on general principle. "Let's go," he says. "Keep your eyes open. I want Kovacs dead by nightfall."

The hunters head into the trees, stalking you again, growing gradually annoyed with Knox's frustration over their failure to quickly dispose of you. This is a hunt, not an assassination, they believe. Knox would do well to remember this fact. Knox should see the value of the challenge in what they're doing.

"I hope that fucker is scared out of his mind," Hamilton remarks as they move into the trees.

But no one says anything to that. In varying degrees from man to man, they are certain you are terrified.

ELSEWHERE THE WILD DOGS move into the vicinity of the hunt, although they are still many miles away. Starving, desperate and mean, they quarrel their way like hoodlums into destiny's ruthlessness.

YOU REACH A LARGE CLUSTER OF BOULDERS at the base of another steep hill. The day is dissolving. A long dusk has commenced and, as if twilight is an additional weight across your shoulders, you stumble into the shelter of the rocks, knowing for the time being you can run no further. Your shoulders ache and you shrug in relief out of the heavy pack. You lean against the rocks, so fatigued you believe you could sleep standing up. Your nylon trousers are virtually dry now, from the sun perhaps or the friction of your flight, and you feel fortunate for this. But your parka remains damp and heavy. It will take much longer to dry. You dig into the sodden mess of your pack and find your second last Power Bar. You devour it greedily, wondering what you can and must do now that night is coming on.

It is obvious you need to build a fire to warm yourself and dry out the heavy coat you wear, as well as the clothes that are wet in your pack. You can find firewood, you know, but a fire is a risky proposition. And you doubt you have the strength to build one with sticks or stones, in the primitive manner you were taught when you were a Boy Scout. What you wouldn't give to be a smoker now, in possession of a lighter or matches. But you quit smoking a couple of years ago, falling in step with a society that disapproves strongly of the habit. You enjoy considering, at this moment, had you known you would find yourself in this situation, you never would have quit. May as well keep smoking, the hunt will probably kill you. And you want to laugh out loud as you toy with this irony in your circumstances. But the humour in the situation evaporates quickly when you realize you would never have run so far on the impaired lungs you owned back then when you smoked half a pack of cigarettes each day.

You get down to business again. You must build a fire or, when night falls, you might succumb to the cold. And you have to build it in the crevice of the rocks, hidden from your hunters, concealed by the boulders gazing back in the direction you have come. You move a further distance around this pile of large boulders, tugging your heavy pack with you. Listlessly at first, feeling hidden in the dusk, you begin to empty your pack, remembering it's been more than a decade since you last took it camping with you.

With growing excitement, after you remove your clothes you find treasures in its pouches, hidden in the pack for years. You discover two storm candles, two lengths of nylon cord. You find an unopened package of metallic thermal blanket, a small kit of needle and thread. When, at the very bottom of the pack, you unearth a small canister of waterproof matches, the discovery feels nothing short of a religious manifestation, as if this last camping trip more than a decade ago was fate's humble seed sown in the past to help you survive at this dangerous moment in time.

Okay, you reflect in delight, cataloguing your few possessions: hatchet, hunting knife, whetstone, matches, candles, cord, sewing kit, metallic blanket. It's not enough to make a stand but these should help you survive the night until you can begin running again in the morning. If your hunters try tracking you at night, you will see the necessary flashlights in the distance. You will know they are coming. You will know it's time to flee again . . . if you can remember from your youthful Scouting days how you were taught to sleep with one eye open.

It takes more than an hour and a half to find the wood you need, to use candle wax and dry leaves to get a decent fire going. The young flames nearly go out when your wet clothing, strung on cord across the budding heat, collapses under its own weight into the hearth. But you drag the mess away before any real damage is done, restringing the clothesline across the flames, anchoring it at each end with heavier rocks.

You eat your last Power Bar. You feed the fire. You

sharpen your knife, finding enough saliva in your perpetually dry mouth to spit on the small whetstone. Strange how it all comes back to you, some of the little techniques a man needs to know in the wilderness. You doze. You feed the fire. You sharpen the hatchet. You wrap yourself in the metallic blanket, astonished that it works and provides warmth. The flames of your fire reflect along its silver surface. With one hand holding the blanket closed over your naked chest, you feed the fire some more, then doze. You feed the fire and sleep. You feed the fire and dream. You feed the fire and rest.

YOUR HUNTERS DO NOT EAT until long after night has fallen. They too have built a fire, hiding it behind rocks as you have done. They acknowledge the direction they believe you have gone. The conclusion that you have probably remained close to the river is unanimous.

"Christ!" complains Hamilton irritably. "Who's hiding from who?"

"Just a precaution," explains Fieldler, aware of the menacing silence emanating from Knox. "Never let the prey know where you are."

"But Kovacs isn't dangerous. What difference does it make if he knows we're close to him? It'll only scare the shit out of him."

"No, John," says Fieldler.

But Hamilton doesn't care and goes on anyway. "Maybe the fire will draw him closer. He might not realize it's us."

None of the men respond to this. As Hamilton grows more desperate, they find it more difficult to answer him. They do not know how to correct him when his desperation obscures what should be obvious improbability. As each hour passes, each of them grows more convinced that J.D. Hamilton is gradually losing his mind.

The men have eaten a freeze dried meal. They have spread their sleeping bags on the ground, as close as they can get to the fire, seeking what is only an illusion of warmth. The fire is small and hidden. It has been built only for cooking and to comfort the man on watch who must sit beside it alone, as they take turns standing guard during the long, dark night.

Knox, the others know, is exasperated that you have so far eluded them. He deals with this in silence, except when he organizes the shifts for their watches during the night. Pirelli first, then Fieldler, then Hamilton, with Knox planning to be awake at dawn to get the others on their feet, to get them moving quickly.

After Hamilton and Fieldler retire, Knox approaches Pirelli and crouches at his side. He doesn't say anything for a long moment or two, which makes Pirelli nervous.

"This whole thing is really bugging you, isn't it?" Pirelli mentions at last, more or less to fill the silence.

Knox doesn't answer him.

"I mean, you know we're going to catch him, don't you?"

Knox nods. "He had a hatchet attached to his pack," he mentions as an afterthought.

"He did?"

"Yeah. I noticed it when we loaded the plane."

"We have rifles, Knox."

"I wonder what else he had in that pack."

"Probably nothing."

"He shouldn't have lasted this long."

Pirelli considers this. "It makes for a better hunt, don't you think?"

"The hunt's foolish. It was a stupid idea. There were a hundred other, safer ways to do this."

"J.D. needs this hunt," counters Pirelli with a shrug.

"Yeah. Keep your eyes open. Kovacs can't be

trusted. Just imagine being brained by that hatchet, if you need any impetus for staying alert."

Pirelli tries to imagine the suggested scenario but fails. He nods anyway. "I want my wife back, Knox. That's enough to keep me awake."

"Okay," says Knox, believing this is probably true at least. "And keep the fire going. Don't let it flare up, but keep it going. Okay?"

Pirelli has been gazing into the flames. When he turns to acknowledge Knox's instructions, the assassin has already slipped away.

IT'S NOT YET DAWN WHEN JOE LEONARD awakens in his bed beside Allison. Fully, instantly conscious, he lies there in the darkness and silence, feeling a sensory completeness washing along his body—the darkness, the scent of his and Allison's bodies, the sound of her sleep-breath on her pillow a few inches away, the flannel sheet against his flesh—all of these feelings circumnavigate his body a quarter-inch above the skin, the way a patient lover's hand does, drawing his senses up to its fingers where they make sensual promises in a slow, erotic pentameter. Overwhelmed by this unexpected bliss, Joe turns on his side and moves his body in close to his wife. One hand tunnels under her pillow and around her neck, reaching for her breast. She stirs a bit and this helps him find her. His other hand reaches across her side and locates her other breast. His face burrows across his pillow towards the back of her head, breathing in the musk of her hair. He transforms her buttocks into a nest he can insinuate his lower abdomen in.

Joe realizes then how hard his penis has become, how much he wants to make love. But he hesitates. Allison is sleeping. And, even more, there is still so much to be enjoyed in merely holding her this way, that provocative, sensory hand a quarter inch above his consciousness, for instance, so subtly stimulating, guiding him into the meadows of a sensuous Elysian pleasure. But Allison is so close, his penis so engorged. It pulsates with insistent blood. So he takes his left hand from Alison's breast and gently uses it to explore between her legs. She is damp even in her slumber.

"Yes, Joe," she murmurs shortly, as she has a dozen times before, when he has arrived at morning needing her so much.

He slides himself inside her as delicately as he would sow a seed into their garden outside.

For all his need, their need, considering how engorged he is, how ready she was for him, their lovemaking is soft and slow. She comes an instant after he does, while he's still pumping semen into her. No one cries out, afraid of disturbing the peace, but there is a chronic kind of gasping, an intermingling of quickened breathing, a heightening of their ecstasy because they want to remain a whisper inside the stillness of this night.

Afterwards Allison assumes the pattern of the breathing in her slumber. But Joe lies beside her, fully awake, not moving away from her flesh, not moving out of her, until, after he has shrunk again, he falls away from her, no longer large enough to remain inside. He lies still then, holding her while she sleeps, fully awake, still relishing this unexpected bliss of peace.

"I think you did it that time," Alison tells him later that morning when she brings her coffee out onto the porch in the autumn chill. She comes to stand beside him where he has been leaning against a post, appreciatively scrutinizing his cherished valley here in his cherished mountains. She puts an arm around his waist.

"I did it?"

"I think you made me pregnant this morning."

"Are you sure?" As a man he cannot help wondering how she can be so certain about such a thing.

"I'm pretty sure," she says.

He would question her further on this but her conclusion is the result of her wisdom, not his. He suspects further cross-examination would be an insult. So he puts his arm around her shoulders and gently holds her closer, looking out over the satisfaction he shares with her about where he lives in this world in a state of effortless authenticity.

THERE'S A RUTHLESS KIND OF SIMPLICITY, a primitive stupidity in the way Leo McKendrick's dogs arrive at the decision to kill and eat the weakest dog in their pack. Their act is the most practical of solutions. It's easy. Uncomplicated. Killing this member of the group will stave off their hunger for another day and, at the same time, it will represent one less mouth to feed. Their leader thinks of this idea first. The victim is the smallest member of the pack and sometimes, during the last day or two, they have had to wait for it to catch up as they have moved restlessly through the wilderness. The Husky-cross is out of patience with it. So the others follow their leader, even though their leader is a stupid dog. The others confuse its meanness with strength, its willingness to make a decision quickly and stick to it with knowing what is best to do. Following their leader's example, they help kill the smallest dog, believing it is wrong to be weak and concluding their victim must die for being wrong in such a way.

When they are done this killing and eating, only five of them remain. With their bellies full, they grow cocky again. They move deeper into the wilderness to discover what they will do next, to keep themselves going, to preserve their shrinking pack.

By the end of this coming day, they will encounter the scent of the gray wolf now engrossed in his own search for food. They will decide—because the wolf's scent is strange to them—their distant wilderness cousin is an enemy of some kind, a threat to their destiny, an impediment to their safety. For all of these reasons, and because they are now used to being mean, they will soon decide this wolf must be hunted down and destroyed.

YOU COME AWAKE BEFORE DAWN in the aftermath of another Sara dream. It's still dark and cold so you feed the fire again, groggy with sleep and a deep fatigue you did not get enough sleep to overcome. Bemused, remembering where you are and why, you conclude you must permit your clothes to dry a little more in the flames during what remains of this night. For a few minutes you are two men: the one waking up to think, the other still asleep and clinging to the receding dream about Sara.

In your dream you were in the woods at the edge of the river where you came ashore yesterday. It was sunny and warm. You were naked, the sunlight lancing through the branches of the trees in precise beams of warmth, as precise as spotlights really, each narrow beam penetrating the foliage to reach your flesh in a focused pinprick of luxurious heat. Through the moving trees, you heard Sara whispering in your direction. And you knew it was her even before she came into view. You turned towards her, not surprised that she was dressed as a nurse. Her uniform was white and strangely formal or antique, its hem three or four inches below her knees, but a nurse's uniform nonetheless, because a stethoscope dangled between her breasts and she carried an old-fashioned medical bag in her right hand. Eventually she knelt beside you and opened the bag. She dipped her long fingers inside and they emerged smeared with paint. She decorated your naked flesh with various colours, with quarter moon crescents, with circles, with solid and broken lines, zigzag characters and bars. Your face, your chest, your thighs, your back. You closed your eyes to this process, to the pleasure in it, dozing, sleeping inside your slumber. Then, when you came awake with a start, you opened your eyes again and Sara was gone. Even in her absence, you felt cured, restored. In the dream you felt transformed. You realized Sara had recreated you into a necessary state of savagery. You stood naked, ready for battle, painted and tall. It was then you shimmered awake out of the dream.

Now, as you crouch beside your fire, aware dawn is taking place, the dream quickly recedes in your memory. You will be going as soon as it is light enough to see. You will resume your regimen of escape, the one you initiated yesterday. You will run two hundred and fifty paces, then count one hundred steamboats. You will cling when you can to the rocks where the hunters will be less certain which direction you've taken. You will veer into the trees when you sense the rocks are leaving you too exposed. You go over these strategies several times as you find consciousness this morning, while you wait for the wilderness to shrug off the last vestiges of its dangerous darkness.

You will need to make a lance so you can hunt. This conclusion arrives in an inspirational burst, like a friend who's just shown up at a disastrous weekend move, bearing a talent for repairs you do not possess yourself. You construct the lance in your mind: a long pole notched at the end, Sara's hunting knife tied securely to the shaft. This perhaps will help you forage for food and food will give you the strength to run two hundred and fifty paces dozens of times this day.

As the fire works to consume the last of your wood, you slink cautiously into the trees, the hatchet in your right hand. It takes several valuable minutes to find a sturdy length of branch. Jack pine, new and needled. You are startled by the harsh sound of your chopping -- you want to run and hide from the noise which seems capable in your ears of carrying for miles. But you persist. You carry your find, not yet trimmed, back to the rocks and your fire, scurrying through the darkness like a diseased, ostracized rat. You would like to see your need to escape as something more courageous, but a rat chased into some dangerous sewer is what you feel like most. Survival first, you decide. Courage in the aftermath.

You feel safer by the fire. Using the hatchet, willing the blows to be silent, you strip the lance of its branches, the pine gum clinging to your hands. You carve the notch in the end. You use your last piece of nylon cord to fasten the hunting knife into the notch. You knot it tightly with your trembling hands.

Dawn has come and the day is getting brighter. You hurry now to be on your way. You take down your clothing, your coat and your pack. They are still damp, but the fire has accomplished much, drying them out enough for you to put them on. Morning is cold. The cold may last all day. You dress. You shiver in the chill. You coil the length of line that held your clothes over last night's fire and stow it in a pouch in your pack. When you shrug into the shoulder straps, you are relieved the pack is lighter now without the clothes you can now wear and no longer have to carry. You scuttle around this bank of rocks, searching for a glimpse of the river you have been following. When at first you don't see it in dawn's hesitant light, you are shaken by alarm. Then, like a coy child, the river reveals itself in the gradually evolving light; you imagine, if it could, the river would giggle in delight at temporarily fooling you.

KNOX GETS THE OTHER MEN UP almost ruthlessly, with a trace of sadistic pleasure. Dawn is coming on, although hesitantly, and he knows they should get going soon. During his turn on watch Knox has been nurturing his annoyance over the way the hunt has gone so far. Sitting by the fire, the last man to take his turn, he's been quietly angry ever since Hamilton woke him up from a comfortable slumber. He's decided Hamilton is deranged or a fool. Probably both. And he's decided you, their quarry, will take longer to kill than he imagined. The hunt is now inconveniently risky. Although he knows your chances remain slim, he has now begun to consider what he will have to do if you find a way to escape.

"Wake up!" he tells each man, using the toe of his boot to endorse the command, roughly kicking each man's ass where it lies slumbering inside his sleeping bag.

He's doused the fire with river water. It's cold this morning. Knox plans no breakfast. These various inconveniences will get the men moving, reminding the hunters they're not on vacation here, that they still have an urgent duty to accomplish.

Hamilton, of course, is the one who protests most about the assassin's boot. "Jesus, Knox, take it easy. I'm awake. Okay? Remember who you're working for."

One by one, grumbling about the morning's chill, the men roll up their sleeping bags, fasten them to their packs and, holding their rifles, gather in a small circle where last night's fire is a smouldering ruin.

"Okay," says Knox, wanting to re-establish that he is

leader here. "He'll stick to the edge of the river. He's liable to have more confidence now. I'm hoping it makes him sloppy. We have to move quickly. Eat your fruit while you walk. Power Bars if you're still hungry. We have to make better time."

The other men nod.

Knox gazes at each man in turn so there's no mistake about the urgency of what he will say next. He's hoping all of them contract the intensity he feels at this moment. "No screwing around," he says. "The instant you see him, the instant you get a clear shot, kill the son of a bitch."

The others nod again, less in acquiescence than in fatigue.

"Let's go," says Knox. "And keep your eyes open. Kovacs has to be history by the end of today."

At this, the hunters move into the face of accelerating dawn. They grudgingly step up their pace as Knox has ordered them to.

A COUPLE OF HOURS LATER YOU FIND A CLEARING at the edge of the river and stagger to a halt. You drop your pack on the ground and gasp for breath. The day has only begun and already you are exhausted and weak. Your guts cry out in hunger. You don't bother counting one hundred steamboats. The effort required to count seems beyond you at this moment.

This time, when it occurs to you the hunters may catch you today, that it will take a miracle for you to survive until another nightfall, your fear is strangely resigned, quietly matter-of-fact. It is no longer a panicky fear. It possesses an edge of reason, an appropriate sense of risk. The hunters are stronger than you and are better equipped. They have food. They can keep going. Their pursuit will be relentless. What else can you assume as you face this second day? Death is probable. To survive you will have to plainly beat nearly catastrophic odds.

"Well, Sara," you murmur aloud. "There's a good chance I'm going to let you down today. I'm tired and hungry. Your father still wants to kill me. The prognosis doesn't look good."

You've been talking to Sara most of the morning, reporting in to her on your progress. It's not that she can hear you, although you enjoy imagining she can; it's more because you're now convinced your efforts to escape death are due in part to her. Like getting away from her father and her estranged husband will somehow honour her. Foolish in a way. Except, out here, running for your life, you feel a powerful partnership with Sara that you've never acknowledged before. You've even thanked her a couple of times, privately, silently, because remembering her has given you strength. You are surprised to discover, with Sara thousands of miles away, she has become the kind of partner you never imagined she could be when you were together in California. She'd enjoy hearing you say so, you expect. But out here all you can manage is a silent, secret oath she will likely never hear. The oath is clear and simple: if you get out of here alive, you will travel all your future roads with Sara at your side for as long as she is willing, if she can forgive your selfish past. At this moment, though, you talk to her.

But Sara, please remember the kind of world we're living in. The bad guys always win in a world like this. It's a world that has its solutions backwards. The posse is convention and it's actually a force of corruption. The fleeing outlaws, hiding from ritualized society, are actually the good guys. I ought to know. Until just a couple of days ago, I was on the other side. I was a member of the posse, dedicated to the status quo. I was wrong and you were right, sweet Sara. You were right about us and them. It's convention that is toxic. It's convention that wants to control everything we are, that is threatened by who we are.

You think these things by the side of the river where you are weak and hungry, not entirely sure if your thoughts are wisdom or some foolishness brought on by the delirium of your fear and circumstances. If you are delirious, it is probably due to extreme hunger, you decide. Certainly, if you don't eat something soon, you won't have the strength to go on.

You wander closer to the water's edge, your pack clutched in your left hand by the shoulder strap, your homemade lance in your right. "I should go fishing, Sara," you say out loud. But after a moment or two spent peering into the shallows, you spot no fish. A river without fish? Unlikely. But there's nothing here. Perhaps further on. If you keep your eyes open. You shrug into your pack, then clutch the lance in your right hand again.

Okay, Sara. I won't give up. I'll keep going. Two hundred and fifty paces. One hundred steamboats. Don't want your BMW to run me down. Don't want your crazy father to celebrate his revenge. Thinking these things in a disjointed fog, you find the will to go on.

YOUR FIRE IS MOSTLY ASH by the time your hunters discover it. They gather around the hearth, all four of them, like worshippers around the site of a sacrifice.

"Son of a fucking bitch," mutters Knox, kicking at the ashes with the toe of his boot.

The others make no remark.

"He built a fucking fire last night."

"Makes sense," offers Pirelli.

"Yeah? Well how the fuck did he do it? Where'd he get the fucking nerve?"

"Okay, Knox," says Hamilton. "Settle down."

"Settle down? We could be chasing this bastard for days."

"So what?" murmurs Fieldler.

"So what? So what?"

Fieldler nods calmly. "That's what I said. So what?"

Knox feels it then, a new, uneasy indication of potential mutiny. And it occurs to him clearly for the first time that there is an even chance, if they don't catch up to you, he will have to kill these other men to make a successful escape. This conclusion that he can and will dispose of the others calms him immediately. He has the airplane. He's planned for this. He has five million dollars, half of his fee, already in the bank. He can disappear, if necessary. He can get away. He can vanish into a world that has no interest in him.

"Okay," says Knox. "You're right. All this means is it's going to take a little longer." He glances at the other men, trying to peer inside their thoughts, trying to decipher how each man feels.

"That's right, Knox," says Hamilton when the assassin glances at him. "It's just going to take a little longer. You're going to have to earn you're fucking money."

When Knox glances at Pirelli, unfazed by Hamilton's words, Pirelli nods his agreement. "I'm with J.D."

Fieldler says nothing. Knox wonders how much this seasoned hunter knows. Has he calculated what must happen—to him and to the others—if you get away? The man's unreadable. Knox cannot tell for sure.

"You're right," Knox tells them then. "Kovacs surprises me. But in the end it won't mean that much. We have all the advantages. We can do this thing. We can take him out."

The other men only look at him inscrutably.

Knox realizes then, despite his professional aplomb and record, he has made an error. He has given too much of himself away. "Okay," he says calmly, to conceal his apprehension. "His fire is an opportunity. Tonight we'll be looking for it. It'll guide us right to him. Maybe the fire he builds tonight will turn out to be a mistake."

The men turn as one unit and return to the woods, moving in the direction you have gone.

"I thought Knox would be the last one to lose his grip that way," observes Pirelli a few minutes later as he and Fieldler lag behind Knox and Hamilton.

"Knox isn't truly a hunter," replies Fieldler. "He doesn't have the patience for it."

"I know. I get the feeling, though, he's trying to adjust to what we're doing here. I think he's beginning to realize he's been in too much of a hurry."

Thoughtfully Fieldler nods. "So it would seem," he says.

THE ROCKS AND BOULDERS YOU DISCOVER a couple of hours later, strewn across the river, form a natural bridge. You stand inside the trees, faint from hunger, trying to fathom what encountering this bridge of boulders can mean for you. You teeter here from weakness and you lean against a tree, tempted to collapse. Your exhaustion is now complete. At this moment it is even impossible to conjure up Sara once again, to sip at the inspiration she has so far provided you. Yet this narrow seam of rocks and detritus across the river seems an act of providence. If you cross the river here, clambering from rock to rock, you will leave no trail behind you. Such an act could conceal your direction from your hunters, maybe even for hours. How much further could you go, if it took them several hours to verify you crossed to the other side?

You stumble closer to the river and the first large

boulder. Ritually, as you have been doing all morning, you gaze into a pool near the shore, vaguely looking for fish. It is noisy here not far from the middle of the river where white water has formed in the narrow channels between the rocks. The sound of the rush of water seems faintly dangerous to you because it obliterates all other sound; you know, exposed this way, you would not hear it at this moment if someone was creeping up on you. Yet you stand here stuporously. Your sense of self seems torn into sections. Your body feels separate from your mind. Your senses feel on their own as well, as if they have nothing to do with your flesh. At this moment, your senses exist in a purgatory, clinging to your body like your body's shadow. You hold up your arms, hold them out in front of you a moment, looking for the strings that would confirm you have been transformed into a fragile puppet.

A strange notion, you decide, the concept of your shadow self hanging onto your desperate flesh. Harshly you rub your face with your hands, to wake up, to come to, to connect the various parts of yourself together again so they can function practically. In real terms, there are no shadows now. The day has grown deeply overcast. The clouds are so dark and thick you feel like you carry their weight on your sagging shoulders. And it's become colder. Your breath is a large fog in front of your face. Wearing still soggy gloves, the tips of your fingers ache with the cold. Your clothing, although partially dry, is still damp enough to chill you. So many simplistic difficulties to overcome just to survive, you realize. So clear and simple, yet so elusive and difficult—food and warmth and the physical strength to carry on. And something else: the conviction you require to make more likely the unlikely possibility that you can escape your hunters.

Unfocused, you gaze into the shallow pool a yard or so away from where you stand on the rocks. Bemused, you linger there for several minutes before you realize there are fish in this shallow pool. They tread water here, fins calmly beating against the pool's gentle current. Impulsively you take a step closer, the lance assuming its position in your right hand. Then you hesitate. You remember what you were taught when you were just a youngster. You set your pack down and retrieve the remaining length of cord from the pouch where you have stored it. With trembling fingers, you tie one end around the shaft of the lance, taking several frustrating minutes to do so, one eye peering now and then at the placid, waiting trout. Finally, you knot the cord around the end of the lance and fasten the other end of the cord to your belt. The exertion of these preparations, necessary so you do not lose the lance and Sara's knife, has made you dizzy and you teeter there on the rocks, tilting this way and that, your sense of balance giving way steadily as your weakness intensifies.

Not enough strength to fish, you decide. Not yet. But your mind has cleared and, again, you retrieve from your past still more strategies you have learned about wilderness survival, taught you so many years ago. With your hatchet you cut off a small branch of cedar from a nearby tree. Moving a few yards upstream from the fish, you gently dip the needles on the branch into the river. You give it a few minutes to soak itself, then you raise the needles to your lips. You suck the moisture from the branch and taste the bitter gum. You suck on the branch until you feel it begin to nourish you. You suck the branch of gum and water, then contemplate how you feel, the bitter taste in your mouth, new strength trickling into your limbs.

Soon you move towards the fish in the pool near the rocks, gratified to believe they have waited there for you. Clumsily, missing more often than not, you finally spear two small trout. This act of taking the fish happens in a kind of hallucinogenic daze, as if drunkenly you are watching someone else perform your actions: the spearing, the gutting, the wrapping of the other one inside the metallic blanket that warmed you during the night, this second fish to serve as your evening meal, should you survive that long, should you find the place and time to build another fire. This man you witness at the water's edge, who is only you in some distant, distended way, eats the other fish raw, sickened by the texture, its tastelessness enhanced by the residue of cedar gum still clinging to your palette. You almost throw up at first, the raw fish is so unappealing, but then you grow resigned to it and, by the end of the filet, you are devouring it greedily, spitting bones onto the ground, using your fingers to pull them off your tongue and from between your savage teeth. You feel new strength immediately, like you have been revived.

Afterwards you count one hundred steamboats, just on principle. Then you start across the bridge of boulders, gingerly hopping from rock to rock, nearly stumbling a couple of times into the roaring chutes of white water below, frightened that you are so exposed on this noisy bridge but believing you must take this chance in case it fools your pursuers for a while. When you jump from the last boulder onto the shore on the other side, you are tempted to rest there out in the open, to turn and look back at the bridge and what it has helped you accomplish. Instead, you dart into the trees where you are less exposed.

It begins to snow before you reach the end of another one hundred breathless steamboats.

THE SNOW IS WET AND SLOPPY, the kind that hangs around on the corner of freezing point like a group of bedraggled hoodlums. At times the flakes come down fiercely and it takes only moments for it to form a film on the ground in open spaces between the trees. So you stay as close to each tree as possible, minimizing the number of footprints you leave behind. It is treacherous going. You must avoid branches that gradually sag under the weight of the heavy snow. You cannot jog. You walk as quickly as you can, moving steadily along, continuing down river but remaining several yards from shore, hidden in the trees. For now, you abandon the ritual of running two hundred and fifty yards then counting one hundred steamboats: the going is too difficult. You must continue on in a dogged and gradual fashion like a determined river barge.

You are already hungry again. The raw fish should linger like a meal in your belly, but it is already gone, replaced by new and even more relentless pangs of hunger. Still, you feel a new sense of confidence about your circumstances. There's no rational reason for this – your situation is as precarious as it has always been. No, the confidence buoying you now resides in the notion that you are fighting back. Your blind terror has drifted away, replaced by small strategies of devious flight from your pursuers. It now seems an eternity ago that you dashed blindly through the woods, that you plunged from the cliff into the river, that you nearly drowned, that you wept in terror on the shore. In less than twenty-four hours you have taken steps to make it difficult for your hunters to kill you. In reality, you know the odds are still fiercely stacked against you, but at least you won't make it easy for them. You owe this much to yourself. You owe this much to Sara.

Gradually you have begun climbing a subtle incline as you remain inside the trees where they abut the river. Your ascent forces you tentatively deeper into the woods as a cliff forms on your left. The river, on the other side of this developing cliff, grows more and more distant as you approach even steeper cliffs in front of you. You can hear white water increasing in volume as the river begins to pass through another gorge. It's like the roar of blood in your ears. It's sound steadily increases. But you struggle onwards, gaining higher ground, keeping to the trees, listening for the river on your left. The river is the friend you hope can lead you home.

By the time the changing terrain pushes you deeply into the woods, you glimpse in the distance the white water gorge that is now so deafening. You emerge into a large clearing and halt abruptly. A new wave of brief but intense fear seizes you by the throat, interrupting the ritual beating of your heart. A large wolf has downed a small doe and it eats from its victim's belly in the now receding snowfall. The wolf is facing you and it has spotted you with the same suddenness you discovered it. The wolf snarls, bearing its fangs, its face and snout covered with blood.

For an eternity, the two of you stand there, gazing at one another. The wolf snarls once more then remembers to eat. It dips its face into the open belly of the doe and tears more flesh away. It chews only for a second or two, then swallows. It watches you and growls again. You have been told a wolf, alone and timid about mankind, is probably not dangerous, but each time it snarls at you, you cannot find the will to believe what you have been taught. It is a relatively larger version of other wolves you have seen before in captivity.

Carefully and quickly you scan the clearing for

other members of a pack, to confirm this hungry predator is on his own. When you see nothing, you conclude he must be alone. You sense his solitude; it exudes a separateness that you can nearly feel. Gradually you decide this wolf is probably little more than another version of you, going it alone, preoccupied only with survival. Your awareness of your similarity is purely intuitive; it has no rational basis. Still, your hunger and desperation are probably mutual—his a factor in his way of life, yours some extraordinary, brutal circumstance you intend to reverse eventually. The wolf is the real cowboy and you are a guest at the dude ranch where he works. He is supposed to teach you to be a cowboy; this is the lore surrounding wolves. They teach and you learn. Then you will go back home to some other non-cowboy world with the knowledge this animal has bestowed on you. Or are these thoughts only the delirium inspired by your fear and hunger? Can you listen to yourself and find the will to believe in what you think?

You badly covet the wolf's food. As soon as this need translates itself into reasonable thought, the wolf seems to sense this shift in the provocation of your presence. It lifts its head again and growls ferociously. The two of you gaze at one another. You do not flinch. You realize you have become astonishingly calm and confident. No one in his right mind attacks a pack of wolves, especially with nothing more than a homemade lance and a hatchet, but this wolf is alone. With all you've been taught about wolves, this solitary predator a few yards away should be intensely afraid of you. You take a deep breath and force yourself to move towards him, your lance held firmly in two hands in front of you.

The wolf growls again but backs away a step or two. You keep coming and the wolf backs away some more.

You feint with the lance and utter some kind of sound that is neither growl nor roar. Your words aren't human and they aren't animal. Whatever you said, though, it sounded like a cry of defiance. You doubt, as you hear your voice in your own ears, that you could ever duplicate its quality. But it frightens the wolf which, this time, retreats five yards or more away. Whatever it is you said in this, your new wilderness language, the wolf has recognized your confidence and resolve. Sensing your desperation, the wolf responds by being cautious. Each step you take closer to the deer is reflected by a response from the wolf and he retreats an equivalent distance. You feint with the lance again and utter something new. It sounds like *yaag*. But the wolf retreats again.

Carefully you unsheathe your hatchet, feinting again with the lance after you retrieve it. When you are beside the carcass of the doe, you position the lance across its flesh. The wolf is now fifteen yards away. It does not growl. It simply watches you as if puzzled, even fascinated by your actions. You bend, one eye on the wolf, ready to retrieve the lance should it suddenly attack. As if you've known all along what to do, you begin to chop off the head of the deer. You are vaguely aware of splattering blood, of bits of dancing flesh, but you ignore these distractions, keeping one eye on the wolf, the other on what you are doing.

At last the head falls away from the carcass. But you are not finished yet. Using the hatchet, you chop away what remains of the internal organs of the doe. With your other hand, you pull these bits and pieces out and leave them there on the ground, blood turning the wet snow into a marbled, pink pudding.

And still the wolf watches you, mystified, like you are a sideshow freak. At one point it moves a little closer, but you reach for the lance and, speaking in your new wilderness dialect, you feint in your adversary's direction yet again, growling, trying to snarl. The wolf retreats. Gratefully you accept the wolf's accolade—you are dangerous because the wolf believes you are dangerous and the wolf lives in this wilderness; he can not be wrong.

At last you are done cutting away what you don't need. The wolf will want to eat what you leave behind. You sheath your hatchet. You retrieve your hood from out of the pouch at the back of your bloody parka and pull it over your head. You reach down and, with a grunt, lift what remains of the deer over your head. Blood splatters onto your face, mixing with the moisture of the falling snow. The carcass feels lighter than you expected, but this is just new adrenaline coursing through your body. The wolf maintains you are strong and dangerous so this is what you are—strong and dangerous. Still, you bend under the doe's weight, the flesh balanced precariously on your neck, held in place by your pack. Eventually you'll have to secure it over your shoulders somehow but, for now, you must take your booty and escape, holding it precariously in place with your left hand. You are relieved the doe was small. If not, despite the respect you've earned from the wolf, you would not have had the strength to even pick it up.

"Okay, big fella," you say in English, just to hear the sound of it in your voice, just to speak again the old language not formed by this new wilderness. "I'm outta here. Okay?"

Giving the wolf a wide berth, you begin to creep out of the clearing, your left hand balancing the deer carcass on your shoulders, your right holding the lance. The wolf moves in an arc as well, away from you and in the direction of the pieces of deer you have left behind.

You enter the woods again, leaving the wolf behind you. Carrying your precarious burden, you stumble between the trees. Gradually astonished and buoyed by a courage you did not know you possessed, you continue on your way, resisting the urge to look back to see if the wolf has decided to attack. If it does, you will have to kill it. Or it must kill you. This is so fundamental a conclusion it hardly bears consideration. But the wolf does not attack. You assume you have left your adversary behind with the generous remains you did not require from the doe.

It has now abruptly stopped snowing but the sky remains sullen. You are aware of these changes only peripherally. Mostly you are preoccupied by your new discovery—a sudden and marvelous epiphany based on the notion you are going to survive. It is a calm excitement, but it remains powerful. You have now concluded that destiny has come to you with a bargain: you are newly capable of escaping your pursuers. You are still profoundly an underdog but you have begun to believe you will find a way to ultimately escape.

THE WET SNOW HAS ALREADY LANDED AND MELTED by the time your hunters reach the bridge of boulders that gave you access to the other side of the river. The hunters have lost your trail in the gradually melting inch of snow. But they believe the snow now rescuing you will betray you in the end. The hunters expect to discover your tracks again when your boot prints show up in the fickle aftermath of the snowfall. Somewhat encouraged and newly confident, the men gather here on the shore to discuss what they should do next. They stand there eating fruit, taking advantage of this moment to rest, but grudgingly, still remembering how apprehensive they were earlier this morning when they found the remnants of your campfire.

"What would you do if you were Kovacs?" Knox asks the group at large. He is careful to sound affable, to conceal the true anxiety he feels because you might be getting away.

Pirelli and Hamilton shrug.

Knox waits. He has been thinking for the past hour or so about what he considers Plan B. At some point he will have to conclude that you have successfully eluded him. Once this decision is reached, he will have to execute the other men, an essential necessity in his personal escape. Fieldler first, because he's the most dangerous; Pirelli next because he has the younger reflexes; Hamilton last because Hamilton is a fool and probably hasn't considered his own hired assassin would need to betray him in this way. After the others are dead Knox will make his escape, working his way back to the airplane, utilizing the directional mental notes he has ritually taken since the hunt began. Once he flies out of here, he will know how to disappear permanently. He will become someone else in this world. He will no longer exist as Eddy Knox.

"C'mon, fellas. Let's compare a few notes."

"How far ahead of us do you think he is?" Hamilton asks.

"Two hours maybe. He was jogging yesterday. He won't be jogging today. Ernie?"

Fieldler nods. "That's my read," he says.

Pirelli makes no comment. He is gazing along the route of the river, trying to control a new and private impatience. He is wet and cold, and, if he spotted you now in the distance, he would feel a deep gratitude to be able to lift his rifle and shoot you dead as a stone. His father-in-law's hunting scheme is wearing thin for him. Maybe Knox was right after all. Wouldn't it have been better to kill you outright, in a more professional fashion? Aren't the risks in the hunt growing exponentially the longer it takes to locate you? Yes, they are. And it's getting cold and damp. For Pirelli, the novelty of hunting you down is virtually at an end, displaced by his discomfort and a new anger he would have difficulty defining. He considers you and life itself must both be punished for letting him down this way.

"We should soon see his tracks in the mud left by the snow," Knox is saying. "We know he's sticking close to the river."

"But which way?" ponders Fieldler more or less to himself. He tosses orange peel into the pool of river near the shore.

"Whaddyuh mean, 'which way?'" This from Hamilton who, like Pirelli, is now disappointed in the hunt; he now only wants you dead. If you exist in a state of panic, he no longer cares as much as he did before. What good is the terror you feel if he is not nearby to witness it personally, to enjoy seeing it on your face? What good is justice if you are not here to listen to the explanation of why you deserve its vengeance? Hamilton possesses little imagination; he can no longer transform the notion of your terror into fuel for his fantasy. Cold and exhausted, he only wants to know that you have died.

Knox detects the tenor of these thoughts from both Pirelli and Hamilton. He is gratified the two men are running out of patience. From now on, he knows, they will listen to him. They will want the hunt to conclude as rapidly as he does.

Fieldler glances across the river, sorting through their options.

"Do you think he crossed on the rocks?" Knox asks, feeling privately clumsy because he hasn't considered this possibility himself until now.

"I would," says Fieldler.

"Me too," admits Knox. "Just to throw us off the scent."

Fieldler nods.

"Jesus," says Hamilton. "Is he strong enough to do that? Is he smart enough?"

"I think so," Fieldler replies. "I'm going to have a look."

While the other men watch him, feeling either stunned or impatient, Fieldler starts across the wet rocks towards the other side of the river. They watch him leap from rock to rock like a much younger man. They watch him until he disappears into the trees on the other side.

"So you think Kovacs gained some time on us yesterday?" Hamilton asks Knox.

The assassin nods. "He ran. We walked."

"Do you think he's going to get away?"

"No. We'll probably gain it back today. He's got to be much weaker today than he was yesterday."

"Will we get him today?" asks Pirelli, moving closer to the conversation. "That's what I want to know."

"Don't know," replies Knox. "We've underestimated Kovacs a little."

"Bastard," mutters Hamilton.

"If not today," says Knox, "we'll have him tomorrow. The elements are on our side. We may find him freezing to death. Killing him will be an act of mercy."

"Not interested in mercy . . . there's Ernie," says Hamilton then as he points across the river.

Fieldler has emerged from the trees. He is gesturing at the other men to join him on his side of the river.

Without a word, taking turns, they move out onto the rocks, disappointed in you and what you are making them do.

"Jesus fucking Christ," says Hamilton to the

universe at large, after he nearly tumbles into the water.

Pirelli helps his father-in-law across, occasionally taking his arm, supporting him each time he appears to be losing his balance. Knox brings up the rear in silence, considering how disappointed he will be to have to kill a man like Fieldler. Under other circumstances, he would enjoy working with such a talented hunter.

THE GRAY WOLF FOLLOWS YOU at a cautious distance, aware you are weak and tired, aware you carry food. Mostly he is curious. At some point just before noon, you left behind your second trout, dropping it along your route, dropping it on purpose, a calculated whim. The wolf knows you left it behind for him. This, more than anything, has made him curious. He must follow you at a safe distance to discover what you will do next. He does not understand you. You may be a dangerous foe, something sinister he should flee. But instinct pushes the wolf on. He intends to stick with you as long as you are willing to share your food.

YOU AREN'T QUITE CERTAIN what prompted you to leave the fish behind for the wolf, but the need to do so was powerful. Impulsive, perhaps, but powerful just the same. You contemplated eating the trout yourself but, this time, the thought of eating the fish raw sickened you. And, by then, you realized the wolf would follow you. You are convinced now that this is what it does. You are not frightened by the prospect. To the contrary, knowing the wolf is behind you is strangely comforting. Although you would be hard-pressed to explain why, the incident with the deer now represents a kind of bonding between you and the wolf, between thief and victim, two different breeds of predator. In your new wilderness-sensitive mind, the wolf has become your partner, someone to share your exile with. A foolish notion, you suppose, except, out here, pursued by hunters, you have begun to lament having no best friend. You have begun to blame yourself for some of your isolation.

Tactically, you see the wolf as a distracting buffer between you and your hunters. This notion is laced with confidence. For one giddy moment, you feel like a wilderness warlock shifting the momentum in your favour, casting magic spells that unify you with this wilderness. The wilderness in turn links itself to you. You can suck its various powers and skills into your weak and fragile frame, increasing your strength, resolve and talent for survival. And the wolf, as your ally, makes this near-magic official, tangible, powerful.

Sara, you know, would laugh at this. And realizing she would laugh, a lucid part of you wonders if the other half of you is gradually going mad. In this way, while you are thinking about your disquieting duality, doubt shows up at the threshold of your thoughts and barges through the door, sitting down in a chair to outline paternalistically what defines you as a fool, describing in some nagging monotone the way you're going crazy, how fear, exhaustion and weakness are driving you out of your mind. You listen to doubt's tirade for several minutes until the argument wears itself out. Ironically, it's your fatigue that carries the day; eventually you're too tired to listen any longer to the doubting side of your nature.

Besides, you decide, insanity is a relative condition. It's only insanity when it finds an appropriate state of sanity with which to contrast itself. Out here, the more conventionally assumed state of sanity holds a dubious definition. The hunters are probably crazier than you will ever be. And thinking this, you find the means to throw doubt out of your house like the true reprobate it is.

You become the wilderness warlock again. Whether you live or die will eventually depend on some final assessment of what or whom is truly crazy in these endless woods and mountains.

You adjust the weight of the deer again, now tied to your pack and across your aching shoulders. Then you strike out again through the trees, hoping the wolf isn't far behind you, hoping he is confusing your hunters, getting in their way, serving in some small fashion as a magical wilderness spell revitalizing you with its power.

THE HUNTERS GATHER AROUND THE BLOODSTAINS and gore where the doe was slain, trying to puzzle out the clues of what has happened here. The snow is melting steadily away. The paw prints of the wolf, the footprints left by your boots: these are now marked in the growing islands of brown, needled earth where the snow melts away. But you have been here and a wolf has been here and there is a trail of blood moving into the trees towards higher ground. The men all stand at the edge of your story, trying to read what it might mean.

"Jesus Christ!" says Hamilton.

Fieldler has crouched on the perimeter of the bloody snow and ground. He gazes at the prints, the blood, what remains of the deer's partially devoured skull and the hide that once housed its neck.

Pirelli moves away from all of this. He stands at some distance, feeling nervous and uncomfortable. The remains of whatever happened here look sacrificial. To him, the signs of slaughter appear like the dregs of some horrible act of witchcraft. Although he will not quite admit it, something about what he has seen here has caused him to be a little afraid of you.

"Well?" says Hamilton, taking comfort in the air of

authority he believes exists in his one-word question.

But this authority evaporates when no one answers him. In the silence he is well aware of how tragically he has put himself out of his element during the first day and a half of this hunt. It makes his belly ache. If not for the inspiration of his deep, unrelenting hatred for you, he would find a way to call the hunt off, to transport himself back to a place in time before the hunt began.

He takes three deep breaths to get a grip on himself. "Do you think something attacked Kovacs?" he asks at last.

Knox and Fieldler glance at him with all the patience they can muster. Again they do not reply.

"Whaddyuh think, Ernie?" Knox asks in a quiet tone. "Give me your read."

"Wolf prints," Fieldler replies.

"But Kovacs was here too."

Solemnly Fieldler nods.

"Whaddyuh think happened?"

"Wolves brought down the doe."

"Yeah."

"But what about Kovacs?" interjects Hamilton.

Again he is ignored.

"How many wolves, Ernie?"

Fieldler glances at Knox before he answers his question. "Can't tell in the melting snow. Maybe just one."

"Christ! You mean we have wolves to deal with now?"

Knox turns to his frustrated employer. "It's the wilderness. Of course we have wolves."

"Well what about Kovacs?"

"He was here . . ."

". . . I know he was here . . . ."

". . . And he went off in the direction of the blood."

"Like the wolf."

Fieldler gazes at Knox and nods.

Knox nearly grins as he realizes the hunt is getting

interesting again, and the subdued glee he feels surprises him. It's not professional. Christ! He's losing himself out here, turning into the kind of adventurer he knows it is dangerous for him to be. He shrugs this self-criticism off, pushes it into a dark corner of his mind. "Kovacs must be starving," he says. "Do you think the wolf carried off the remains and Kovacs went after him?"

"If he was nuts," replied Fieldler. "He wouldn't have the speed or stamina to catch a wolf. If he wasn't desperate, he would know that."

"Desperate from fear," cries Hamilton in triumph "Right?"

"Or the reverse," says Knox to Fieldler.

"The reverse?"

"Yeah. He takes the deer and the wolf follows him."

"Highly unlikely," says Fieldler, sounding a little like a pragmatic Mr. Spock.

Knox nods, although he enjoys something about his theory, is attracted by the adventure in it. Not professional, Eddy, he thinks privately. Get a grip on yourself.

"Anyway," says Fieldler, grunting as he rises from his crouch, "I think we're gaining on him. And the trail is still easy to follow."

"Yeah. We should be going." Knox turns to Hamilton and the still silent Pirelli. "Keep your eyes peeled. We think he's closer now. We may soon have him cornered."

"But what about the wolf?" whines Hamilton.

Knox and Fieldler gape at him.

"Whaddyuh mean, J.D.?" asks Pirelli who has now skirted the carnage on the snow, wanting to leave this place.

"What do we do about the wolf?"

"Nothing," replies Knox.

"What if it attacks us?"

"Shoot it, for Christ's sake."

"Fuck," says Hamilton, less out of fear of the wolf than not wanting to shoot anything but you.

This meeting over, the hunters all turn away from one another. Soon they depart, following the receding trail of blood further up the side of the mountain in the direction of what remains of their waning afternoon.

YOU LOSE THE RIVER. It gets away from you, slipping through your fingers. Your lifeline. The linear manifestation of your escape. You turn your back on it and it slips away. Sight. Sound. Everything.

This knowledge of the river's loss comes to you as a wicked surprise, as evening descends on you. You thought the river was with you, but now you know it is gone. Twilight is silent, filled with despair and provocation. You can remember the sound of the river churning through the gorge a couple of hours ago. You can even remember the sound receding steadily as you climbed towards some faraway rocks and precariously clinging trees in the distance. But you cannot recall the precise moment when this silence indicating the river is gone fell so completely around you. The silence feels like the destruction of sound itself, the arrival of nuclear winter, a vacuum of vaporization. Losing the sound of the river is somehow much worse than the way you lost sight of the river. Without the watery artery as a companion you feel hopeless. You are left only with the weight of the venison across your shoulders and the ragged gasp of your breathing here in the gradually deepening dusk. Everything else—your life, your hope, your faith—is covered by a nihilistic shroud.

You cannot go back to find the river. To do so would mean running the risk of encountering your hunters. And eventually you would run out of light. You would stumble around in the darkness, forlorn and in danger. Besides, the river probably still lies somewhere to your left. If you can resist the way the terrain tends to force you to the right, you can gradually work back towards where the river should be. Maybe tomorrow. Maybe tomorrow when there is more light. Of more importance at this moment is some appropriately concealed cleft in the rocks where you can build another fire.

Your mouth waters. A fire means food. The food you have carried much of the day has caused your shoulders to ache. A feast of venison over the flames of a fire is more than just a meal; it is a fitting reward for your efforts.

You set off again in the direction of a cluster of large rocks that have been your destination for hours. You cannot move quickly. The carcass around your neck is now heavy and it makes a bloody mess of your coat, even dribbling down on your nylon trousers. And you are still climbing, albeit gradually. It is only reasonable to assume your hunters are gaining on you today, if they discovered the bridge of boulders you used to cross the river.

Contemplating your pursuers, you realize your terror has given way to a steady, relentless version of itself, a gnawing fear. If they continue to follow your tracks, if they have found them in those places where you crossed soggy, needled earth, then they are gaining on you. And at least two of them are extremely experienced. Which one does the tracking? Fieldler or Knox? Or is it both of them? Your fear increases in intensity a moment, like a relapsing illness. These men are formidable. If they spot you, they will kill you with ease. It is only intelligent to be afraid.

Oh, Sara. I think they're coming for me soon. Your eyes mist up and a couple of tears trickle down your cheeks. Whether from fear or from thinking about Sara, you can not say for sure.

You must get moving again. Your shoulders cry out in agony, your legs numb and trembling. You stumble towards your destination, the rocks in the distance that will shield your fire. You force yourself to hurry with all of your remaining strength. Night is coming towards you and your hunters are gaining on you from behind. You are trapped somewhere in the middle of a miserable, shrinking room composed of death and darkness. Motivated by your intensifying fear and your instinctive will to survive, you push on. If there is a moment in time when you are supposed to die, you sense that moment is approaching soon. Death, for someone as young as you, breathes a kind of halitosis. You smell the stench of this moment as death prepares its passionate kiss for you.

Yet you remember to believe the wolf is following you, tempted by the food you carry across your shoulders. It's lunacy perhaps, but you are strangely comforted by the notion that the wolf moves through this wilderness somewhere between you and your various hunters. You feel less lonely with the thought that you have a wilderness companion. The concept of the wolf and the notion of Sara knowing how you struggle are similar somehow. In a way you do not understand—but embrace anyway—the wolf and Sara join forces somehow to make sense of your circumstances, to express some kind of wisdom in your precarious dilemma of survival.

"I love you, Sara," you murmur aloud, just to hear the words, just to keep on believing in their truth.

KNOX MOVES SOME DISTANCE AWAY from the fire he shares with the other men. He spends several long moments in the deep pitch of darkness, squinting into the distance, looking for some indication that you have built a fire of your own like the one you built last night. For all of this time spent gazing into the night, he sees nothing. And the smell of the smoke from the hunters' own fire is indistinguishable on the air from the one you may have built.

For a moment, Knox feels at sea and—although he would never admit it—even deeply apprehensive. He is disturbed by the sense that you have been adopted by this wilderness, the same one that seems now to push him away. A stupid notion, he knows. The wilderness isn't alive; it isn't an entity unto itself. It can't like or dislike him. It can't choose. It can't root for one side over another. No, he's just uncomfortable after the short debate that ensued a time ago when the hunters realized they are running out of food.

Hamilton, that pompous, old fuck, was the one who started the trouble, of course.

"Jesus, Knox," he said. "You were supposed to outfit us for a hunt like this. Now you're telling me tomorrow's our last day to eat?"

Knox glared at him. "Kovacs is supposed to be dead by now. We're supposed to be back home. Don't talk to me about food with Kovacs still alive."

"Well, what are we gonna do?"

The question echoed in the silence, exaggerating its message of helplessness.

Then: "We hunt our food," Fieldler said.

"If necessary," amended Knox. "Tomorrow Kovacs is dead. We gained on him today."

"Yeah, but we still have to walk back out of here after we're finished with Kovacs." Hamilton frowned at his assassin, apparently enjoying his conclusion that all failures connected to this hunt were the professional's fault.

Knox bit back his anger. "Like Ernie said, 'We hunt

our food.'"

"Jesus," muttered Hamilton, visibly in agony over the pain in his belly. It showed on his face that he also had to deal with an ever growing fury and disappointment specific to his life and Kovacs' trespasses.

"You wanted a hunt," said Knox. "You've got a fucking hunt. You'll have to make the best of it."

Hamilton seemed prepared to argue further but there was little more he could say. He turned and stalked away from the other men. Petulantly, he stood off by himself for a while. Knox considered then the changing odds of how many men he would have to kill if they failed to catch up to Kovacs.

Now Knox goes back to his own fire. They have set up the same watches they used the night before. He desperately needs some sleep. Tomorrow you must die before someone makes a mistake, before fatigue and frustration take their toll.

Eventually Knox dreams of a hunting wolf, a vaguely misshapen giant coming for him in the distance, its fangs glinting as large as butcher knives, its eyes red coals of ruthless demonhood.

EVERYTHING IS DONE. AGAINST ALL ODDS, you have survived safely into another night. Exhausted, smelling of your own grime, of deer blood and raw fish going rancid where you had wrapped it in your metallic blanket, you lean in a stupor of near slumber against the rocks, tolerating this stench because your belly is full and you are still alive.

Your fire is safely sheltered within the rocks. You had difficulty finding dry kindling but eventually the fire caught. It was virtually dark by then and firewood was hard to find. But you built your fire and cooked up a couple of pounds of venison, devouring each piece greedily as soon as it was singed and done, growing drunk afterwards as the feast tranquilized you. You cut up more of the doe, butchered it by the flames of the fire, putting the pieces into your pack. The result of your labours bears no resemblance to steaks or roasts or even stew. It's just meat, chunks of it, misshapen but edible, important and lighter now inside your pack, no longer to be lifted across your shoulders.

Like a religious sacrifice, you picked up a severed foreleg of the deer, then you spun in circles by the fire a couple of times before you tossed it like a hammer throw as far as you could into the deep recesses of the darkness. You heard it land somewhere out there with a distant thump. You need to believe your wolf still follows you. If so, he must be hungry. You need to believe the wolf will be enticed by your offering. Here, tempted by food, he can stand on watch for you, sounding the alarm if your hunters come near in the darkness, his loyalty purchased by the food you share.

You were tempted to fall asleep immediately; you nearly succumbed to exhaustion. But there was more to be done. You sharpened Sara's knife on its whetstone, the business end of the lance you carry. You sharpened the blade of the hatchet you carry around your waist. You fed the fire more wood. Now you feed it once again, unable to fight sleep any longer, struggling to complete your chores for the night.

The last thing you remember doing before you fall into a deep slumber is informing Sara silently you have made it a little further in your attempt to escape. And, yes, you are still alive. You believe she needs to know this. You need to imagine she can hear your various messages to her telepathically. You need to believe, out here in the woods, that you and Sara are connected by fate or God or love, that this connection will not fail you now that your life is at risk.

LEO MCKENDRICK'S DOGS, HUNGRY AGAIN and ill-tempered because of it, pursue your wolf. They encountered the scent of their quarry last night and, jingoistically impatient, they have decided for the moment to kill it. The dogs are frenzied now, some fierce, frightening amalgam of misplaced pride and fury at a world they cannot truly conquer but wish to subdue regardless. They are still some distance from you and it will take them the better part of a day to catch up to you and the wolf. And just before they do catch up to you and the wolf, they will insinuate themselves into the path of the hunt, between you and your increasingly desperate hunters. They will inadvertently assume a role in the drama of death and revenge being performed between you and the men from Los Angeles who grow steadily more frustrated because you have not yet been found and killed.

YOU WAKE UP BEFORE DAWN, groggy but feeling somewhat stronger than you felt the day before. You wake up in time to feed your dying fire with the remnants of your firewood. The clouds that sulked against the sky last night as you fell asleep have dissolved or moved away, replaced by a blue-black fabric of sky embossed with disappearing stars. It seems warmer on the cusp of this new day and this transition in temperature comforts you. It appears yesterday's snowfall will be followed today by sunshine.

For one delirious moment, you are convinced you cannot die on a sunny day, despite your precarious future. If death was ready to take you, yesterday's sullen sky of clouds and snow would have been a more appropriate time and setting. You do not understand your faith in this conclusion; it is instinctive, nothing more. When you suspect this is delusion, you spit that verdict out of your mouth; you will not die, you swear, on a sunny day.

You skewer four small pieces of venison on the stick you cooked with last night. While the meat sizzles in the flames, the stick propped between two rocks, you notice the fear and nervousness you've felt receding now in your psyche. The possibility of escaping your hunters has increased each day they have not caught up to you. Although you have no means of measuring it, you are aware you are growing stronger. Your resolution to survive is deeper now, not so frantic, not so characterized by panic. Your first day of terror and flight reflected an inverted death wish. Back then your death seemed inevitable, even justified. But you were a different man then. There was a desperation in your unconscious conclusion that your vacuous life was somehow worth clinging to and defending. Now you have changed your view. The transformation in your attitude took place invisibly. You don't recall noticing the transition. Today you are aware of several new conclusions about your life: first of all, it is a journey rather than a destination; secondly, being afraid of being dead is too much like being afraid to be born—a waste of precious time. Thirdly, you love Sara. Sara, yes, Sara is worth battling for. She clearly represents a fine and provocative enough reason to escape these mountains alive. Just knowing these things now, as you sit at the edge of your campfire, is an unexpected gift. You must make a choice. Whether to live or die. Whether to remain a shell or not. Whether to take from the treasury of life or give back to it for a change.

You rub another day's growth of beard with your

hand. You are a mess. You stink. Your parka is covered with deer blood and emits a pungent, tangy aroma. Even more powerful is the stench of fish still clinging to the metallic blanket that kept you warm overnight. Bear bait, you suppose. But your clothes are now dry and you are not so chilled. This oncoming day seems filled with promise, bequeathing you a vague yet necessary turning point. Today, if you are lucky, if you can veer back to the left and find the river, your instincts inform you it is likely you can save yourself.

Eventually, as dawn begins its tentative illumination, you eat the pieces of partially cooked venison from the stick. The food warms you and provides you with additional strength. Afterwards, the way you did last night, you share another portion with the gray wolf you believe you bribe into serving as your companion, tossing a morsel as far as you can into the emerging dawn surrounding you, hoping it is the wolf you feed and not some grizzly bear who can eventually do you harm. Then, as soon as it is light enough to see, you move into the trees that survive in a desperate way here at this elevation—sentinels, Spartans, monks— dedicated, indomitable mountain men. You angle to the left, moving quickly along the crest of this small mountain, searching for the river you didn't mean to lose when you were fleeing your hunters yesterday. You have the strength to run again. You have the strength to count the steamboats measuring your periods of rest. I'm coming home, Sara, you swear in a silent oath. I think I'm coming home alive.

HAMILTON HAS WILLED HIMSELF TO RISE BEFORE KNOX can use the toe of his boot to wake him up the way he did yesterday. At least he thinks he does. In truth, Hamilton has had a dream and this is what awakens him. Despite the chill of this new morning, there are beads of sweat on his forehead, a cloying sheen that erupts from the bulging cords of his neck. He shivers from the autumn mountain cold and from the details he has already begun to forget about his dream.

The characters in his dream were plastic dolls. Their heads and bodies were mismatched. Sara, most of all, was naked and glamorous even in plastic flesh, but her head was attached to your body and your face grinned mischievously atop her nude, provocative body. This tasteless anatomical error nearly made Hamilton nauseous. Knox's body was there too, dressed in parka and jeans, but he was headless. He flailed blindly at everything, even at the stubborn desert of the dream itself, stumbling here and there in search of someone to be while he was a guest in Hamilton's nightmare. His head lay on the ground. Knox staggered towards it, then inadvertently kicked it with the toe of his boot. Recognizing it, he bent to retrieve it, picking it up in two hands to place it on his neck and shoulders . . .

. . . But Hamilton woke up at this point to find himself again inserted into an unpleasant reality not much better than the dream.

Now he lies shivering in his sleeping bag, fully dressed, letting the nightmare recede. His belly is torn with suffering. He knows intuitively the illness in his stomach bleeds. He can almost feel the hole in the wall of his belly where the blood seeps through, burning the tender flesh it touches.

Stifling a groan at the intensity of his pain, Hamilton drags himself out of his sleeping bag and feels deeply sorry for himself. He is convinced he has been right about everything for much of his life and that the weight of his certainty has just about broken him. He believes at this moment that he has never been wrong, not even that night nearly twenty years ago when he first discovered without guilt or even dismay that he wanted everything about his daughter to belong exclusively to him. Since then he has decided the world has been too often resistant to the fact that he is right. You in particular, Kovacs. You have been stupid. Hamilton hates you less than he hates your stupidity in not knowing he has never been wrong. Your stupidity and your temerity, these are what he despises. You are not a man to him. You are an impediment. You are dull-witted and you stand in the way of what is right about everything he does and still intends to do. When Hamilton kills you, he suspects he will be unaware he is killing a man. No, he will believe he is killing an idea, a brainless obstacle, a trespasser on the property of his life, which has been right and true and inviolate virtually from its beginning.

Standing now, feeling exposed in the dissipating darkness, noticing Knox on watch by the fire, Hamilton endures a spell of weakness. The pain in his belly accumulates alongside his ever-increasing fatigue and a need for food that Knox will not be able to satisfy when tomorrow arrives. This morning he and Knox and the others will eat the last of their fruit and some cheese. Tonight they will eat the last legitimate meal they carry with them in their packs, some freeze dried stew Knox has planned. Tomorrow, in not arranging enough provisions, Knox will be exposed as a fool.

Staggering into the darkness to have a piss, Hamilton realizes he now hates Knox nearly as much as he hates you. Knox too, to a lesser extent, is becoming an impediment to the success of the hunt. For this reason, he has earned Hamilton's enmity. This is how it is done—earning Hamilton's enmity: one lets him down, one fails him. Failure, more than anything else, inspires his enmity. Knox is doing this. Knox is betraying him. Knox is failing in his assignment; he is making an enemy of himself.

Squinting into the weak light of dawn, Hamilton grows aware that the other men are clawing themselves out of slumber too. His Sara-loving surrogate, Pirelli, is tying up his sleeping bag and attaching it to his pack. Fieldler is over by some rocks, urinating powerfully with the kind of force enjoyed by a much younger man. Hamilton can hear his piss splashing loudly against the ground at the base of the rocks shaping this shadowy, evolving morning. It irritates him how some men are so much more physically powerful than he is himself.

Hamilton approaches Pirelli. He has nothing specific to say to him. But Pirelli will fill this conversational gap. He is an underling. He fills all awkward silences. It's more or less his job.

But when Pirelli speaks, there is no obsequiousness in his remarks. He even sounds, in a way Hamilton cannot clearly define, like an entirely different man, transformed by the frustration of the hunt. "I don't like the way this is going, J.D.," Pirelli says. "I don't like it at all."

"Whaddyuh mean?" asks Hamilton blankly, still surprised at his son-in-law's unexpected frankness.

"I'm getting fed up. It's cold and we haven't seen Kovacs for two days. I don't like it. We should have spotted him by now."

"You want to give up?"

Pirelli is surprised by the question. "Of course not. I'm just saying this whole business was supposed to be easier than this."

"Well," says Hamilton, lowering his voice to a mutter. "I'm as disappointed as you are."

Fieldler joins them now. Just for a moment, catching fragments of their conversation, he is tempted to believe they are discussing a business deal, especially when Pirelli and Hamilton fall silent, conditioned by habit to be secretive. The awkward silence lasts a full minute. The men are groggy and tired. Even Fieldler. It's difficult, in their state, to know exactly what to say. Although no one wants to admit it, they are silenced by an unacknowledged possibility they are going to fail.

"Today?" asks Hamilton bluntly, when the silence has worn on too long.

Fieldler nods. "I expect so. If not, tomorrow then."

"Jesus," says Pirelli.

"Kovacs is more resourceful than we thought."

For the moment Pirelli and Hamilton merely ruminate on Fieldler's observation. Fieldler has less of a personal stake in the outcome of this hunt. Both men, remembering this, gently resent him for it.

"Maybe hunting him wasn't a good idea after all." This from Pirelli.

But Fieldler only grunts. Although the hunt was his idea, he is unwilling to take any responsibility for its failure. Like Hamilton and Knox, Fieldler is convinced he does not fail and is never wrong. Fieldler is a member of a club exclusive to him and a few others, the "us" that is superior in the equation of "us" and "them."

"Ernie, that business with Kovacs and the deer and the wolf . . ."

"Yes?"

Hamilton looks down at the toes of his boots to finish his question, his hand positioned over the agony of his belly, gently stroking it in case this caressing actually helps. "What do you think it means?"

"Nothing. Don't trouble yourself."

"But it was spooky."

Fieldler considers this. "Things happen in the wilderness," he observes at last. "It's a different world.

Difficult to conquer. It doesn't explain itself."

Knox has doused the fire and now approaches them. "Let's go," is all he says, covering up his concern that the other three men no longer invite him to their meetings. Perhaps they toy with some idea of mutiny. Today, for tactical reasons, he will allow a part of his mind to contemplate the means by which he will kill them all so he can make his escape. He must be ready for when the hunt fails. If it fails, he must kill the others so that there are no witnesses.

Without a word, each man carries his own unfortunate set of secrets. The hunters gather up their rifles and strike out in single file into yet another dawn.

BY MID-AFTERNOON OF THIS, YOUR STRONGEST DAY since the beginning of your flight, you realize you cannot find the river which, until yesterday, guided you through this wilderness. In its own uncaring way, the water represented the most significant component in your hope for escape. It has now been nearly twenty-four hours since you lost sight of the gray current or the white river's rapids. The cliffs hold back the stream like the necessary wall of an artery. Without the river to accompany you, you must acknowledge the disturbing conclusion that you are quite lost. Except for the sun and an idealistic notion you can measure its autumn arc from east to west across the sky, you face the possibility you are wandering without a clear sense of direction or destination. The river, you believed, flowed somewhere toward a settlement of human beings. Now that the river is gone, so too is the likelihood of a society of rescuers living somewhere along its banks.

Yet you resist your despair. You still have food. You feel stronger today. You still carry the notion of Sara as an important destination worth surviving for. And perhaps the wolf from which you stole the venison still accompanies you, back there in the distance, a buffer between you and your hunters, an alarm system, a rearguard sentry, a wilderness clone of what you must eventually become to survive out here in the mountains alone. Your hunters? Strangely enough, it occurs to you at this moment you fear being lost, a victim of the elements, as much or more than you fear your adversaries from L.A. This reassessing of dangers is not enough to cause you to let down your guard, but it is enough to cause you to wonder whom your actual enemy is. Not the wilderness itself, you decide. But time. Time and its alliance with the wilderness, that is. Several days out here, another week or two perhaps carrying a homemade lance and a hatchet, is all the time that remains for you. Beyond a week or so, the elements will lose patience with you and your intrusion. They will conspire to remind you of the fragility of your life. What is it that people say? Mother Nature bats last? Words to that effect. In the end Mother Nature will swing her bat of winter and knock you over the wall of her inhospitable park.

You consider these truths like a skip in a record as you hurry as best you can through this endless wilderness. You consider them when you find level ground, and again when you reach a clearing to jog across. And you consider them some more as you skulk through a thick stand of wilderness evergreens, counting the necessary steamboats you use to measure out your hope as precisely as an atomic clock measures time. To measure time in this way is to control it, spacing it out until you can find a better setting where you can pretend to be in power over your life again.

Afternoon gradually wanes. Doggedly you head for higher ground, hungry, tired, but stronger in some small way, married to hope and resolve but married also to despair, in a bigamistic dilemma you now suspect defines the human condition itself. In this strange, dual fashion, and in other ways too, you feel connected to your instinct as you've never been connected to it before. You feel yourself to be human in a new and powerful way. Despite your apprehension. Despite your despair. Cheating death in the way you have so far, inspires you to believe you have never been so alive.

THEIR LAST NIGHT WITH FOOD. The hunters hold a meeting to discuss what they will do tomorrow to bring the hunt to an end and to set about feeding themselves. The men are deceptively calm following another day of failure, but their calm is a blend of fatigue and each man's canny, secret resolve to reach a goal necessary only to himself, only to his own survival.

"I thought we'd find him today," says Hamilton wearily. The stew that was his supper gnaws into his belly like a voracious parasite, where it chews at the flesh of his abdomen. When he permits himself to think about it, he imagines teeth in his belly like those in the mouth of a piranha.

"I thought we'd get him yesterday," says Pirelli.

"Fuck," says Knox. "We should have had him yesterday before dark."

All of the men glance at Fieldler who is staring into the fire. It is his turn to comment. He's like the last man to throw his money into a pool of wagers over a sporting event. Knowing this, he makes the other men wait for him.

"Ernie?" This comes from Knox.

Fieldler gazes at him then shrugs to buy himself more time. He has been considering other worries, other strategies. He has known all along that Knox will become his enemy, should they fail to hunt you down. Knox has the most to lose if you appear to slip through their fingers within some appropriate time limitation. Knox then must implement the only means he possesses to escape from this hunt and its failure. He must kill everyone here, the colleagues with whom he shares this philosophical campfire conversation, taking his five million dollars and vanishing from the face of the Earth to hide from the wreckage he has left behind, living without the other half of his fee due—according to Hamilton—when Kovacs has been killed. He must leave behind no witnesses to the failure to hunt you down. Now convinced there are two hazards about which he must be alert—the remaining search for you and the awkward, dangerous moment when Knox decides to take his life, along with Hamilton's and Pirelli's— Fieldler has concluded, hours before this disingenuous moment of peace before the campfire, that it is likely he will have to kill Knox before finally getting the opportunity to dispose of you.

"Ernie, for Christ's sake," whines Hamilton. "Do you want to share your thoughts with us?"

"We have two problems now," Fieldler replies at last. "We have to hunt our food and continue looking for Kovacs. Hunting food will slow us down. If we shoot game to feed ourselves, we also run the risk of alerting Kovacs that we're close to him."

"Do you think we're close?"

"Yes, I do. But not as close as we thought. Not as close as we should be."

Pirelli sighs in exasperation. "Wait a minute," he says. "Here we are out of food and Kovacs isn't as close as we thought. So how has he kept going, for fuck's sake? I mean, what's he eating tonight?"

Intently Fieldler gazes at him. "He's eating venison."

"What?"

At the word, "venison," Pirelli's mouth begins to water. He's never eaten venison in his life; it dismays him that he desperately wants to eat it now, so soon after eating stew. Kovacs has found something succulent out here in the wilderness that, by rights, should have been his.

"Whaddyuh mean, 'he's eating venison?'"

But it's Knox who feels compelled to reply. "You mean the remains of that deer we found yesterday?"

Fieldler nods.

"But what about the wolf prints?" Pirelli wants to know.

Everyone gazes at Fieldler, awaiting his latest theory.

"The wolf could be a red herring," the tall hunter says. "Maybe the wolf happened along the remains after Kovacs took what he needed."

Knox guffaws. "So how did Kovacs kill the deer? Talk it to death?"

"Or," adds Fieldler, ignoring Knox's remarks, "Kovacs chased the wolf away from the kill."

"Oh c'mon, Ernie. How the fuck would he do that?"

"I don't know," the hunter replies. "I wasn't there. But Kovacs is a desperate man. Either way, he's eating venison. Who stole it from whom isn't the issue. I know it in my gut. Kovacs is eating venison."

All the men fall silent, pondering their version of a scene in which you won some imagined argument with something as ferocious as a wolf over the vital flesh of a deer.

"You trying to spook us, Ernie?" Pirelli asks shortly.

"You wanted to know what Kovacs is eating. I suggest he's eating venison. Beyond Kovacs' surprising resourcefulness, how he came by something to eat is of no concern to us."

"Okay," says Hamilton impatiently. "He's resourceful. We keep talking about that. So what? We've got all the time in the world. When do we catch him?"

"Tomorrow maybe."

"Maybe?"

The men grow silent again. "Maybe" echoes in the darkness on the fringes of their fire. Surveyed now, most of the men would abandon the hunt at this moment, if you were not their quarry. They are cold and tired, and tomorrow they will be hungry. If not for you and the possibility of your escape—the story you would tell the authorities afterwards—they would soon give up on this quest to find you. But the men are trapped now by the limited opportunities within their original plan and by their subsequent failure to see it through yet. They must soon kill you or face unacceptable consequences. Only now are they realizing that a freedom of choice they never acknowledged they had has slipped away from them as the hunt prepares to enter its third day.

It is Pirelli who is most irritated by this apparent transformation in their circumstances. It bothers him that he and his colleagues are now prisoners of this wilderness hunt in much the same way that you are. Now, like you, they are fighting for their survival. "When did it happen," he wants to know, "that a slime bucket like Kovacs put us into this position?"

But no one answers him. No one wants to admit they are as trapped by their quarry as their quarry is by them.

"Listen to me," Knox orders at last, emitting a powerful sigh. "All of you have to remember to keep up your morale."

"Morale," scoffs Hamilton. "We're out of food, Kovacs has vanished and you're talking about morale? School spirit? Esprit de corps?"

"Knox is right, J.D.," says Fieldler carefully.

"Jesus," says Hamilton with all the patience he can

muster. "We're out of food, for Christ's sake. And I don't even know where we are. Kovacs has led us away from the river. Even if we find Kovacs, even if we kill him, how do we get back? What do we eat? You can't seriously be worrying about morale, can you?"

"I've memorized our way back," Knox tells them calmly.

"Me too," adds Fieldler. "I've been marking the trail. Knox too. He knows as well as I do that he has to get back to fly the plane."

Silence.

"Don't worry about how we'll get back," repeats Knox to make it perfectly clear. "I'm keeping track of that. It's been part of this mission all along. When we're done here, obviously we have to get back to where we landed."

Hamilton and Pirelli both nod. Both hope Knox's remarks reflect more than empty assurance. Both want to be relieved by some kind of truth in anything he says.

"And tomorrow we're going to have to hunt for food."

"Are we going to split up?"

"Probably." Knox gets to his feet. "We've talked enough. Time to get some rest. Same watches as last night." Abruptly he walks towards his bedroll, disappearing into the darkness.

Shortly, one by one, resenting Knox with an almost comfortable predictability, the other men relent. Pirelli takes his watch. Fieldler and Hamilton, now strangers to one another, no longer truly trusting one another although they would be hard-pressed to explain why, set about bedding down to sleep.

PIRELLI MOPES AROUND THE CAMPFIRE, vaguely unhappy with himself. His sense of inadequacy has been growing for the past day and a half. He is aware he needs some kind of redemption. He feels weaker than the other men—Knox who has slain human prey before, Fieldler who is so at home on a hunt in any wilderness setting, and Hamilton, his employer and father-in-law who continues to intimidate him in the same manner he always has, by means of his power and wealth even this far from Los Angeles. He would like to show them all, the other men, that he can be a professional too. His craving for success is at the root of his need for redemption. He wants to be the one to bring you to your knees, to make you cry for mercy or, failing this, to line you up in the scope on his Remington and blow your fucking brains out.

For him, the hunt isn't as much about Sara as he once thought it was. Pirelli has realized he doesn't truly see her as a victim in this scenario of retribution. He now believes she is your unfaithful accomplice. Maybe, he muses, it would have been better to kill Sara. A bad idea, he knows, but something that comforts him like any other improbable fantasy would. It's just that his father-in-law—at some point during the aftermath of Sara leaving him—gained control over their shared disappointment and over their mutual quest for revenge and satisfaction. It was more important to Hamilton that Sara return to her husband than it was to him. Over time, Pirelli knows, he might have let Sara go. He might even have given up on resenting you as her lover, especially if Hamilton left even a fair portion of his corporate empire to him, his former son-in-law. But now it's too late. Now he's trapped by what needs to be done for his father-in-law and by the promised wealth, power and prestige Hamilton's corporate empire represents. Now it's gone too far. Now he must be—and must continue to be—as vengeful as his benefactor. There is a great deal at stake. Pirelli must once again acknowledge he has no choice.

He labours under the weight of the secrets he must keep. He cannot tell his father-in-law that Sara was a pain in the ass—demanding, over-sexed, too independent for a man like him. He cannot admit there were occasions before she left when he sometimes hated her, when she reminded him somehow of inadequacies about himself, various kinds of impotence he didn't want to hear about, sexual and otherwise. Now, when Kovacs is dead, the theory that Sara will return to him inspires ambivalence. He wants Sara in his matrimonial bed less than her father does. Knowing this, Pirelli realizes he is trapped by J.D.'s irrational love for his daughter and the vast wealth of the Hamilton corporate empire which, with Sara back, is Pirelli's to own someday. He is equally trapped by you, the interloper who managed to stagger inside this fragile and complex house of economic cards with no business being there.

Pirelli wants to kill you; he really does. Most of all, though, he knows he must. Must is different than want. Must is something outside himself, a motivation originating in the outer world. Want is a need from the inner world he owns. It strikes him that must has grown more important than want throughout much of his life. Pirelli wonders when and how this exchange took place between what is vital to him and what is vital to the world. Sitting alone by the fire, chilled, tired and anticipating hunger tomorrow, he is aware he has lost his passion for the hunt. Sport was integral to the plan. Now two doors stand waiting in front of him: one represents all he can win for himself; the other reflects all he can lose. He must choose one over the other. Either choice is reason enough to be committed to your death.

Nothing personal, Kovacs, he muses into the night.

It's a dog eat dog world. Satisfied with this prehistoric homily, Pirelli waits out his watch, his Remington cradled across his thighs, its comfortable weight, at this moment, seeming to be his only friend.

HAMILTON HAS SUSPECTED FOR MONTHS that the pain in his stomach will eventually kill him. Out here in the silence and the cold—now that Pirelli has bedded down and Hamilton is on watch—Hamilton realizes the wilderness does not apologize for itself nor to wealthy industrialists either. Here, he has been learning to accept his inevitable, even imminent death. In case his days are numbered, the preparations a man must make for when he is gone were made some time ago. He has taken care of all the business that must be tidied up when a man prepares to leave this world. He has dotted every errant "i" and crossed every necessary "t." He has arranged his estate in a way that leaves Marjorie secure, not that she deserves it necessarily, but so that he will not be remembered as a man who did not provide for her. The rest will go to Sara, although she must remain married to Tony to claim her inheritance. If not, if she decides to divorce her husband, the bulk of his corporate holdings will go to his son-in-law.

He's set it up this way, not so much to ensure Sara resumes her marriage with Tony but to prevent her from marrying anyone else. It was fine that she married Tony—he more or less selected Tony for the job. But marrying someone else, some asshole like you, for instance, would represent an intolerable infidelity to him. While Sara is married to Tony, Hamilton is convinced she remains married to him. While he cannot prevent her from marrying some other ignominious you in the future, Hamilton knows he can reach out from beyond the grave to make certain his daughter lives in comparative poverty should she betray his love and wishes. Yes, the poverty Sara will know is relative. It won't be true poverty. But it will be poverty by comparison to what she will have if she stays with Tony who is rightfully her husband. She will pay in vast riches if, in not going back to Tony, she does not remain with his marital selection for her and therefore with her father.

All of these edicts have been taken care of should Hamilton die, should the pain in his belly ultimately murder him. At this moment, gazing into the fire, as Hamilton waits out his watch and occasionally feeds the flames with wood, only one outstanding debt remains to be paid. This debt, of course, is you. You must die for despoiling Sara and for standing in his way. Once you are gone, Hamilton believes he can happily die. He is weary, deeply weary, and he is filled with some vague but large disappointment that life was not the joyful experience he once believed it would be. He can't say why exactly, but the feeling of letdown is staggeringly deep. Looking back, he cannot think of any major changes he would make in how his life has been lived. Yet he faces his astonishing disappointment anyway, now realizing its immense depth has haunted him for many years. Joy deprivation, he supposes now. No wonder he feels such spiritual exhaustion.

He supposes someone lied to him about the true nature of life once upon a time, way back then when, as a child, he didn't know any better. He supposes the lie surrounded the nature of life's rewards and the cumulative choices a man makes as he climbs the arduous ladder towards the rafters of his satisfaction and the peace defining his death. But he doesn't know who or what lied to him. Or why. Who told him joy would not matter? Or that joy would be readily accessible once his ambition had satisfied his conventional goals? How much he should care about the lie and how it got told? He's worth more than a billion dollars. And, more than three decades ago, he conceived Sara, the woman of his dreams, out of the unexpected creativity in his lustful loins: Adam helped God with the birth of his personal Eve.

But his disappointment with life exists nonetheless. Someone lied to him at birth about what life would be truly like. He likes to think it was a conspiracy of some kind, but he cannot see his conspirators' faces; he has no idea who they are. The disappointment now gnaws at the flesh in his belly. Maybe he wasn't truly led astray. Maybe a man goes down the road set out for him, robbed of any choice. But something hard and hurtful and heavy he has named disappointment, whether his fault or someone else's, claws at his belly like a hot poker. He is absolutely convinced it must eventually take his life.

But Hamilton intends to kill you to make up for everything else that may have failed. You, he believes, are his only true mistake, the way he let you inside his family's sacred fortifications. He will kill you to correct this mistake before he allows his pervasive disappointment to steer him unprotesting towards the inevitability of the grave.

Knowing all of this, but going over it endlessly in his mind, Hamilton passes his watch in reflection and a kind of tragic wonder. Life has disappointed him and he has no idea how the disappointment could have been avoided. At some point he glances at his watch and discovers he is ten minutes into overtime, as if he's been enjoying his thoughts and has been gilding some kind of philosophical lily on company time. Surprised, with a groan he can barely stifle, he struggles to his feet and stumbles towards the spot where Fieldler sleeps. "Ernie?" he whispers hoarsely. "Get up. It's time for your watch."

FIELDLER IS AWARE HE COULD USE A WOMAN about now. Someone young and relatively innocent, he muses. Merely thinking about this need inspires a lonely erection in the stench of the lower extremities of his unshowered body. Even out here, hundreds of miles away from any satiation, he needs a woman, maybe more than one, to antagonize and then quell an endless hunger inside him he has known for years. He thinks about his need calmly, despite the intensity in its endlessness. He's been a man like this forever and he can no longer remember a time when he felt even a modicum of shame about his preoccupation with sex and the pain he feels must accompany it. He can control the need for now—it's impractical way out here—but he lets it take hold of him anyway because it distracts him for a time from the urgency of the hunt. For a while he contemplates a young and innocent woman and the pain he would inflict on her before impaling her on his restless need.

And time passes for Fieldler under the star-strewn night of this mountain-festered wilderness.

Eventually, though, he turns away from these thoughts to wonder when Knox will decide you are out of reach—that the hunt for you has failed—and it is time to kill his fellow hunters so that he can make his own escape. Fieldler is already prepared for the moment when Knox comes to this decision. Even tonight, when he wakes the hired assassin for his turn on watch, he will be ready to kill him if Knox gives any indication that he is ending the hunt. When Knox assumes his position on watch, here at the edge of the fire, Fieldler will remain awake in the darkness, his Remington lying beside him at the edge of his bedroll, touched by the palm of his hand, so that he can kill Knox before Knox tries to kill him.

Fieldler has already decided to assume responsibility for protecting Hamilton and Pirelli from Knox. For two reasons. Firstly, Fieldler knows when Knox decides to kill his colleagues, Knox must try to kill him first—as an experienced hunter Fieldler is the most dangerous man. Secondly, if he were to warn the others about Knox's intentions, Knox would notice their dismay. So Fieldler must act alone as he protects all three of them. Enjoying this notion, comforted by his altruism, he assumes a subtle nobility in this solitary responsibility. His nobility nestles like a gem inside the larger, gaudy necklace that is his commitment to survival.

Fieldler doubts Knox will betray them tonight. He will want to be part of the process of one more day of hunting you and the game they will have to kill for food, before he truly gives up on finding you. But should you remain alive tomorrow night, Knox may then decide the hunt for you is a bust. Then Fieldler will have to kill him to keep the hunt alive. Even so, just in case, when Fieldler turns the watch over to Knox tonight, he will not sleep until morning. He will remain awake to prevent Knox from betraying them earlier than expected.

FOR NOW, KNOX IS MORE PREOCCUPIED with his need for food than he is with his concern that he will soon have to dispose of the other hunters. As he sits by the fire, awaiting dawn, he wonders how best to accomplish both the continuing search for you and the new need to hunt for wild game. He has worked out all the ramifications of Plan B: his survival, his escape from here to a safely anonymous somewhere else. Plan B simmers on a back burner for now. He has already endured an early anger that he was stupid enough to take part in Hamilton's hunt. He has already worked his way through the frustration he feels that he must radically change his life, if the need to kill the others and escape is ultimately required. But for now he must think about game, about hunger. After this need is satisfied, he can turn his attention to what remains of the hunt and the moment he should conclude you have escaped, becoming a danger to him.

Plan B, as he likes to call it, already exists. It means killing his co-conspirators, returning to the airplane where there is more food—canned goods mostly—stashed away in a cargo compartment, then flying out of here to assume a new identity. He knows he can get by with five million dollars, with living by another name, taking up residence in another country. But he knows he will be bored without his career to keep him occupied. And he knows he will have to develop new appetites for life to replace what has been his only preoccupation for so long: the professionalism he brought to his career and the necessary solitude this professionalism required. He has to achieve more than his escape from the failure of this hunt. As the modern colloquialism suggests, he must learn to get a life.

Still, even knowing all of this and having planned for it, Knox has not given up yet. Another day or two, he thinks, before the conclusion you have slipped through his fingers becomes inescapable. Fieldler, he believes, will know how to bring down a deer or moose, something they can butcher and eat. Once his belly is full, Knox will keep an open mind. He doesn't fear killing his colleagues and he doesn't fear failing to find his way back to the airplane. He does fear the possibility of changing his life, of becoming another man when he enjoys and is used to the man he is right now.

THE DOGS KEEP MOVING into the middle of the night, driven by new and maddening scents carried by the currents in the air. The appeal in what they smell is irresistible, a satiation for their two major cravings: hunger and what is quickly becoming an endless need for violence. The dogs move like shadows through the mountainous wilderness, close to the landscape's surface, like bumps under a blanket in a childish game of fidget. They smell the wolf and hate him. They smell what remains of the slaughtered deer you share with the wolf and they covet it. They trot steadily in the darkness of this deep mountainous night, purveyors of anarchy.

They smell your campfire smoke too, aware it is tantalizingly different than the campfire built by your pursuers. Your campfire is the one visited by the wolf. Your campfire is the one that promises the drippings from your venison. These various scents, these various delights, drive them on blindly. Anarchy is a frenzied compound of both illness and its cure. The dogs do not know the difference. They are like soldiers too used to war. They see the ongoing problem of strife as the ongoing solution to life itself. They are out of options, out of new ideas. They are canine ideologues. While doing what they've been doing in the several weeks since they fled domesticity, without knowing why they would want to, they have concluded they must keep going, keep doing the same things. This conventionality is their ideology of narrowed options; the ideology of narrowed options leads to anarchy. It transforms the endlessness of their problem into a perceived endless solution. A cure. And each time it turns out there actually is no cure for their tiresome existence, the conundrum of illness and cure intensifies. Fuelled by boredom and anger, the dogs cling to their anarchy. They love and despise within and outside themselves. They are the finest of ideologues: reduced to hunger and viciousness, they know no other motivation.

In this way, they hurry through the darkness, dogs of war and retribution. And the smells that drive them on, inspiring them to salivate, grow stronger and stronger as they draw closer to what they have come to think is their destination.

THE WOLF LIES RESTING on a rocky promontory fifty yards from the gentle glow of your fire. He has eaten your latest offering, although he feels no gratitude. Instead of being thankful, he is mostly puzzled. He considers that you might be a new breed of wolf and man he's never encountered before. Although he remembers you chased him from the fallen doe he has come to believe you probably mean him no harm. But what are you doing here? And where do you think you are going? What is your purpose in his life? He wonders these things in the way a wolf wonders, not thinking about it exactly but sensing these questions in vague, instinctive abstractions.

Then suddenly these feelings evaporate. He enjoys a last few seconds of calm reflection before a moment of change arrives, an onslaught of lunacy he has been expecting for more than a week that now is clearly inevitable. The wolf drifts quickly to his feet, in silence and deep caution. Apprehension prickles along his flesh and aspects of his fur stand up and tingle in response.

He hears the dogs before he smells or sees them. He knows immediately these are dogs, a mutation in his species, because they announce their arrival in a way he never would, with threatening growls and snarls that compromise the necessary surprise the wolf knows is integral to a successful attack. The wolf could run from these wild dogs. He is physically superior, faster, stronger, healthier. But this place so close to your fire, where he has eaten and waited for what comes next, now belongs to him. He decides he will stay here and fight to keep it, this tiny wedge of territory. To run from what belongs to him in this wilderness would degrade or belittle him. And the dogs would chase him for days, hounding him ceaselessly. In silence, the wolf waits to be encircled, every muscle and sinew taut in the few seconds remaining before battle.

Soon, when Leo McKendrick's dogs attack the wolf, he is ready for them. He plunges down on them from the rocky height where he has stationed himself. The wolf believes he has no choice. Because these dogs are crazed, an anarchy here in the wilderness, the wolf knows he must battle them to the death.

IT IS FORTUNATE YOU ARE SLEEPING not far from your fire—sleeping sitting up underneath your metallic blanket, the way you do these nights—when Leo McKendrick's dogs attack your wolf somewhere in the darkness not far away. It is good fortune to be rudely awakened in this way because you regain consciousness before you have time to think. Instead of reflecting on your options, you come awake with little more than the gift of inherent instinct. You hear snarls and growls and yelps of pain, but you take no time to be cautious. Instinct inspires you to reach for your lance then plunge into the darkness where there is no question you will do battle with some new and unknown breed of antagonist.

Although it is very dark, you discover you see quite

well. You have not yet allowed yourself to doubt whether you will be able to see. You have not yet had time to consider common human doubts about the quality of your vision. Still, although your eyesight is surprisingly keen, it takes a moment or two to make out who is whom among the undulating shadows emitting noisy snarls of battle. Eventually, though, you recognize the larger shape of your wolf, then the smaller dogs or coyotes—you cannot be sure exactly what they are at this moment—that encircle and attack the wolf.

You answer only to your instincts. Even now you do not take the time to reason out your options. Instead you are driven only by some primal need to be part of this unexpected sorting out of what is right and wrong. You plunge into the melee—not quite gleefully but celebrating a need for justice that is new to you. You pick out one of the dogs that has turned in your direction—it looks like a dog by now, a collie of some kind. It hesitates, confused, before it decides to attack. Before it can come at you, you thrust down and then up, the large blade at the end of your lance penetrating its chest, killing it instantly. There is a gentle yelp, then the gush of escaping air before the dog falls away dead from the blade at the end of your lance.

You plunge deeper into the skirmish, snarling invectives of your own. You hold the lance out in front of you and kill another dog, twisting the blade into its throat. All this growling and snarling—yours, the wolf's, the dogs'—arrives at your ears with a calamitous volume, but this only encourages you more as you slash and spear at the dogs alongside your battling wolf. The altercation is all frenzy now, bloodlust and retribution. You and the wolf attack, meting out the justice that lives inside the purity of a necessary instinct. There is a vicious husky that soon turns on you. It turns its back on the wolf to lunge at you. But the wolf lunges in and under, and the husky shrieks in pain as it is disembowelled by the wolf. Only one dog remains and it stands there stupidly, alone with itself and the knowledge that it has been so easily led. You use your lance to spear it in the chest, not an act of war this time, but the gift of some sweet mercy . . .

. . . Until all the dogs are dead. Until, realizing they are dead, you stand exhausted in the darkness, gasping for breath.

Your throat is raw from growling and snarling in the heat of battle. You stand there in the carnage, blood on your hands and clothing, a gash on your knuckles, scratches along your wrists. Then, because you cannot help yourself, you raise the lance aloft, holding it over your head, holding it in both hands like a ceremonial staff. Because you cannot help it, you scream into the night, feeling triumph, elation and freedom, all these emotions unleashed, set free in the primal sound of your cry.

Cautiously the wolf moves away from you. Then, knowing he must, he disappears into the darkness to find a secluded place where he can lie down to lick his wounds. He has suffered a bite along his shoulder and there is a slight tear in his right buttock. But the damage is relatively insignificant, due in part to your intercession.

You check your hands and arms for further evidence of wounds. There is a cut on a finger of your right hand, but you do not remember when it you sustained this injury. It doesn't matter. It is small, hardly worth noting.

After the wolf is gone, something civilized in you gradually takes hold of your personality again. You stand alone in the darkness, panting, letting human reason return. Trembling now in aftershock, you slip cautiously into the darkness back towards your fire. There, after a dazed and motionless moment devoid of thought or feeling, you feed the smoldering embers the last of your wood. Aching, you pull the metallic blanket over your stiffening body. You sit there warming yourself, gazing into the flames. Although it remains dark, dawn will soon be coming on. You don't know how you know this, how imminent dawn actually is; you only know you know and you do not question the knowledge. The dogs, you decide, are really no use to you as food. They may have been diseased. Rabies or some other angry affliction.

The battle less than fifteen minutes ago feels like a dream in many ways, now that it is over. It seems to have happened to someone else. Or in another life. Or in some dimension you hardly know that drifts along behind you like your shadow.

You recall suddenly that everyone back in Los Angeles believed you would make a million dollars this year. You smile into the flames at the incongruity of this memory with what has just transpired: your alliance with the wolf, your instinct, despite the danger, to save its life and your own. L.A. and the money you were going to make seem so far away now. Memories of that time seem like artifacts of someone else's culture, historic events you shared with scarcely remembered strangers.

Seeking your favourite solace, you embrace Sara in your mind. Sara, you wouldn't believe what I've just done . . .

Clarity arrives, inspired by memories of Sara and some instinctive nobility you now feel, having battled the dogs alongside a wolf who feels strangely like your friend. Nobility and competence. Besides, it now seems clear to you the dogs would have come for you after they had killed the wolf. It is better to meet an adversary head on, you decide, than it is to wait for your adversary to come to you. Thinking this, believing it to be true, you realize at this moment, gazing into the fire, that you have reached the point where you are done running away from your hunters. You come to this conclusion with the same wisdom and clarity that tells you dawn is now approaching. A new day of life and survival is on its way.

You will not let them kill you running away. They will have to kill you on a field of battle where they will have no choice but to face their fear, the way you face your fear. You will force them to face you. You will force them to look at you with all the vacuity of their empty morality. And you will try to take one or two of them with you on your way to hell, just so that they know whom they're dealing with.

You doze at first inside the comfort of these conclusions, then feed yourself new pieces of roasted venison you skewer on your lance blade. When dawn breaks, you put out your campfire with the toe of your boot. Turning in the direction you have already gone, you slip into the morning grayness, determined to find a way to face your hunters.

SYNTHESIS

"I THINK IT'S GOING TO SNOW," Joe Leonard tells his wife in Senaki as he gazes out the window, anticipating this will be the last day they need to finish harvesting their garden.

"We'll be done just in time then," she says.

He turns to her and nods.

In the ensuing silence, Allison moves to the wood stove where she can warm her hands. Joe remains at the window, contemplating the day and its weather, noticing purple, white and gray clouds moving in, dense, jagged creatures changing shape as they gather around and embrace the mountain peaks in the distance. They will linger on the mountains a few hours before pushing towards his and Allison's valley later on this day. Joe knows everything there is to know about this time of year. He knows the snow these clouds carry will arrive this afternoon sloppy and wet, heavy with moisture, the same kind of snowfall that dusted the valley a couple of days ago, melting away in temperatures trapped a few degrees above freezing point. Autumn will be several weeks long this way, too cold for rain but still too warm to freeze the garden soil, preparing it to welcome the significant accumulations of snow winter will eventually bring to this place.

Joe enjoys knowing this valley and its weather intimately. He enjoys knowing its animals and its mood. In this place he borrowed from the Earth on behalf of himself and Allison, he has discovered a world of plenty. Here there is calm. Here there is peace. Here he finds knowledge and a delicate, egoless wisdom. Here Joe is and can continue to be authentic which, for him, is probably the most important quality a man or woman can possess. With authenticity he has found overwhelming peace. He is grateful for it and cherishes it. He does not have to look ahead in a search for who he is. He does not have to fret about why he is alive. Because he is authentic, it is enough to just live. It's not that "why" isn't an important question, Joe believes. It's just that when a person is authentic the answer to that question arrives more easily and calmly.

When he turns away from the window, feeling a quiet sense of gratitude, Joe catches Allison's eye and smiles. She smiles too. They made love last night, and she has convinced him of the exciting certainty that she is pregnant, although it is far too early for her to know for sure. Still, this news, combined with the knowledge they live here jointly in an uncomplicated and rewarding way, knits a feeling of easy joy to bind them together this morning in a gentle and lasting afterglow. Smiles this morning cannot help but be easy and uninhibited. There will be other smiles today, no doubt. It does not occur to them to contemplate any harm in what is celebrated between them, an apolitical, natural love and sexuality. They have found their necessary innocence and there is no one here to define or decry it as selfish or naive. Here, authenticity is harmless. They do not use some version of it to wage war. They do not build a society of like-minded peers. They have no need to amass riches, to have more or less than someone else. They are nurtured by the simplicity of everything they require. When Joe thinks about their perfect state of needlessness sometimes, he realizes how happy he is to live without envy, how happy he is to have no reason to feel contempt.

KNOX IS GRATEFUL FOR THE OPPORTUNITY to be tracking you on his own. It's good for his confidence; he feels like a professional again. The other three men—his colleagues—now worry him constantly. He no longer trusts them. They do not communicate with him in the respectful way they did when the hunt began, asking him for his thoughts or what he expects to do on their behalf. They no longer appreciate his leadership. They have forgotten how all four of them are supposed to operate as a team. As Knox sees it, the other three men have transferred the failure of this hunt—its shaky foundation and its pointless risk—onto his shoulders. Knox resents their presumptuousness, regretting the way he inadvertently permitted them to foist the blame on him. This error now looms in his mind as the most glaring professional mistake he has ever made. Regardless of the means he finds to correct this mistake—by killing you or by killing them—Knox anticipates the amending moment happily. It will provide the required opportunity for him to escape the chaos that began with his initial misjudgment of this project. He should never have agreed to the hunt as the way to take your life; the inherent risks were too great. When he corrects his error, though, his life will never be the same. It will have new risks for him forever.

For now, though, it's business as usual. He has dispatched the other hunters, under Fieldler's lieutenantship, in the direction of a valley they noticed in the distance earlier this morning. They have their instructions. They are to bring down enough game to feed themselves for a day or two. While they are engaged in this assignment, not wanting your trail to get any colder than it already is, Knox tracks you across the westernmost ridge that helps define the valley's perimeter. When he hears gunshots, Knox will return to the valley, leaving a marker behind indicating which way you've passed. The gunshots will mean Fieldler has brought down something to eat. With food, they can resume the hunt in earnest and, with luck, begin to gain on you again.

Or else Knox can implement plan B and embark on the process of escaping the remainder of the hunt altogether, correcting his great mistake in judgment and getting on with the unhappy proposition of starting his life anew. This latter possibility continues to be a sour prospect for him. Yet something innately moral in his character has accepted that he deserves this punishment of being forced to change his life, specifically because he agreed to this assignment of hunting you down in the first place. He knows greed was his motivation. Greed placed him in this untenable situation. He must show his mettle by accepting responsibility for his initial weakness. There is a price to be paid; the time he will have to pay it closes in rapidly. Knox approaches being a hired assassin the way any devout Protestant would—he will not shirk the responsibility of what needs to be done.

None of the other hunters objected to splitting up this way, although Knox speculates it must have bothered Fieldler that he was going off on his own. In the past twenty-four hours he and Fieldler have grown increasingly wary of one another. In a way, strategically, the two men read each other's minds. Knox knows Fieldler realizes that he must leave behind no witnesses to the failure of the hunt, once the point is reached where the hunt is clearly deemed a failure. And Fieldler probably knows that he is the first man who must die, if Knox is to make a satisfactory escape. Knox has concluded intuitively that the big game hunter has surmised most of the ramifications in his diminishing options by now. It's something Fieldler would do. Fieldler, after all, is a worthy antagonist. Nor is it a remote possibility, he has decided, that Fieldler will succeed in killing him first.

Again, Knox assigns these speculations to a back burner in his mind and concentrates on finding and following your trail. He has grown increasingly competent at wilderness tracking. Or maybe it's because you are getting sloppy. Overconfidence perhaps? Maybe, because you've survived this long, you believe you have escaped. Knox enjoys pondering this possibility. If you continue to leave behind such a readily discernible trail, he is convinced he or one of the other men will finally bring you down.

Yet, while this conclusion is promising, it is undermined for Knox by continuing evidence of wolves reoccurring in places at the edge of your trail. Already this morning he has found wolf scat—shit in fur-twisted turds—in piles along your route. Now and then he has noticed paw prints too, some of them small, others disturbingly large. If he did not know better, he would conclude you are collecting companionable beasts to serve as your comrades-in-arms, as you move more deeply into the wilderness. Do they pursue you because they mean you harm or do you conscript them as allies? The further north and west you flee, the more Knox asks himself this question. He would be content to find your carcass along this route sometime soon, your flesh half devoured by wolves. He would not be very happy, though, if he discovered the impossible alternative: that you've inspired a lupine platoon to help you do battle with your pursuers.

Knox keeps to himself this wild imagining about you enlisting allies. If he shared it with the others, they would think he'd lost his mind. While Fieldler says there are no recorded incidents—outside of captivity, that is—of wolves attacking humans, Knox has absorbed this information with more than a grain of salt. It appeals too much to him to embrace the notion that you have been stalked, then felled by wolves. Your death in this way would make resolution of the hunt so much simpler, so much more satisfying. And he would stop wondering once and for all if you have joined forces with this wilderness world initially conceived as the perfect location for your hunters to take your life easily.

Knox stops gazing at the ground long enough to peer at the swollen clouds collecting on the faces of the mountains immediately ahead. He hopes it snows again. Snow will enhance the various footprints you leave behind. Clear footprints represent an overdue shortcut to your death.

WHEN YOU SMELL WOODSMOKE wafting on the breeze, you hide at the edge of a stand of jackpines, trying to locate the source of the smoke with your gaze. As morning has progressed you have been growing more and more ambivalent about your decision to turn back to face your hunters. The scheme—now reflecting some potentially absurd notion of faith in yourself and some ill-defined principle of courage—has begun to drift away in your mind, replaced by an intensifying, much more rudimentary fear you are more familiar with. One half of you feels inspired to be turning around this way into the face of danger. The other half argues that interrupting your desperate flight represents commitment to some kind of honourable recourse. A principle. An ideal. Stacked up against your fear, this ideal of no longer behaving cowardly is beginning to dissolve. Killing the wild dogs last night no longer feels like the epiphany it seemed at the time of the skirmish. You feel stronger now in this pervasive mountain setting. You feel at home with its various dangers. Still, it would be foolhardy to believe your flesh has now grown miraculously impervious to rifle bullets.

Thank goodness for the smell of the smoke; in its own encouraging way it implies rescue could be at hand. The smoke you smell does not belong to your hunters; of this you are convinced. It's late morning now, too deeply into this day for the smoke to be a noticeable remnant of their all night campfire. No, what you detect at this moment tantalizing your increasingly sensitive ability to smell belongs to someone else. It is clearly an additional justification for continuing in the direction you've chosen, even though you are likely nearing the danger posed by your pursuers.

You are convinced your sense of smell has improved dramatically in the past few days. For one thing, the lack of olfactory clutter here in this mountain wilderness—no vehicular exhaust fumes, no urban storm sewer stench, no dog shit along the sidewalk, no vomit in the gutter, no cigarette butts pockmarking the pavement—makes it easy for you to separate the scent of anything specific from the collective wilderness odour that surrounds you here each day. But your ability to sort clearly through the various scents and odours, you suspect, reflects much more than the purity of the air. Your new ability represents the coming back to life of a long dead sensory talent.

It's as much the return of your memory of your senses' acumen as it is that your senses are more acute. Newly receptive to all your senses, you are willing to listen to what they tell you, knowing there probably was a time you refused to listen. Your circumstances as the hunted—defined by so much danger in this overwhelmingly vast and sensory environment—have slimmed you down somehow, removing dozens of distractions and irrelevant preoccupations, leaving you much more focused on the handful of urgencies your presence in these mountains demands you ultimately address. You think of your new instinctive wisdom, the keenness of your senses as basic knowledge, inherent wilderness intellect. Mute to this point in your life but whispering hoarsely now in an attempt to get your attention, your enhanced faculties remind you of primitive capabilities you previously couldn't discern.

Still smelling the smoke but unable yet to discern its source, you take a deep, encouraging breath and move cautiously out of the trees. You think of Sara again, as you so often do, and call on her silently to convey her usual inspiration. Apprehensive, even fearful, but committed nonetheless, you slip quietly through this wilderness morning in the direction of the source of the wood smoke tantalizing your nostrils, praying it belongs to someone who can help you save your life.

AROUND MIDMORNING, MORE OR LESS BY ACCIDENT, Knox comes across the torn remains of Leo McKendrick's dogs. It is rocky in this clearing and, if not for the remains of the fire you built last night among the boulders, he would not have discovered this was your location a number of hours ago. But the bloody carnage of dead dogs he discovers a few yards from your fire tells him a deeply disturbing story. He bends and examines the dogs, trying to figure out how you've managed to survive what was clearly their attack.

Ravens have been here, other scavengers too perhaps. But there are still enough remains to piece parts of the puzzle together. One of the dogs, a husky, has had its throat torn out. Another, a collie, sustained mortal injury when something sharp was thrust into its chest. Still another dog, a mongrel of some sort, apparently fell because of a series of blows to its head with something sharp. Methodically cataloguing the various injuries, Knox grows increasingly troubled by what they tell him about your resourcefulness. And, as incredible as it may seem, it appears you've made an impossible alliance with a wild animal of some kind. The tracks he has followed all morning explain a great deal about how this tiny battleground came to be.

His examination complete, Knox gets up from his crouch in this graveyard of dead dogs and scans his surroundings. He does not expect to see anything but the habit distracts him—in view of the evidence that lies before him—that he could be losing his mind. He has begun to blame this wilderness for chipping away at his previously immutable faculties. He has come to realize this mountainous setting is a wilderness radically different from the wilderness of political society where he normally plies his trade. This wilderness makes no sense to him. It defies his attempts to control it. inexplicable events can happen here. For all he knows, people here can talk to gods in whom he has never believed. Or they ride the backs of wolves from mountain peak to mountain peak, confounding every cynical reality with which Knox has shaped his life. Where is he at this moment? Who is he here in these mountains?

"Okay," he says aloud, comforted by the sound of his own voice. You have weapons of some kind: an axe, a primitive lance perhaps. And yeah, okay, something tore the throat out of the husky: a wolf perhaps, maybe a bear, or some scavenger who happened along when the coast was clear. Yeah, that's more likely. A scavenger after the fact. Either way, Knox knows he should remain troubled. Comforted by the solution of a scavenger, he frets that this would mean you had the capacity to kill all the dogs yourself.

Knox curses in frustration: he'll never know for certain what actually happened here. But he must soon leave this world. He has to get back to the airplane. He is desperate to fly out of these mountains. He underestimated so much. He wants to return to a world where he feels he actually belongs. In two or three more days he will lose his mind in this place. He will be swallowed up and destroyed by something pervasive here he does not understand, an environment all around him that wants to burn his mind with acid.

He marks this spot where you have triumphed over the dogs with a fluorescent piece of rag he pulls out of his pack; he ties it to the branch of a spindly pine clinging desperately to the rocks. He told the others he would do this; the marker is part of the plan they arrived at earlier this morning, if he picked up your trail. When the other hunters are escorted to this spot, they will realize the odds of you escaping alive are much higher than they thought. They may even realize that they are now the prey and he, as a professional, is about to become the only hunter.

FOR A WHILE THE REMAINING HUNTERS conceal themselves at the top of the ridge and peer down into the valley where Joe and Allison Leonard harvest the last of their October garden. Pirelli and Hamilton are restless and impatient, annoyed that they are hungry and have no food. But Fieldler makes them stay put while he considers what they should do next.

"Christ, Ernie, what are we waiting for?" croaks Hamilton at last, losing patience with the silence. His belly is in agony now. Today's version of his chronic stomach pain has worsened steadily as the morning hours passed.

For his part, Fieldler barely hears the question. He keeps gazing at the woman in the distance, unable to see her features clearly but aware she distracts him in some deep and familiar way just the same. She is a woman, any woman—out here she is every woman— and she unwittingly beckons to his need and to some deep disapproval connected to her, connected to need itself, that he doesn't know he feels.

"Ernie?"

"Obviously they have food," Fieldler remarks at last, more or less to shut Hamilton up.

"Yeah, but we can't just walk down there and take it, can we?" This comment belongs to Pirelli but his question actually reflects the opposite of what he truly feels.

Pirelli has been thinking they should take the food. But he needs to know Fieldler and Hamilton agree; this morning he feels too alone with his growing desperation to believe he can be of much value in making a decision or contributing to a plan. He feels defeated by these mountains and he wants to go home. He can hardly remember your face, although he continues to believe he still hates your guts. But you're less a person now than some idea he once had. Although he still wants to kill you, killing you won't be any fun.

For the moment, Fieldler merely sighs. Perhaps it's the woman who makes him sigh. Perhaps it's because he and the others hide in the trees behind some rocks in the middle of a vast, mountainous nowhere. If there are any rules preventing them from doing what must be done, he cannot understand why these rules haven't been set aside, the way they normally are when one is rich and powerful. Yes, his unexpected wonder over nature's rules and how they shut him out inspires him to sigh again. Something unjust is happening here. His belly is growling in hunger and there is a woman in the distance who belongs to someone else. He must work for a moment or two to remember how much he matters in this world, much more than silly homesteaders who work their silly garden in this silly piece of no man's land. They have tucked themselves away in this secluded valley, hiding from a more realistic world where they wouldn't make the grade. People like these anger Fieldler. They own something he'd like to own himself, if only he could determine whether it is worth owning. He's never liked the world's slackers; he's judged them harshly. But dislike turns to hatred for Fieldler when he finds himself wondering if they, the slackers, have managed to possess something valuable that he does not.

"Look," says Hamilton. "I think we should go down there and talk to these people. Maybe we can buy some food from them."

Fieldler glances at him, dismayed at the absurdity of Hamilton's words. "Yeah, maybe they take Visa or American Express. C'mon, John, it's no longer hunting season. Hunting season is over. If we don't come up with a good story, they'll probably figure out we don't belong here."

"Maybe they won't give a fuck either way," counters Hamilton.

Pirelli too has been thinking the couple won't care, but he doesn't say anything.

Fieldler realizes at this moment that everything is too late. This conclusion occurs to him with a certain suddenness, yet he is calm in accepting it, as if he's known everything is too late for some time, without knowing that he knew. It's too late to scheme, he realizes, too late to believe in the perfect crime your death would represent. Maybe he believed two days ago. Maybe even yesterday. But today it is too late and this fact reflects the inarguable conclusion that life, destiny, fate, whatever a person wants to call it, is only the way things go—the way happenstance transpires. It has no deeper meaning or value than time dribbling away the way time does, unshackled, even free. He and the other men are now too hungry and desperate. And today there is a woman down there in the garden, insulting everything he needs and doesn't want to need. And you? Who knows where you are, or whether you actually survive, or, if you do, how much longer you can survive. All of these considerations—food, time, the woman, you—merely reflect the way things go, nothing more.

"Ernie? For Christ's sake, man. What are we waiting for?"

"These people are witnesses," Fieldler replies tonelessly, as if speaking only to himself.

"I think we should talk to them."

"Me too," says Pirelli, although something loitering at the fringes of his thoughts is virtually duplicating Fieldler's conclusions. He too is nearly convinced it is too late for any perfect crime. Things are futile now. The hunt, specifically the scheme to terrorize then hunt you down, at least as his father-in-law once conceived it, is all nonsensical now. And besides, it's too late to rectify the choices of a traitorous Sara. Her affair with you was ultimately more insulting in the end to the incestuous proclivities of her pathetic old man than they were to the man she married. What Pirelli doesn't understand, though, is why he enjoys his conclusion that it's too late somehow. Being here and being too late fills him with a calm, passive, and familiar delight.

"Ernie?"

"Well," the big game hunter says finally, "it doesn't look like we have any other option."

"No."

"Like Vietnam," Fieldler says, the comparison slipping out of his mouth before he can hold it back, surprising him as much as it surprises the others.

"What? Whaddyuh mean? Whaddyuh mean, 'like Vietnam?' I didn't know you were in Vietnam."

"C'mon," Fieldler says in embarrassment, ignoring Hamilton's remarks. "Let's go see what happens."

Was he in Vietnam? At this moment Fieldler truly can't remember. There's something pathological about his past. He can't quite extract the truth from the mythologies swirling around his culture. He will never again remember what is and isn't true about his world, his country, his life. He will be glad to forget whatever is or isn't true about himself. And about his place in society's great big, greedy lie, which he has loved until now.

Shit . . .

Thinking these things, Fieldler finds a way to blame the woman working in her garden. It's too late to turn around and go back the way they've come. He and his colleagues are hungry. Fieldler blames the woman for all of his unsatisfied appetites. Feeling justified for intruding on her valley, Fieldler discovers he blames this woman, this her for virtually everything.

Not quite knowing yet what they are going to do,

the men from Los Angeles creep out of the trees to begin their descent into Joe and Allison Leonard's world of innocent plenty.

JOE GLANCES UP THE MOMENT HE DETECTS the hunters' intrusion. By then they are very close, stumbling to the southern edge of his garden. Joe turns towards Allison and more or less grunts her name, some kind of intuitive call of alarm that doesn't quite come out with the intensity he intended. Then, sensing everything about the sudden arrival of these men is going to turn out wrong, Joe dashes in the direction of his rifle several yards away, leaning against the wall of his porch, not far from his front steps. These men should not be here. These men do not belong. He recognizes the danger signified by their intrusion.

"Hey!" one of the hunters shouts.

But this cry of authority only verifies Joe's alarm. He runs harder still, legs and arms pumping, adrenaline pulsating through his body.

Another shout, unintelligible this time against the blood rushing in Joe's ears. Maybe "hey!" again, or maybe something else. But he runs as hard as he can towards the porch and his loaded rifle.

Then a bullet tears through his flesh, painless for a moment, like it's intended at first as a helpful shove, a push propelling him more quickly towards the porch. But an instant later, he feels a burning agony as the sound of the gunshot arrives. Destroyed by the pain and the sound of the shot, a murderous marriage of human contrivance, Joe tumbles to the ground. A deep current of inky darkness begins to suck away his life. The last sound he hears, as the current of death envelopes him and carries him away, is Allison's heartbroken scream.

"JESUS," CRIES PIRELLI. "What'd you do that for?" He stands at the edge of everything that has suddenly happened, his mouth open, his forehead beaded in sweat.

Fieldler lowers his rifle but only slightly. "Grab the woman," he says with a calm the others find unsettling.

Hamilton merely stands frozen a few yards from the other two men. He inches away a bit, not consciously, but because his body is embarrassed somehow by the shooting of the young man at the edge of his garden. His belly screams in pain. He feels diminished by his astonishment at what has happened. He's now shrinking here in the company of more important men who have always comprehended life's deepest secrets so much better than he has comprehended them.

"Jesus, Ernie," whines Pirelli. "What're we gonna do now?"

"Shut up! Grab the woman, I said."

Pirelli is tempted to refuse, so shocked is he that Fieldler has shot the woman's man. But when Allison begins to run in the direction of her husband, Pirelli feels a strange mixture of fear because she flees and exhilaration in doing battle with fate in a way he did not expect. He dashes after her, forgiving Fieldler as he runs, remembering his earlier conclusion that everything is too late. At this point he is grateful so much has been taken out of his hands. Everything is too late. He is merely required to do as he is told.

He tackles the woman around the legs as she emerges from the garden, and she tumbles to the ground. Before she can prevent him, he sits on her there, holding her belly down against the wet grass. She struggles at first, surprising him with her strength, but soon she goes limp. She seems so suddenly lifeless at this moment, Pirelli wonders if she has abruptly died. But soon he hears her gasping for breath and realizes she is alive. As he detects her terror, something unexpected in him grows relieved—even delighted—to feed on it. A moment ago, as she struggled, he was desperate to tell her how sorry he is. Now, inexplicably, he regrets any such inclination.

"Hold her," orders Fieldler. "Hold her down, Pirelli."

Fieldler makes his way to Joe Leonard's body and crouches, quickly checking for signs of life. When he discovers none, he gets to his feet again.

"Is he dead?" Hamilton asks from the edge of the garden where he has been standing all this time, afraid to move in any way, not knowing when he'll ever again be capable of figuring out what to do. Or when he will ever again believe he isn't lost irrevocably inside these antagonistic mountains.

Fieldler ignores him. "Hold her!" he cries instead in Pirelli's direction when he notices the fallen woman has begun to struggle once again. He approaches quickly, aroused by her helplessness, by the satisfaction he feels in knowing everything is her fault, even the death of her man a moment ago, the man who knew enough to run from his garden to protect his wife from harm. The man, at least, realized clearly that everything today is—and was—potentially altered forever. He, at least, realized right away that he was powerless, and that powerlessness is an inevitable precursor to death. Fieldler likes that in a man. He likes an inferior man to recognize his place.

"You want some of this?" Fieldler asks Pirelli from an unseen spot beyond the younger man's left shoulder, gazing down at the woman sprawled out on the cold, damp grass.

"Do you?"

"Yeah, I do, I guess. I'm getting a bone on just watching her squirm right now."

Upon hearing Fieldler's words, Pirelli is now aware that he is excited too. He doesn't want to be, especially with what Fieldler just said—it seems adolescent and tacky in some way like a moment out of high school or college, some party in a dorm that is about to get out of hand—but arousal is coming on him anyway. He can smell the oniony scent of the woman's fear and it seems in some muddled way to be evidence of her sexual need for him. And he recalls the times during his marriage to Sara when he wished he could show her a thing or two. He liked the scent of Sara's fear of him, but it didn't happen much. His mouth goes as dry as a desert fissure, whether from want or fear or from closure, confusion or resignation; he doesn't know any longer.

"Pirelli?"

He cannot find the words to reply as he turns to glance at Fieldler who is now unbuckling his trousers. Instead he vaguely nods as the other man exposes himself.

In a moment the two men set upon her there, in hatred and in disgust. They seek, during the torture of Allison's soul, the first available rationalization they need to justify what they have become. Unwittingly they manage to do so easily. Rationalization is a drug and it isn't difficult for them to consume it once again. They have rationalized successfully so many times during their respective pasts. They have known Olympian heights of justification. This woman they rape and assault has brought it on herself. Pirelli and Fieldler don't care about anything else but license. License is all their world has been for a very long time.

While Pirelli and Fieldler each take their turn with the woman, Hamilton remains rooted to his small piece of ground within this modest valley, although he turns away from the rape in embarrassment. He now meekly accepts what the other two men already know: that everything is now too late. He supposes he turns away from the rape of Allison Leonard in case he recognizes something in her that will make him think of Sara. Whether in the context of need or anger or closure, he cannot imagine for certain. He does not recognize what he has become during the many treacherous years in which he has been Sara's father, but he does not want to imagine any condemnation in his daughter's eyes—whether deserved or not—for all that has been so wrong between them for so long, for which she would take no blame, for which he would be exclusively at fault.

THE GUNSHOT CRACKS SOME DISTANCE AWAY but it startles you nonetheless. From where you are, it sounds like a tear in the drape separating your new wilderness world from the old urban one you once happily occupied. The curtain hangs tattered and fragile between then and now. At the sound of the gunshot, you dive headlong into the trees, colliding with an exposed root. There is a brief cry of pain across your shoulder, but the blow has been glancing and the pain soon begins to subside. There isn't even a bullet to give purpose to the sound of the gunshot. Soon the silence that follows the explosion of the distant rifle grows very clear and deep. The wilderness is appalled once more by the sound of the rifle's intrusion. Its disgust hushes this setting completely. For a long time the wilderness sulks in a deep and violated silence.

You lie on the ground for several moments, wondering what the gunshot means. Was it one of your hunters who pulled the trigger? And what was he aiming at? You sniff at the tantalizing wood smoke you've been hoping belongs to some potential rescuer, but you don't know anything for certain. Your world remains filled with risk. For a moment you want to shrink into a fetal position here on the cold, hard ground. This world of new gunfire and happenstance into which you will be born against your will, a birth inside fate's careless orgasm, is filled with too much risk. You want to let the world work things out for itself. then, in the aftermath, the world can embrace you safely again as its innocent child. Strange how, knowing so much more than you once did, you would like another crack at being born. You'd embark on life differently, employing the wisdom you now possess.

Then your feeling of terror passes like a hangover after a binge, drifting caustically away, leaving behind only its trail of fetid judgments and your inherent knowledge that you must go on. Even tired of so much danger, you feel the passion in your will to live.

You count one hundred steamboats then get gingerly to your feet. You sniff at the wood smoke on the currents of the air then move cautiously deeper into the trees. You see a wisp of smoke in the distance at last, high up in the trees. You recognize a valley below you, still a significant distance away, but you begin to speculate there must be a chimney in some cabin there, spewing out the hospitable smoke.

Yet you move in this direction carefully. You are part of this wilderness now. You and it are silent together. You are committed now. You will follow this smoke in the valley to see what it ultimately means. The wilderness is your ally; these days it goes with you everywhere. You belong to it; it belongs to you.

THE GRAY WOLF HUNKERS DOWN when he hears the gunshot. He gazes into the woods where you have vanished a few minutes ago. As it so often does, his eyesight lets him down. But the wolf can smell your scent and hear your feet whispering across the needled ground as you pick your way through the trees in the direction of Joe Leonard's valley. For reasons of his own, the wolf keeps track of you. He lifts his nose and follows your progress along the wind currents surrounding you as they drift in his direction. Soon he too is up and approaching the wilderness valley that was Joe Leonard's home.

KNOX HAS VEERED TO THE RIGHT in his journey back towards the valley and his appointment with the other hunters. You have gone to the left. By the time Knox hears Fieldler's gunshot, he has unknowingly moved some distance away from you. While you both head in essentially the same direction, Knox is intent on what the gunshot means—the game Fieldler has brought down—and he no longer searches for your tracks or other indications of your passing. Indeed, he does not even consider the possibility that you have decided to double back—why would you do that? A man being purposely that stupid would reflect a chaotic miscomprehension.

Knox thinks instead about what Fieldler has shot, venison perhaps. His mouth waters at the notion. His belly aches from hunger. And, married to his hunger, is the need to weigh the pros and cons of giving up on finding you, Sorting through the odds of success, he decides at last to kill the other men and successfully make his escape. He will abandon the quest of finding you. He has lost interest anyway in achieving a retribution he has never truly understood.

"WHAT DO WE DO WITH HER?" Hamilton asks, gesturing at the woman.

Fieldler and Pirelli have moved away from Allison

Leonard and have turned in the direction of her cabin. "Leave her for now," Fieldler says, intent on going into the cabin and finding something to eat.

Hamilton glances at the woman. She has covered herself where the other men ripped her clothing away, but her trousers are torn and smeared with mud, and they do not entirely cover the flesh Fieldler and Pirelli have violated. Now she sits in her dark blue parka like a statue, so still she resembles an ornament someone has placed on the ground in a corner of their suburban garden. She gazes at a place a million yards away where dignity, delight and peace have left her brutally behind. She seems lifeless to Hamilton. While he watches her, her eyes don't even blink. They merely gaze off into space. She has left a world she used to know; it lies all around her in shattered ruins.

Absurdly, Hamilton wants to ask her if she's alright. He doesn't though; in view of what she has suffered he knows it would leave him looking foolish. And he has no concept—not even the slightest—of the rubble these few short minutes have made of the rest of her life. He could never conceive of the depth of abandonment she feels. The last few minutes of time have obliterated everything she has known and loved.

Fieldler and Pirelli are climbing the steps onto Joe Leonard's porch. Feeling exposed out here all by himself, standing not far away from a raped woman and the remains of her dead husband, Hamilton scurries in the direction of the other two men. He winces as even this minor exertion unleashes new agony in his belly. By the time he catches up to the others, they are both inside the cabin, opening cupboard doors, casting what they don't need onto the wooden floor, behaving like thieves who don't realize yet there's little need for hurry.

Hamilton clutches Fieldler by the arm. "Won't the woman run away?"

"Where's she going to go?" replies the other man.

"Yes. I suppose," Hamilton admits more or less to himself. "There's no place out here to go, is there?" He's talking to himself. He's talking about himself. Now he's the only man who will ever listen to what he says, who will ever pay attention to what he thinks.

He keeps trying to remember what it was like in L.A. As the man he was when he lived there, people listened to him, reacting to his every remark. But it's too difficult now to recall his former life—today L.A. seems a millions years ago. In L.A. it seemed this hunt, everything, in fact, would work out much better than it has. And he was a man of belief back then—people believed in him, he believed in people. The system they sustained together, him and his colleagues and peers, was so readily believed in, so easily believable. Now, out here, everything back there seems imagined, a life directed by the most insipid of myths: the tooth fairy perhaps, the Easter Bunny, even Santa Claus. Now only here seems real. Back there is . . . unbelievable.

Hamilton shuts down his thoughts to watch the other two men greedily stuffing their mouths and packs with food, with vegetables and venison and some kind of smoked meat he can't identify. He stands there immobile, glancing around the functional cabin, vaguely surprised that it's so tidy, vaguely disappointed too. If the cabin had been a mess, it might have helped him in some way to justify the respective death and rape of the man and the woman outside. He doesn't know why this is so. But he senses his conclusion reflects an important tenet he has always needed to believe. He is aging, even old, and now he can no longer remember when his various judgments became so severe. Nor can he recall when he didn't make judgments based on stereotype or when he didn't feel fear. He discovers he is and has always been a vague all-encompassing cliché.

"J.D.? Toss me your pack."

"What?"

"I'll fill your pack."

Pirelli comes forward. Delicately, as he would if he were dealing with an overgrown infant, Pirelli removes his father-in-law's empty pack.

"What do we do now, Tony?" Hamilton asks.

"I don't know. Think of something, I guess."

"I'm going to die, you know."

"Huh?"

"Soon. I'm going to die soon. If we don't take care of Kovacs soon, I won't live to see it happen."

Expecting to do well in Hamilton's will and embarrassed by a melodramatic timbre he hears in his father-in-law's words, Pirelli takes a long time to respond. "Whaddayuh talkin' about?" he says eventually, conjuring a great new artificial hatred for you, his wife's lover, and feeling a powerful new immortality and power developing rapidly in his heart. "I'll see to it that Kovacs is dead. I'll see to it that it happens soon. You're not gonna die, J.D."

"I don't think we're ever going to get out of these mountains, Tony."

But Pirelli, still feeling strong and empowered, cannot manufacture any more politically correct kindness for his father-in-law. Suddenly he is deeply embarrassed by this wreck of a man who once mentored him, who once seemed so powerful. So he turns away in silence, preoccupied instead with stuffing more glorious food into his father-in-law's pack. "God," he observes out loud, his mouth watering. "Our first morning without food and I'm already starving. Not used to it, I guess."

Fieldler nods. "We get soft," he replies.

Pirelli hands Hamilton a small length of dried meat. Hamilton takes a bite, but his stomach is screaming in outrage and he spits out even this tiny morsel.

When all of their packs are full, the three men move out onto the porch. "What now?" Pirelli asks. "Do you think Knox is on his way back?"

"Probably," Fieldler says.

"He's going to be pissed at what's happened here, in spite of the food."

"He'll try to kill us," Fieldler announces with disturbing calm.

"What? What are you talking about?"

"He has to kill us to escape the failure of the hunt."

"Why would he do that?" Hamilton can't believe what Fieldler is saying. There's more money coming Knox's way after they finally hunt you down . . . another five million . . . he'd have to give that up. Fieldler knows about the balance owing; has he lost his mind?

But Fieldler gazes at him, looking certain. "He already has five million dollars and the hunt has failed. He can kill us all, return to the plane and disappear forever. Five million is more than enough for him to start over."

Bemused for the moment, neither Pirelli nor Hamilton can think of anything to say. A deal is a deal. To receive the rest of his money, Knox must live up to the terms of his contract. Pirelli and Hamilton still cannot accept that ten million dollars did not entirely buy them their very own assassin. From a corporate perspective, ten million dollars buys just about anyone. This is the way it has always been in the world they have chosen to embrace, a world dedicated mostly to amassing wealth for the purchase of everything.

"Think about it," Fieldler says when it is clear to him the other two men do not believe him. "Put yourself in Knox's shoes."

"I don't get it," says Hamilton.

"I don't get it either," adds Pirelli.

Fieldler sighs, then clasps Hamilton's shoulder. Noticing him wince in pain, he removes his hand but, beyond this, he has no interest in the other man's suffering. "What would you do if you were Knox and Kovacs got away? Huh? What would you do?"

"Keep looking for Kovacs," murmurs Hamilton. "We all have to worry about that. We all have to worry about what he might tell the authorities if he gets out of here alive."

"Okay," says Fieldler, trying to control his impatience, perturbed the other two men cannot see what is so obvious to him. "What would you do with a dead man on the ground and his woman sitting nearby at some cabin way out in the woods?"

Hamilton nods. Admittedly he is distressed that the situation has gotten so deeply out of hand. Yet there has to be a way to fix things. Knox is the kind of man who knows how to fix things. That's what he does in this world. "Look, Ernie," he remarks at last. "All of this is theory. Knox is pretty shrewd. He's a professional. When he gets back, he'll have a plan. He'll come up with something, I'm sure."

"That's what I'm afraid of," mutters Fieldler.

Hamilton shrugs and turns away. He stands there a moment, trying to think. He notices the woman has crawled to a place a few yards away where she can sit on the ground next to her dead husband. She touches his chest with one hand, gently at first, then begins striking his corpse in resigned, halfhearted anger. Hamilton would tell her to stop, except she is soon exhausted and abandons the angry sadness that punishes her husband's dead flesh. Now he must stand and watch as she begins to cry.

"What do we do with her?" he asks Fieldler. "Do we have to kill her?"

Fieldler shakes his head. "That's a job for Knox. When he finishes her, if he finishes her, we'll take care of Knox . . . if we have to, I suppose." His calm is so deep and complete, the other two men are both mesmerized and annoyed by it.

"How do we get away with all of this?" Pirelli demands. "I mean, we're in a shitload of trouble." He gestures towards Joe Leonard's body. "The skinny guy's dead and . . ." He falters for a second . . . "and we haven't even caught a glimpse of Kovacs for days."

Fieldler nearly smiles, so proud is he of everything he's thought through. "Never mind about Kovacs for the moment. Just hear me out. Listen carefully. Imagine all of this is Knox's fault. He killed the indigenous—hey, do you think they're indigenous?—couple. He burned them and their cabin to the ground. He's the guy that killed Kovacs. You see? We had to shoot him in self defence. See what I mean? It's just a case of working things out after we deal with Knox."

"Yeah?" says Hamilton. "Then how do we get out of these fucking mountains? Let's say you're right about Knox and we have to get rid of him. None of us can fly a plane."

"But we can work a radio. We can send out a mayday once we've got all our ducks in a row."

Hamilton nods. He wishes Fieldler was a pilot. If Fieldler was a pilot, he would have never needed Knox. He wouldn't be standing here now, not knowing whom to trust.

"Jesus," says Pirelli in a nearly giddy falsetto. "Are you telling me, no matter what, we just might get away with this?"

"Yeah, if we use our heads. All it'll take is a little creativity."

Hamilton studies Fieldler for a moment, deeply aware of his own waning influence. "This is still my hunt," he says at last, feeling weak but trying to regain lost ground in the eyes of the other two men. "You still haven't convinced me Knox intends to break the agreement. You haven't convinced me that we can consider him expendable."

"Of course it's your hunt, J.D. It's always been your hunt. I'm just saying we have to be careful. How do we know Knox just won't dispose of us and then fly out of here? That's all I'm saying. I'm just suggesting we have to consider the possibility."

Hamilton nods. "So what do you propose?"

"Well, for one thing, Tony's right. When he comes across what's happened here, he's going to be pissed off. We'll know then what he truly plans to do."

"You mean," says Pirelli, "if he intends to kill us, it'll be then."

"That's right. When he has to deal with the woman, that's when we'll know how far he'll go and what he intends to do about us as witnesses."

"Witnesses?" echoes Hamilton.

"To the hunt for Kovacs, the hunt that has so far failed."

Hamilton's belly screams again, nearly doubling him over. He believes he can feel himself bleeding again somewhere inside his body. "So what do you propose?" he gasps, holding his stomach with the fingers of his right hand. "What do we do right now to sort everything out? That's what I want to fucking know. Eventually, and I mean soon, I've got to see a doctor. My stomach's killing me. There's something wrong with me."

His face is white with anger and pain. The other two

men retreat half a pace from him, like he's a plague victim and dangerously communicable.

"Okay," says Fieldler. "How about this? One of us stays here for when Knox gets back. Out here where he can be seen. The other two make for the trees over there at the edge of the valley. When Knox shows up, we just keep him in our sights until he disposes of the woman and we know what he intends."

"In other words," murmurs Hamilton with a tired sigh, "if he tries anything, he's dead."

"Yes."

"I should be the one here when Knox gets back. I hired him. I'm the one who's . . . not well . . . a liability. You, Ernie, as a marksman, should be in the woods. Right?"

Fieldler nods.

"And Tony?"

"Pirelli's with me," says Fieldler. "In case anything goes wrong."

Hamilton nods. The plan makes sense to him. And he'll have a chance to remind Knox about the terms of his fucking contract. "What about Kovacs?" he asks now that he has agreed to wait out in the open for Knox, now that something seems settled for a change.

Fieldler shrugs. "You know what I think? Intuition tells me Kovacs is probably dead. C'mon, we'll worry about Kovacs later."

"Okay," says Hamilton. "One problem at a time."

For the moment, for the first time in a very long while, you don't matter to him. Hamilton is in so much pain and is so certain of his impending death, he can hardly remember the features of the man he has hated for so long, the interloper who has brought him to this strange place where he might die without anyone caring about his death. He doesn't feel the need to consider you much today. No, he's more preoccupied with his own dying. He keeps thinking about dying without feeling any fear. Then again, it's just a fuzzy notion, this dying he considers, a game his mind can't resist playing with itself, like toying with the concept of suicide just to get through a particularly bad and lonesome night.

The three men step down from the porch and begin to slip across the field in the direction of the trees where Pirelli and Hamilton intend to hide. They pass within a couple of feet of Joe Leonard's body and his violated, grieving wife. None of them glance at her—she is forgotten. The hunters are too preoccupied by the pressing matter of their plan.

"What do I tell Knox?" Hamilton asks just before the other two men leave him here alone in the open.

"You mean about us?"

Hamilton nods.

"Tell him we're scouting around for Kovacs, wondering if what happened here at the cabin might have flushed him out."

"Do you think he'll buy that?"

"Make it sound convincing," Fiedler says as he and Pirelli turn away to find their hiding place in the woods.

FOR A COUPLE OF MINUTES, where you hide in the trees on the crest of a steep hill, it is all that you can do to prevent yourself from running joyfully down the slope towards the cabin you now see in the distance, shouting out your triumph and relief. You are so excited at your discovery, your eyes well up with tears. Sara! A cabin! Sara, I think I'm saved. Sharing your relief and the potential for rescue with Sara only increases its emotional intensity. Before you can get hold of yourself, a couple of tears sneak down your cheeks unchecked.

But you have come too far to carry on without

caution. The rifle shot you heard several minutes ago must be considered carefully. So you stand hidden in the trees for a long time, deciding the safest way to descend into the valley unseen.

The stand of white spruce in which you hide at this moment stretches all the way down the hill and virtually up to the cabin on your left. The rest of the area around the cabin has been cleared. But here, on the left, there is an opportunity to approach the building by clinging to the coverage provided by the trees. Clearly this would be your best approach. You take a deep breath. You sniff the air like a hound. You adjust your pack. You clench your lance in your fist. You notice the first few reticent flakes of wet snow that suddenly begin to fall, visible against the dark contrast of this large stand of trees stretching on and on into the valley. You take your first step, not daring to pray there is someone in the cabin who can help with your rescue, so afraid are you of disappointment. You fear hoping for your rescue will incur fate's wrath and put a whammy on the concept of rescue itself.

Then the keening wail of Allison Leonard's voice echoes through the trees. It's sound is so shrill and unexpected, it clutches your heart with icy fingers and tingles along your flesh. Instantly you dive headlong to the ground again, gasping for breath, alarmed at what you've heard.

"JESUS," CRIES HAMILTON WHEN HE HEARS Allison's long shriek of misery.

He hurries outside the cabin where he has been trying to eat bits of smoked meat he found on the counter and one piece he picked up off the floor. For the moment he can't locate the woman who uttered the loud and terrible cry, but when she wails again he spins around and notices she has moved to the corner of the cabin, tugging on her husband's body. Her hands are locked under his armpits, pulling on him. She tries to creep backwards with him, her torn trousers falling down, catching in a knot at her knees. Hamilton watches for the moment, fascinated by the tragedy of her torn trousers. She at last falls to her knees, betrayed once more by her damaged clothing. Frustrated, she wails her grief.

"Hey! Shut up!" yells Hamilton, snapping out of his reverie, frightened by the despair he hears in her cries.

She gazes up at him, responding mostly to his voice. He senses she can't really make him out through the fog of her misery and tears. God, Hamilton decides, someone should put her out of her misery soon—it would be an act of kindness.

Of course he knows he can't let this kind of compassion show. "I mean it," he tells her menacingly. "Don't do that. No more screaming." He takes a deep breath, knowing what he intends to say next will sound strange in his own ears, out of character with the person he believes himself to be. Still, out of character or not, he recites the lines he has absorbed while watching so many movies and television programs during his life. "I don't want to have to kill you. So shut up. Okay?" This said, he begins to warm to this new menacing tone. "Shut the fuck up. Or else!" he adds deliberately, pointing his rifle at her, waving it like a baton, trying to convince her he means business.

The woman cries, but gently now, as if at least part of her understands the risk she runs in crying out, as if she actually believes there is a chance she could go on living if she behaves herself. But this chance to survive is so tenuous, she finds herself contemplating the proposition that she may not want to live. The life still remaining to her—so stripped of all it once promised just a while ago—might not even be worth saving at this point.

She keeps sobbing quietly as she works to straighten her torn trousers, crying out in frustration each time her fingers fail her. The trousers temporarily gathered to where they should be around her waist, she stands up to resume pulling her husband's body towards the edge of the porch to Hamilton's left. She does this until her trousers give way again; then she falls to weeping once more at the futility of what she is trying to accomplish, this harsh but needful compulsion to drag her husband's body into the sanctuary of the woods.

Hamilton suspects her intentions and supposes he could prevent her. Perhaps he should prevent her, but he is too sick and tired to try. Just as long as she stays quiet. Just as long as she doesn't start keening again. Then he'll find the patience to wait for Knox. Knox, he still believes, will know what they should do next. Knox is a professional—results define the value of his job, maybe even the purpose of his life. Even at this moment, believing he might imminently die, Hamilton remains a corporate kind of man; he gauges the value and purpose of Knox's life by its usefulness to him and the world he has created within the parameters of his ideological definition. Even this close to death and the wisdom normally packaged inside the act of dying, Hamilton cannot discern any other criteria than function or wealth for measuring the value of a human being's life.

THE SNOW IS GETTING PERSISTENTLY THICKER as it tumbles out of a white sky. You hurry towards a small slope overlooking the cabin so you can see what's going on before even heavier snow obscures your vision. You can make out a woman in the distance, although just barely. She is tugging on a man who seems to be unconscious. Even at this distance—a couple of hundred yards at most—you can detect the woman's frustration. You can feel it reaching you, providing you with a miniscule glimpse into the heart of what she feels. You are now about to understand the tragic pain she has apparently suffered here.

Regardless of what you do not know yet about what has happened here, your wilderness senses are filled with outrage and empathy for this woman's anguish. This empathy comes over you in a fury until, for the moment, it seems the only motivation you understand. There is no question in your mind that you must make your way to this woman's side because she has been injured in some way. Like last night when the dogs attacked your wolf. You knew then what you must do. In your world up here in these mountains, how much simpler your choices are. But this time, your decisiveness about the woman feels much deeper, even more profound. Something to do with Sara perhaps— the way you now honour her, the way you now understand that there must be a doing when something needs to be done. You now know that a person's life can find new purpose when it holds some small and private inspiration of valour, integrity and authenticity.

You know your pursuers are the reason for this woman's despair. You believe they should pay for this. You know how important it is to save her from whatever else they have planned.

The snow falls more and more thickly. A squall is trapped here in the valley by the wooded, mountainous walls normally sheltering it. Sleet falls angrily with the snow, slicing into your face and eyes at a bit of slant, although you can detect no wind. The storm acts like someone's fleeting temper tantrum; its outrage is confined inside the valley walls, preventing it from moving on.

You creep more deeply into the trees in the direction of the woman and her fallen man, squinting against the wet snow now reduced in intensity by the umbrella-like canopy of trees overhead. Your feet cross the earth in wilderness silence. You breathe without making a sound. The woman has become your essential mission. It no longer occurs to you to be afraid. This is your wilderness now. Here you understand completely—in a way you never have before—what you are capable of, what defines your value.

"JESUS, ERNIE," WHISPERS PIRELLI from the place where he and the big game hunter hide in the woods. "I can't see a fucking thing."

"No. The snow's heavy," Fieldler admits.

Since their rape of Allison Leonard, the two men have drawn closer, like soldiers who have shared a near-death experience in the heat of battle. They kneel on the ground behind a tree and their shoulders touch in an unexpected comradeship. The wet snow is falling so heavily it threatens to bury them. It is cold where it insinuates itself into crevices in their clothing, seeking places where it can reach and touch the heat of their bare skin.

"What do we do in all this snow? If Knox shows up we wouldn't even know it."

"We wait it out," says Fieldler. "It can't last that long."

Pirelli gazes at him a time, admiring Fieldler's capacity for patience. He supposes patience is the quality that best defines a hunter. Maybe, in learning this quality himself, he decides, he can learn to be a hunter too.

"HAMILTON? WHAT THE FUCK IS GOING ON?" Knox's

question. Knox's return to authority.

On the porch, Hamilton whirls at the sound of his voice, then watches as the assassin emerges the rest of the way out of the thick, falling snow, passing from some other world into this one like a ghost walking through the wall. Knox is already brushing snow from the shoulders of his coat as he climbs the two short steps onto Joe Leonard's porch. Snow has gathered thickly on his hat and his ears are red from the cold.

"Jesus, Knox," gasps Hamilton. "You scared the shit out of me."

Knox does not respond to Hamilton's words. He removes his hat, gives it a solid whipping against the thigh of his trousers, then replaces it on his head. He glances instead around the partially open door to the cabin, noting the mess on the floor, the result of the ransacking it suffered. After he studies this evidence a moment, contemplating what it probably means, he turns at last to face his employer who looks as white and pasty as this snow-infested day.

"You sick?" he asks, not really giving a damn either way.

"Yeah. My stomach. It think it's bleeding. You know, on the inside?"

Knox couldn't care less. "Pirelli and Fieldler. Where are they?"

"Out looking for Kovacs."

Knox says nothing to this. No way for him to decide at this moment if he believes this information or not.

"Probably lost in this snow, fucking assholes," Hamilton adds for good measure, uncomfortable with the insincerity he thinks he hears in his voice.

Some of his words are overwhelmed, though, by a new outburst from the native woman who cries out again in frustration as she tries to tug her husband through the slippery snow and into the woods at the edge of their cabin. Again her trousers fail her and tug her cruelly to the ground.

Knox studies this woman critically, assessing her sobbing collapse not far away from where he stands on the cabin porch. He heard her earlier cry too, not liking the sound of it or what it might require of him soon. Now, as he notices the bare flesh exposed above her torn jeans, he realizes—as much as he is able—what has been done to her. Filing this information away for the moment, he gazes at the man the woman has been dragging arduously along the ground. Not much blood. Whoever he is, he's been dead an hour or more. A shot carrying over the distance, he remembers. Fiedler hunting, he thought, saliva on his tongue at the thought of venison. Now . . .

"Jesus," he mutters under his breath.

"We have food now," blurts Hamilton when Knox turns to him again. He feels like a guilty child caught doing something he shouldn't, and he searches frantically for any information, any kind of a report he can provide Knox that might ameliorate his guilt or stay the nasty punishment he now suspects could be on its way.

"Who did that?" Knox asks, gesturing into the falling snow in the direction of the woman and her dead husband.

Hamilton only shrugs in futility, his palms open to Knox in supplication.

"Who shot the fucking Indian?"

"Fiedler. What difference does it make?"

"That was the gunshot I heard, wasn't it?"

Hamilton nods.

"Jesus fucking Christ!"

"He was running for his rifle as we approached. That's all I know. Maybe Fiedler panicked."

Knox glares at him. "And the woman?"

Hamilton can't look him in the eye. He shrugs.

"And the woman?" Knox repeats.

"Fieldler . . . and Pirelli . . . yeah, Pirelli too. Fieldler and Pirelli. Both of them."

While it's late in arriving, Hamilton begins to feel a deep disapproval of his son-in-law. If they get out of these mountains safely, out of this place alive, he'll want to reconsider his feelings for Pirelli. Pirelli's shown a new capacity for poor judgment, a characteristic Hamilton cannot respect in the son-in-law he virtually adopted as his own son. He isn't sure fucking the woman was justified in any way. He wouldn't do anything like that. Because of Sara. Sara's probably the reason he wasn't even tempted. Sara remains a tribute to his self control. He knows this now, standing here on this porch in the middle of someone else's fucking mountains, caught by someone else's fucking mirror exposing for all to see what he has always been. He doesn't feel comfortable right now inside the prison of his own skin. He feels he's arrived at a destination he does not recognize. If today is a day of truth, everything he has believed about himself has actually been a lie about someone else.

For his part, Knox merely nods. His anger doesn't dissipate; instead it merely makes him tired. The situation is academic now. Plan B is all that remains to him. You—at one time the only purpose for this hunt— no longer matter in the slightest. Knox knows what must be done, whom he must kill, the way back to the airplane, how he must now make certain he, at least, escapes.

"I guess you were right about Fieldler," Hamilton admits in the long minute of Knox's silence.

Knox just glances at him without saying a word.

"You know, that business you mentioned about his

appetites, I mean."

"Yeah, yeah." The assassin feels so weary now he can hardly remember what it was he was right about or even the nature of the world where it mattered if he was right or wrong. Out here everything has come undone. Pirelli, Fieldler, Hamilton, a raped woman, a murdered man. And you up there somewhere in the mountains, apparently cavorting with wolves, slaying starving dogs, getting somehow stronger while he and his fucked up cohorts have been growing steadily weaker. This is a crazy place. This is an impossible place. This place is a blemish on the world he has previously considered perfect because he understood it so well. This place in the mountains insults everything he's done in an otherwise perfect world, the things he's done to keep it functioning in a clear and simple way, maintaining its perfection, its usefulness, even its inevitability.

"Knox?"

"This is a fucking mess, John. That's the nub of it. The whole operation here is a goddamned mess. You see that, don't you?"

"Yeah, of course I do. But I told them, you know, Pirelli and Fieldler... I told them you'd know what to do."

"You told them I'd know how to clean everything up."

"Yeah. Of course I did. You're the expert, Knox. You still work for me. I still respect your professionalism, the deal we have. I still believe you know what you're doing."

"So where are Fieldler and Pirelli now?" asks Knox once more, not caring what Hamilton thinks. Barring some kind of unexpected miracle, Hamilton is only a few minutes away from being dead. Time to bring order back into this world of chaos, Knox has decided. That's usually what has to happen—order returns from chaos only after the right people die. And he is the instrument that maintains this needed order. He cleans up chaos with the appropriate ruthlessness ending chaos requires. Knox knows ultimately he is the one who makes sure the right people die.

"I don't know where Fieldler and Pirelli are," the industrialist is saying. "Out there in the snow someplace. That's all I know. So what are we gonna do?"

Knox turns away without replying. He slips his arm into the strap of the Remington he has been carrying in his hand, positioning the rifle over his shoulder. Knox is very calm now that he has accepted what fate has ordained for him. Plan B. One step at a time, the way he's always done it. Coolly. Calmly. Like a professional.

"Knox?"

Still ignoring the other man, Knox enters the cabin in search of a length of cord. He finds a spool of brick-coloured nylon twine in a crude drawer of the cabin pantry.

"What're you gonna do?" Hamilton asks the assassin when he comes back outside, the cord stretched taut between the knots he has twisted around his wrists and holds firmly in his fists.

"Whadda you think?" he replies, stepping around the other man as he leaves the porch to take care of the woman who intermittently struggles with the body of her fallen man.

Peripherally Knox notices the heavy fall of snow has begun to let up and he can see a little further when he gazes out to the perimeter of the land cleared to build this cabin. He is now convinced Fieldler has no choice but to kill him, so he hurries around the corner of the cabin to get the menial task of strangling Allison Leonard out of the way before he focuses his attention on much more dangerous enemies.

Behind him, Hamilton turns away, not wanting to watch as Knox prepares to dispatch the native woman into a spirit world where he has decided he would like to believe her husband waits for her.

WHEN KNOX BURSTS OUT OF THE SNOW to strangle the woman you believe you believe you are here to rescue, to you it is as if he has charged out of some well-disguised bathroom shower, suddenly pulling aside a flimsy curtain of wintery white gauze you didn't know concealed him. The famous shower scene from Psycho? He doesn't even notice you as he moves towards the woman, reaching out with both fists into which he has knotted a length of nylon twine.

But you have time to recognize him, to overcome your surprise at his sudden arrival through the curtain of falling snow. You have time to transform him in your mind's eye into one of the dogs you battled in the darkness last night. Then your imagination fails you and this cold, efficient beast with the menacing nylon cord is transformed back into Knox again. And you know this is a man it would be propitious for you to kill. So you take one hurried step forward, the lance held point upwards in both of your hands, prepared to do what you must do before some ill-conceived morality changes your mind.

Knox notices you then, hesitating a moment before it entirely dawns on him. A stupid reality. Your miscomprehension. Then, cursing, his astonishment abating, he shrugs his rifle free from his arm and shoulder, trying to swing it upwards in these close quarters of trees and cabin to lash out at you.

But it's much too late for Knox to take your life. Too much has happened to you since the last time you saw him, days ago now, an eternity ago—the way it seems now in the peculiar way wilderness measures time. You've become someone else since then. You've shared food with a wolf and helped it kill its enemies. And you've discovered this obviously indigenous woman needs your help. You've even discovered how complex you can be now that you understand society's reductive simplicity, the way it has insistently limited your being to keep its collective wheels turning. But now you feel yourself to be a man with a nobler purpose, committed to a new and clearer liberty that houses your important choices. Knox, you realize, cannot so easily kill the man you've now become. He is a cog in society's wheel. You are different from him. You are governed now by the force of individual freedom.

Being different now, someone else, some new brand of savage, you jam the blade of the lance—with a kind of urgent calm—into Knox's upper belly, just under his rib cage. It punctures a corner of his lung. The sharp blade of the knife Sara once gave you while you were having dinner in a strangely different world, Carmel-By-The-sea, then twists upwards to tear a corner of the assassin's heart. As Knox falls backwards at the force of this mortal wound, blood forms quickly at the corner of his mouth. There is a loud wheeze of air—his dissipating life—that escapes his twitching lips. You hear it like a sad, final remark, a pointless observation, a plea you must ignore as you pull the lance free of his chest.

You reach for his rifle . . .

"Knox?" J.D. Hamilton's voice, only a few feet away.

. . . but Knox has fallen back on it; the rifle is caught beneath his body.

"Knox? You okay?"

You own so much clarity now, so much clarity here in this wild place. You remember everything. You tug up the assassin's pantleg. You slip the revolver strapped to his calf out of its holster. You aim at Knox's face, not having used a revolver like this before, not knowing if it is loaded or whether it will even work, its weight a surprise to you because you assumed, remembering how it was strapped to Knox's leg, it would be lighter . . .

The revolver fires. It blows away some of the front of Knox's face, establishing that it works, that it is loaded, that it has become a device you can use in your battle to survive.

The woman screams so loudly in your ear you hear the sound of her voice ringing afterwards. Her scream or the revolver pop, hard to say which was louder, but one or both of them have nearly deafened you.

"Knox?" Hamilton's voice breaking through the ringing in your ears again, clearly frantic now, no doubt confused by the sound of the pistol going off, the sound of the woman's scream.

The snow is thinning quickly. It's working its way down to flurries. Hamilton recognizes you the instant you veer around the corner of the cabin. He is not ready for you. Although he holds his rifle in his right hand, the barrel is pointed down towards the floor of Joe Leonard's porch.

Your eyes meet. You think, for one crazy moment, that you are going to be able to order Hamilton to drop his rifle. For one moment, you actually think you have this option, that he will hear your command and obey, that you can take him prisoner or arrest him like some cop in a weekly television drama where everything will now work out in time for the series of commercials at the end of the program. Yes, just for a second, you believe you are in a make believe world where your once powerful antagonist will see the light and drop his gun.

But Hamilton begins to raise his rifle, his face strangely white and contorted with the effort, and you feel foolish for considering, even for a moment, that he would surrender. You can see he is exhausted. But you remember he is and has always been a dangerous man.

Holding Knox's pistol in both hands, you fire all the remaining bullets it holds into J.D. Hamilton's diseased and dying carcass, knowing you are killing him but firing anyway and hoping Sara will forgive you. Each bullet leaves the gun accompanied by your silent chanting of her name . . . Sara . . . Sara . . . Sara. You don't know why you chant her name like this, but you do until the gun clicks empty. Sara . . . Sara . . . Sara.

And then you turn away as his body slumps backwards onto the railing of the porch, eventually crashing to the floor. Now you must retrieve Knox's rifle. Now you must explain to the screaming woman that you are here to rescue her.

"JESUS," WHISPERS FIELDLER AS, through the scope on the top of his Remington, he watches Hamilton's body jerk backwards and fall. "I think that was Kovacs. And J.D.'s down."

"Huh?"

"Kovacs. I think we've flushed Kovacs out."

"It wasn't Knox?"

"It could have been Knox. It should have been Knox. I expected it would be Knox. But I think it was Kovacs."

Pirelli squints towards the cabin in the now quickly easing snowfall. The world is white from ground to horizon to sky. He feels like he is piloting a submarine as he moves to lift his rifle, like he is inside a great white tube inexplicably out of control in a perfectly colourless sea. He feels deep fear—or anticipation—two sensations so similar to him he cannot sort them out. What now? he wonders. What do we do now?

"Damn," says Fieldler calmly, as if all this time he's been hunting moose or elk. "I can't get a clear shot. He's gone behind the cabin by those woods over there."

But Pirelli still can't see anything. The world is too

white and bland. It has virtually no definition. He might just as well be peering into a gigantic glass of milk.

"Use your fucking scope, Pirelli."

"Yeah. Okay."

Clumsily Pirelli lifts his rifle the rest of the way into position. He squints into the scope, noting only the cabin porch and a fallen J.D. Hamilton.

"If it's Kovacs, he must have got Knox too," Fieldler is musing. "I don't see Knox. Son of a bitch! Kovacs must have gotten Knox."

"How do you know? How can we know for sure? What if it's Knox? He'll be coming for us. I mean, do you really believe Kovacs would be strong enough to take out Knox? And take him out with what?"

"Never mind. No matter who it is, Kovacs or Knox, it doesn't matter as long as we take care of him. We have to circle around behind the cabin. You go to the left and I'll go to the right."

"Okay," replies Pirelli, although he doesn't move. Although he would prefer to crouch right here inside the delusion of safety this white and wintery womb inspires.

"And keep to the trees. C'mon. Hurry up. If it's Kovacs, we can't let him escape after all we've been through." Fieldler begins to move away but soon reconsiders and halts. "Oh, and Pirelli?"

"Yeah."

"He probably has Knox's rifle. Okay?"

"Yeah." Pirelli's voice is hesitant, exposing his deep trepidation. He tries to conceal it but knows instinctively he can't fool Fieldler. He realizes now he has never been the kind of man who really fools anyone.

"And Pirelli?"

"Yeah?"

"The secret here is making sure we don't shoot each

other. Be sure, be absolutely sure before you pull the trigger."

Fieldler studies him a moment longer, accepting Pirelli's nod of acknowledgment, then moves off to the right, further into the trees.

Bemused, trying to figure out what he's doing here, why everything about this gunfight is so different from how he anticipated it would be, Pirelli watches his mentor go. Then, remembering you, remembering what he is here to do, he begins to inch through the trees to the left, as Fieldler has instructed. The wet snow squishes under his boots. This nearly commonplace sound is the only insistent reality he can discern in his ever more fanciful circumstances. Making his way more deeply into the woods, Pirelli is disturbed to realize he can hardly remember exactly what he's supposed to be doing, what the point of everything actually is, what life was supposed to ultimately achieve for him, what this hunt would ever have accomplished, had it worked out exactly as planned.

WHEN YOU REACH OUT TO THE WOMAN with your hand to calm her, she flinches violently, barely controlling another urge to scream.

"I'm Kovacs," you whisper. "I'm here to help you."

But the woman continues to back away from you, terrified, until she encounters the wall of the cabin and can back up no further, pinned against the wood of what was once her home. Now trapped, she stares at you in alarm, her eyes as large as uninhabited planets.

"We have to get out of here," you begin to explain. "There are two more men. We have to go someplace safe."

The woman does not respond.

"What's your name?" you ask after an eternity of helplessness inspired by her silence. "I won't hurt you. I'm here to help you. What's your name?"

She doesn't reply. Yet you feel her trying to focus on your face. You sense she might be trying to break out of the prison of her pain. You can feel her making the effort. You can sense her struggling within herself, with her pain, with finding something about you she might be able to trust. You wish you knew some better way to reach out to her, to offer her a strong and reassuring hand, but the woman's pain is so deep, her injuries are so profound, you feel a miracle would be ultimately inadequate.

"Is this your husband?" you ask gently, gesturing in the direction of the man now lying contorted on the ground a couple of feet away.

Although she doesn't answer, her eyes glance at him and say, yes, as best they can, shedding a pair of tiny, tired tears.

"I'm sorry," you whisper. "These are evil men."

She gazes at you, agreeing to nothing.

"Did they hurt you?" Dumb question. You know they did. Her torn clothing tells the story. You know what the other men did.

"Do you know how to get us safely out of this valley?"

No answer.

But you expect she probably knows a way back to civilization, to the police, to some kind of respectable society that will deliver both of you from any further harm. You know she has a name and will eventually tell you what it is. You know, when Fieldler and Pirelli have been dealt with—if they've been dealt with—if, indeed they must be dealt with—there will be a time for sympathy for this woman, a time for exchanging names with her and working out the means of returning her to safety.

Still, you ask her one more question. "Do you have family around here? People you can turn to?"

No answer. And this confirms for you that it remains too early for questions such as these. For the time being, this broken, damaged woman cannot help you help her. You sigh and turn away. Cautiously you tug Knox's body onto its side, freeing up the rifle that was trapped underneath. Carefully, you pick it up and examine it. You locate what you think is the safety. You make certain it is unlocked.

"Stay here," you whisper to the woman. "There are two more men. I'll be back."

Nothing.

"Please," you whisper. "Just nod your head if you understand. Can you do that?"

There is a nod, although it's almost imperceptible. For all you know, it could be only a twitch, not some acknowledgment of your words. Nothing seems certain or clear at this moment. Clarity has grown hopeless again, even as a concept. Waves and troughs. You are certain, until you can find a way safely home, clarity will roll in and out like breakers. You feel involved in a minor accident right now, in a state of shock, unable to interpret what comes next as something meaningful, helpful or purposeful. It's not quite like dreaming, but it's not like being entirely conscious either.

"I'll get you out of here," you tell the woman now. "I'll be back to get us out of here."

She doesn't move and she doesn't react to your commitment to her. Her eyes do not blink. You wonder if she's gone away again to some other more forgiving place where she can be injured no further, where she doesn't have to deal with the confusion around the promise you've just made. You doubt she's in the mood for believing in anything. You doubt she's in the state of mind for any kind of faith.

FIELDLER BEGINS TO BELIEVE HE HAS WAITED most of his life—been preparing most of his life—for this sacred opportunity to hunt and kill one of his own kind. To him, you are a thinking, desperate man, the only being on Earth who knows for certain that he has the capacity to die. To hunt a being like you with a true sense of what it is to be prey, Fieldler has dreamed of this possibility. He has imagined many times what it will be like to hunt and bring down a thinking, cognizant human who understands mortality, who, knows he does not possess an unlimited forever. A man is prey that understands—with an incredible range of fear and desperation—what will never be experienced when life comes to an end; what cannot be undone, what hasn't been felt; what amends can never be made. Whenever death arrives, a human must accept that life is too late because death has arrived too early. A human being knows what procrastination he cannot justify, what inexplicable opportunity he has never been offered or accepted. A human being is someone who knows all the things he's missed or done wrong, someone who can sort all these various disappointments into regret and dissatisfaction. A human is someone who knows—as a victim of the hunt—the extent of the injustice surrounding what death steals from him when it inevitably arrives. To Fieldler, these are the reasons why hunting a human being is so exhilarating.

This is the most dangerous quarry of all for a man like Fieldler, a man who loves to hunt. Lions, water buffalo, elk, deer, moose—these are not desperate creatures. They live an infantile life, ignorant of their inevitable mortality. But you, a man, know exactly how much is at stake. Even if Fieldler kills you easily, he is convinced you will excite him immeasurably as a quarry, purely because you embrace a cognizant concept of your future. You will know, if only for an instant, that you are dying prematurely. You will already know that death is a great mistake, regardless of when it arrives. But when Fieldler hunts you down, you will know you are dying early when you shouldn't even have to die at all. To Fieldler, this transforms you into an unique hunting trophy he has only recently determined is vital to his life's experience.

Fieldler now believes he is having quite a day. The woman he has had sex with, her man whom he has killed, and now you. By the time he is done today, he is going to celebrate at least one tiny moment when he has caught a superficial glimpse of what it is like to be God.

IN POSSESSION OF KNOX'S RIFLE and feeling the odds are a little less against you, you nonetheless aren't exactly certain what you should do next. The gunfire. Two men dead. Fieldler and Pirelli must be on their way by now. They have no choice but to come after you. There's no way, with Hamilton and Knox dead, with this woman raped and her husband dead, that Fieldler is going to change his mind about hunting you down. And as long as Fieldler is committed to your death, Pirelli will be committed too. So Fieldler remains your most dangerous adversary. Fieldler is the one you must figure out a way to outsmart.

You have moved into the woods away from the woman but you keep peering back at her to make certain she's all right. It has stopped snowing but the wet snow that fell previously now clings to the branches of the evergreens in which you hide, creating a false dusk that surrounds you everywhere. It is a viscous darkness inside this giant, natural igloo in which you find yourself. You gaze up into the trees which look like a complicated network of spindles forming the skeleton of a giant umbrella. If only you could fly, you now conclude, you would soar up to the treetops to study the view such a vantage point would provide.

You are nervous but calm. A few days ago you would have run away. But today, running is no option. The woman must be rescued. No matter what, keeping this woman alive has become your chief concern. You suppose you continue to fear death, yet you feel on the verge of being in control of your own destiny. Certainly, things have progressed too far for you to feel panic. While so much continues to lie outside of your control, much more is in your hands than what once was. Mostly you are going to fight the other two men because you must—to save your life and get the woman safely away from here. Your decision does not reflect a foolish choice you made at some foolish moment. No, strangely enough, you have become a wilderness savage, blessed with a sense of inherent justice, the kind of justice you have learned no other collective society seems capable of.

If only you could fly.

Then it strikes you, a bolt of inspiration. While you will never fly, it's possible you can climb.

Yes. Up there near the ectoplasmic canopy of collected snow and tree branches and needles, perhaps you will be able to glimpse the other men coming for you. Perhaps, with Knox's rifle, you can skew the odds in favour despite Fieldler's need to hunt you down. You continue to believe it's Fieldler you must worry about. Perhaps up there in the dark canopy of branches and sticky snow, you can see Fieldler coming before Fieldler discovers what you have done.

You slip into the shoulder strap of Knox's rifle. It snags on your pack a moment, but you force it into place along your back. Then, satisfied that you can keep your balance, you pull yourself upwards into a tree. You hesitate a moment on the first limb, feeling strange and childlike to be climbing on the branches of a tree; then you begin to move carefully upwards through the dark canopy overhead. The snow is a complication—it leaves tracks, it's slippery, it's wet and cold—but you are stuck with it. You climb.

PIRELLI CATCHES A GLIMPSE OF MOVEMENT out of the corner of his eye. It flashes so quickly and silently, by the time he turns whatever it was he noticed is no longer there. He feels a rush of fear hot in his chest. He spins, gazing into the thick confusion of the trees, seeing nothing. He has no idea what he thought he saw. But his nerves feel like they've been burned with acid. Given enough time on his own this way, especially in view of everything he's already been through, he knows his decaying mind could imagine anything out here. Doggedly, mostly to prevent himself from thinking, he moves very slowly in the direction Fieldler has instructed him to go, staring so intently into the gloom of these woods, in search of human movement, his eyes ache with the strain.

No wonder he has been seeing things. He's unsettled over the proposition that you, instead of Knox, may have killed his father-in-law. If true, it would mean you have a rifle, and that your persistence—no, even your talent—at survival has placed him in unexpected danger. In these woods, fearing them and fearing you, it is no surprise to him that he imagines movement out of the corner of his eye; antagonists and threats that aren't really there represent the tedious hobgoblins a man must endure at times when an unkind world turns against him.

Because it's true: Pirelli feels betrayed by circumstance. Fate has connived to make everything dangerous for him. His luck has left him. Fate has removed his right to win.

Pirelli feels depressed. None of this wilderness escapade has worked out all that well. There are people dead and none of them are you so far. And no matter who dies next—you or Knox, whichever one of you is out there, or Fieldler, for that matter—he has no idea what story can be concocted now to make everything all right in the end, once the escapade is actually over. Pirelli only has Fieldler's word that Knox is dead, that it was you who shot Hamilton. For all Pirelli knows, he is actually now hunting down a professional assassin, Knox, a man who could kill him easily.

At least his father-in-law is dead. And now, no doubt, Pirelli is a fabulously wealthy man. But Pirelli knows it's not going to do him any good if he doesn't get out of these mountains alive or, if he does, he doesn't come up with a foolproof story maintaining his innocence afterwards. For the most part, though, he cannot wrap his mind around the complexities of his situation and the complexities of a plan that will make his innocence plausible. And what if he and Fieldler don't find their way back to the airplane?

And if the woman is still alive, well, there's no doubt she must be killed. What was it Fieldler said? Burned to death in her cabin? Christ, he wonders now, what got into them? He and Fieldler actually came inside of her. Now Pirelli feels disgusted with himself, with sex, with what Fieldler shamed him into doing. His penis feels sticky, soiled and cold. He would give anything for an opportunity to wash himself. And he knows he'll feel better about what he did to the woman after she is dead, when recollection of his self-debasement isn't so fresh in his mind, when it's begun receding into denial.

There, off to his right at the edge of the woods,

didn't he see something move? Out of the corner of his eye? Wasn't there something there? He curses silently in frustration. Nothing now. Jesus, he concludes, this is no time to be seeing things.

FIELDLER HAS BEEN DETECTING MOVEMENT as well out of the corner of his eye. Something swift and silent. Something nearly seen, then mostly unseen: a chimera, a mist that moves so rapidly in and out of his eyesight, it isn't there at all. By the time he focuses on what he thinks he's seen, there's nothing there and the implied movement manifests itself somewhere else. At this moment he resents the unnecessary distraction of his overactive imagination and the mirage it has created. He's hunted in the wilderness before without worry over ghosts or demons, without being distracted by imaginary movement at the edge of his peripheral vision. These mountains are getting to him. This wilderness is too large, too endless. Soon, if he's not careful, he won't remember true civilization, the perfect social universe this wilderness does not need but to which Fieldler would like to return for its comfort and endorsement.

Still, he has been making progress through these woods, circling around in the trees in a wide arc in the general direction of the cabin. Now, if only that asshole Pirelli doesn't shoot him by mistake, then perhaps he can get to you—he still thinks it's you rather than Knox, as incredible as it may seem—before any more damage is done.

YOU FIND A PLACE TO SERVE AS YOUR PERCH in the tree that you have climbed. It's eerie up here, ten yards above the ground, and darker still. You feel pinned against some giant ceiling that, should it discover you hiding there, will give way to whimsically release you to the deep crush of gravity, urging you into a dizzying fall towards the unforgiving earth. Fear of heights. Even now, more desperate, more powerful, more at home in this wilderness, you cannot escape the acrophobia you have suffered much of your life.

There is no wind and you are deeply grateful for this. Up here, perched on a branch so thin it can barely hold your weight, you have one arm around a tree trunk that is disturbingly slim. Any kind of innocuous breeze could pluck you from this branch and toss you to the ground. Still, with respect to Fieldler and Pirelli, you maintain a powerful hope that neither one of them will think to look up towards the treetops as they track your progress into these woods. You have left tracks. They are there at the base of the tree. But, by then, by the time your footprints are discovered . . .

So you bite back your deep fear of heights. You ease Knox's rifle from your back, grunting as it snags on your pack. Precariously, you labour to free it from your shoulder while maintaining your balance. You cling in desperation to this tree, painstakingly positioning the rifle, inch by frantic inch. Don't drop it, Kovacs. Whatever you do, don't drop it!

When at last the rifle is free after a virtual eternity up here so many feet above the ground, you take a deep breath and cautiously lean the barrel on a limb. You use your elbow to lock yourself in place. Your balance is precarious. It will take both hands to aim and pull the trigger. It occurs to you helplessly that it is even possible the recoil will fling you from this perch.

Yet hiding up here to spot the first hunter you must kill is probably your wisest plan. Yes, you can do this for the sake of the woman fate has determined you can rescue. And thinking of the woman sitting beside her dead husband against the wall of her cabin, you feel connected once again to her brutal suffering. A now familiar outrage returns. Outrage reduces your fear. Outrage even eases your acrophobia a little.

Feeling a little stronger now, grateful to be quietly angry, you remain focused where you reside in the upper penthouse of this tree. One hunter. Just one chance from up here. After this single victim is disposed of, you will be exposed. You will have to climb down as quickly as you can so that your second assailant doesn't pick you off.

PIRELLI KEEPS SEEING THINGS. And the things he sees aren't things because he doesn't really see them at all. He can't make out what they are. Just little microseconds of movement in the trees. Like a bit of fluff in the corner of the eye, seen for such a small fragment in time, it isn't really seen at all.

Pirelli's frustration over hallucinating grows deeper. His eyes water from the damp chill of the day and the deep darkness in the woods underneath the canopy of snow, and from the intensity of searching this half light for a glimpse of you—or Knox. He thinks that you are Knox, the Knox he still believes in, while you are some imagined troll he now can barely remember from his childhood. All these things do not matter as much as his frustration that this mountainous place is making him crazy. He's hungry again. He wants to return to the place where he belongs. He wishes for civilization, the city, L.A. Back home is gloriously safe and familiar, a conventional hearth that welcomes him. There, not here, is where he is desperate to be.

Yet, feeling all of this desperation, all of this need, weeping steadily over his desperate circumstances, Pirelli continues to arc through the trees in the general direction of the rear of the cabin. His body is divorced from his hurt feelings and has a will of its own. There isn't much else to do. There's no better plan than doing what Fieldler told him to do. And maybe it'll be all right, if he does what he's been told. Maybe he'll stop crying. Maybe he'll stop seeing unexpected movement here in the woods with him, some as-yet-unseen spectre caught in the corner of his eye where his wild imagination apparently begins.

IF FIELDLER BELIEVED IT WAS KNOX he is stalking, he would feel more apprehension than he does at this moment. But he is convinced it was you he saw revealed for a brief moment in the scope of his rifle, after you killed Hamilton. So he feels a tremendous exhilaration as he moves through the trees towards the corner of the cabin where the woman weeps silently over her fallen husband. The notion that Knox is no longer an adversary is gratifying enough, but the resolution in your death will make everything easier. After you're gone, it all will work out fine. He'll get rid of the bodies—yours, Knox's, Hamilton's, the murdered indigenous couple's—and no price will have to be paid for his and Pirelli's bad behaviour. No bodies, no murders. The story he and Pirelli fabricate will then be transformed into unarguable truth. There will be no one else alive to expose it as a lie.

Fieldler stops now to peer into the trees ahead of him. He notices movement again out of the corner of his eye. Flicking his gaze to the right, he cannot see anything. He's imagining things. Glancing ahead once more, he can make out the rear of the cabin in the near darkness in these trees, but the cabin is still some distance away.

Where are you, Kovacs? Fieldler wonders. What would a

man like you do to try to outsmart a man like me?

Fieldler eases his back against a thick white spruce and gazes systematically into the trees. Higher ground perhaps? An ambush from higher ground? An ambush from the trees?

Fieldler begins to glance upwards, but he is interrupted by more mysterious movement on the ground a few yards in front of him. He turns and this time captures more than merely a glimpse of movement. This time the intruder is revealed to him as a large animal. A dog? he wonders at first. A wolf?

Jesus, a wolf, a large wolf. The animal stands there fifty yards away, gazing at him.

Fieldler feels an unexpected chill run down the back of his neck. It is intense and deep and very civilized. Hating the fear he feels, hating the wolf for inspiring it, he slowly raises his rifle...

YOU KNOW THE MAN FRAMED IN YOUR SCOPE is Ernie Fieldler. You even know you should put a bullet in his chest. Still, you hesitate. It feels like cold blooded murder.

Then Fieldler begins to lift his rifle, as if he's begun to sense your presence. Is he going to glance upwards, maybe even in your direction? And you remember the wild dogs that had to be killed last night, the woman assaulted by the hunters to whom you've given your promise of rescue, her dead husband lying near her on the ground. You remember all of these things. And you remember Sara too. You remember your need to return to her to let her see the person you actually are, the person you've clearly become.

Remembering all these factors, tallying them up like debts, you check your sighting in the scope then calmly squeeze the trigger before you can change your mind.

This man you hardly know, this stranger here in the mountains, hesitates a moment before he goes down. Your bullet has had to slip through a rip in time. He seems to break into an expression of hopelessness, arms outstretched, legs spread, his rifle exploding out of his hands like it too has been shot. Then Fieldler falls backwards in a silent heap as the sound of the rifle shot ricochets through the trees.

Shocked at what you've done, you cling to your desperate perch in the trees, wondering what to do next.

"Fieldler? Did you get him? Was that you, Fieldler?" It's Pirelli's voice. You recognize it even though it sounds broken, desperate and frantic, some distance away to your right.

But it spurs you into action. You must climb down the tree to check Fieldler's body.

"Fieldler? Answer me, will you?"

You can't tell where Pirelli is. The frantic quality in his voice seems to echo from everywhere at once. You descend from your tree as quickly as you can. Death's ultimate judgment of this hunt is marching steadily in your direction. You sense, as you climb back down towards the earth, that you have a vital appointment with justice itself to decide what may or may not be and who may or may not live or die.

PIRELLI SCREAMS FIELDLER'S NAME THIS TIME. He cannot help himself. He is horrified that his only remaining ally will not answer him. "Fieldler? Tell me you're okay."

Silence and terror. And knowing, always knowing, he doesn't have much choice. If Fieldler is gone, everything is too late and no matter how he paints it, it's been too late for most of this day.

Impossible to believe that you have shot Fieldler.

Too impossible, Pirelli must conclude. Something else perhaps. Knox. Knox could kill Fieldler. Not you. It must have been Knox. And the thought of Knox's cold experience, the ease he finds in killing, fills Pirelli with a fresh wave of terror. Then again, maybe Fieldler is alive. Maybe Fieldler just can't talk. Maybe there's some other benign reason for his silence that Pirelli will soon uncover. Maybe Fieldler has his own reasons for opting to be mute.

Frozen, weeping against a tree, Pirelli takes a deep breath, trying to get hold of himself. He's a man with so few choices left – this is how it feels to him. He checks the safety on his rifle, peers for a frightened moment or two into the darkness of the canopied woods. This place is its own planet now and it doesn't like him much. But at least he's still alive; at least he has instructions from Fieldler; at least he has someone competent to obey, reducing the risk he must admit he poses to himself.

He takes another deep breath, holds it, slowly lets it out. Pointing his rifle out in front of him, Pirelli plunges more deeply into the woods, moving in your direction.

FIELDLER ISN'T DEAD YET, although he wonders if he's going to be. His body feels a curious mixture of pain and numbness. He can taste blood in his mouth and intuits, if he bleeds heavily internally, he will shortly drown. He even suspects the unexpected bullet that knocked him down a couple of minutes ago invaded and did damage to his lung. It's so difficult to breathe, even lying here on the ground, resting against a tree, not having to do very much. Each breath is an exhausting wheeze. Something—his wound, the bullet—is sucking the oxygen out of his atmosphere.

And, Jesus, he doesn't want to die. It feels like a great mistake, his lying here on the cold, needled ground, twisted a little on the hard roots of the tree nestled against his left shoulder. Maybe his wound isn't as bad as he thinks. If he turns his head slowly or delicately enough, everything about this woods appears the same as it was a few moments ago, dark and endlessly brown, punctuated here and there by startlingly white patches of snow made from opportunistic snowflakes that have found a way to penetrate this thick stand of trees.

He can't see the fucking wolf he was going to shoot. And he senses, as a hunter, he made a fundamental mistake when he allowed it to distract him from his primary target. The wolf wasn't the trophy he was after; he should have ignored it. And he shouldn't have succumbed to the fear the wolf inspired in him. It's a fear he can still remember with a puzzling intensity even though it's now a couple of minutes old. Was the wolf his bitter enemy all along, some symbolic culmination of pure enmity? Bleeding on the ground, he transforms the wolf into a disappointing idea—the sentry at the intersection where his own tame world abuts its wilderness alternative. On second thought, he should have killed it just to make a point about who runs this fucking world, about what the world's currency is—namely whatever a cloister of human beings needs it to be.

Kovacs!

Gazing up at you, Fieldler coughs, what passes for a laugh at this appointed moment in the process of his dying. He tried to laugh because you smell so much worse than you look and because he found your stench surprising. Maybe, Fieldler wonders, he should have used his nose instead of his eyesight when he was trying to track you down inside these endless mountains. Maybe then he would have smelled you coming and you, rather than him, would now be lying on this bloody patch of ground, wishing desperately for a breath of purer oxygen.

"You were lucky, Kovacs," mutters Fieldler breathlessly, a sore loser to the end. Bitterly he imagines himself in a dark closet where death waits on a rusty hanger to wear itself on him.

You don't answer the big game hunter's words. He is dying in a large ocean of his own blood. You can't really think of anything to say to him at this moment. You don't feel any remaining malice towards him but you don't feel any compassion either. And everything you've figured out about yourself these past few days in the mountains reflects values you are certain he would never understand, regardless of how well you explained them. So you just crouch by this fallen man, Knox's rifle across your thighs, waiting for him to die, waiting perhaps for even a small glimpse of the wisdom of compassion Fieldler might appreciate the moment before he dies.

ASTONISHED AT HIS GOOD FORTUNE, Pirelli nearly cries out loud when he moves cautiously between two trees and witnesses you crouched by Fieldler's side, less than twenty yards away. He has you dead to rights. Your back is turned to him. He stifles his cry of delight, the astonishing depth of his relief, because all he has to do is silently lift the rifle, peer into its scope, and line you up in the device's precise hairlines. Then, after he pulls the trigger, his nightmare will be over. He will find his way out of here somehow, out of these stupid, endless mountains. His story about your violent rampage on this hunt—about everyone you killed—will be terrifying to tell.

Yes, this is most important of all: the instant he

pulls the trigger, the instant he takes your life, he will get away with everything. The raped and soon to be murdered woman he saw again a moment ago, leaning against the cabin wall. The fortune bestowed on him by his father-in law. The return to him of the woman he married, Sara, who has put him through this hell and will ultimately live to regret it. In a moment, if he is careful, if he takes his time, he will win a lottery purely by pulling the trigger that matter-of-factly takes your life.

He lifts his rifle slowly and gazes into the scope until the back of your head is framed in the scope's hairlines. God, he wants to gloat. He hesitates because the need to gloat is so powerful at this moment, for himself, even for J.D., who did not live to share this moment. He would like to call your name, compelling you to turn to him in surprise. Then, when he was certain you knew you were going to die, he would pull the trigger. He wants you to be aware, at the moment of death, which hunter is killing you. But this need for triumph passes. Better to be silent. Better to kill you now before anything else goes wrong, before . . .

. . . The deep and prolonged snarl is astonishingly loud. And it's right there, right on top of him. Pirelli turns, his finger pulling the trigger, the reflex of surprise. He hears and feels the rifle's report. At the same instant he notices a large gray shape lunging through the air towards his face. There is a sharp, high-pitched yelp and something heavy, a furry blur, changes its direction slightly at the force of his bullet. Then the shape glances heavily off his shoulder, propelling him backwards against a nearby tree. He grunts at the force of the wolf's collision with his body, then again with the force with which he is thrown against the tree. He feels a bolt of pain in his shoulder where he has hit the tree, but he doesn't lose his footing and he doesn't drop his rifle.

For the moment, you are forgotten. Still swallowed up by the rush of his surprise and fear, Pirelli leans against the tree, gasping, trying to catch his breath. He gazes at the large, twitching, furry animal he must have shot. Like a dog, only much larger. Like those wolves he's seen on television, the ones American ranchers fear on behalf of their livestock.

Then he remembers you, how you were supposed to die for everything to work out, for everything to be perfect for him. Pirelli turns in your direction, groaning with the pain of what he knows must be a dislocated shoulder, trying to lift the rifle now so heavy in his hands.

He sees you gazing back at him, your rifle pointed in his direction. Your eyes meet. This is Pirelli's last glimpse of anything, his last seeing. This is the final second he exists before the bullet you fire at him tears into his heart, instantly and mindlessly stealing his life from him.

YOU CROSS TO PIRELLI'S BODY CAREFULLY, holding Knox's rifle up in front of you in case Pirelli moves again. But Pirelli is down and dead, you discover, when at last you reach his side. His eyes stare sightlessly upwards at the umbrella of this woods, at the natural wilderness dome sheltering the unfortunate, stupid war that has taken place here.

You move to the wolf and crouch beside it. It too is dead. It has the same sightless stare as Pirelli, whose body lies nearby. You remove your glove, sodden with sweat or snow, and touch the coarse strands of fur, beige, brown, black and gray. Your uneasy ally. You are moved to mourn a little, a mourning that tip-toes across your chest. Fancifully, it crosses your mind that you and the wolf are even, now. The dogs that attacked him and the dogs that were intent on killing you are a fair trade, you suppose.

You will gather up all the dead men here, and you will ask the woman if you can use her cabin as a temporary crypt. You will also ask to take the wolf inside, so it too is not devoured by passing scavengers. Perhaps the police will ask you about this decision at some point, why you treated the fallen wolf with the same care as these ruthless, fallen men, when the authorities arrive to sort out everything that's happened. But you have time to figure out something understandable to say.

Which reminds you somehow of Fieldler, last seen dying several yards away.

You rise from the wolf and walk back to stand looking down on the big game hunter. Fieldler too has gone. The last moments of his dying must have taken place while the wolf was attacking Pirelli or while you were shooting Pirelli or while you knelt by the wolf, sorting through your way to a new and gentler wisdom. Somewhere during all of these important developments, Fieldler died alone, failing to find a way to purchase that one last breath that would keep him alive.

Never mind; there is much for you to do. The woman, the gathering of the bodies—human and lupine—and the journey out of these mountains to return you safely to Sara. So much for you to do to survive this overwhelming wilderness and get the injured woman the help she needs.

So many things to explain when you leave these mountains, to people who will not want to believe you, to others who only might, to a final important few like Sara who probably will and must. The indigenous woman has seen just about everything. She is the one who knows the truth. You will need her help as much as she needs yours.

For the moment, you leave the dead where they lie.

In these mountainous woods now coming alive once more with sound, forgiving yet again your intrusion here, you move in the direction of the woman. You gaze at her but do not try to touch her. You don't want to frighten her.

"I'm Keith. What's your name?" you ask gently.

You wait a long time for an answer and a relenting of her fear. When at last she replies, you can barely hear her.

"Allison," she says.

"We're safe now. We have to go home. Can you get us to your family?"

She thinks about this and shortly nods.

When she is ready, together you will make your way through the civilization of nature to find your respective paths to safety.

"I'm sorry about your husband."

She says nothing but manages to nod.

You think a moment and your eyes well up.

"My husband's name is Joe," she says.

"The woman I love . . . her name is Sara."

ABOUT THE AUTHOR

Barry Grills is a former chair of The Writers' Union of Canada and the Book and Periodical Council. His short stories have appeared in various literary magazines and anthologies, including *Best Canadian Stories*. His critically acclaimed memoir, *Every Wolf's Howl*, won an Alberta Book Award for its publisher, Freehand Books. His first Fluid Grouse Enterprises book, *Roadkill*, was a finalist in both the Next Generation Indie Book Awards and the Whistler Independent Book Awards. He is also the author of three musical biographies on the lives and careers of Anne Murray, Alanis Morissette and Céline Dion. His work on an updated version of Dion's life, co-authored with Jim Brown, was the source for a CBC television movie. In 2019, he was appointed a life member of The Writers' Union of Canada. He currently lives and works in North Bay, Ontario, Canada.